C000132160

STEAM GEARED

Victorian Steampunk Erotica

ROBINETTE WATERSON

This is a work of fiction. Similarities to real people, places, or events are entirely coincidental.

STEAM GEARED

First edition. January 20, 2019.

Copyright © 2019 Robinette Waterson. ISBN: 9781798289259

Written by Robinette Waterson.

Table of Contents

1. Second Chances...1

2. Down the Primrose Path 39

3. On The Boardwalk 61

4. The Dinner Party, Part I 73

5. The Dinner Party, Part II..99

6. My Fair Lady, Or Pygmalion Re-Versed 115

7. Try, Try Again 123

8. Mogambo, Or The Red Dust................................141

9. A La Carte 149

10. Wouldn't You Like To Be Beside The Seaside?.............159

11. Insatiable 169

12. The Correspondent 183

13. Albert and Minnie, Part III, Or The Consummation......195

14. The Divine and Ali Baba 207

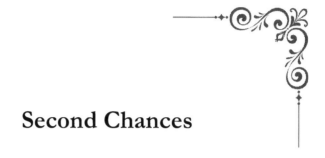

Second Chances

Second Chances

A STATUESQUE WOMAN wearing a highly fashionable dress sailed down the cobblestone street like a proud frigate with top-gallants and studding sails aloft. Her hat was extravagantly plumed and her dark hair was elaborately coiffed. Beside her, trotting briskly, was a trim gentleman in a dapper bowler, seemingly shorter than her due to the height of her millinery splendor. Every few steps, he half skipped to stay abreast with her. She stopped at the corner of Spaulding and Runcible Streets and turned to him.

"Harold, please don't dawdle, you know how I hate to be late." Lavinia opened her reticule and reread the circular to verify the address. "The shop is in the next block. Now let's review what we will do when we get there."

Harold hopped the final distance between them and turned to face her. "Yes, m'dear Vinnie?" He reached out his gloved hands to her, his eyes alight and his expression besotted. He had the look of someone stricken by love at first sight, in spite of their many years of marriage. Unable to restrain himself, overexcited by the grandness of their current venture and the overabundance of his feelings for her, he leaned forward, aiming to kiss her cheek.

Lavinia's hand darted out to his shoulder, providing the restraint dictated by their public circumstance. "No, no, not out here in the open! And you must not muss my hair after I had such a time coaxing it to fall in this seemingly artless way." As if to temper her refusal, she nudged his hat to tilt at the perfect angle and brushed a stray strand of his pale hair behind his ear. "We do want to appear well-turned out and well-heeled for the landlord's inspection. Although we don't want to appear too anxious." She darted a quick glance down at her own apparel as she continued to speak. "Don't gush as you are wont to do.

2

But don't appear too blasé either. The landlord will know it is an act and inflate the price on us."

"Quite right, m'dear. Just so." Harold smiled cheerfully, waiting on her spate of words to subside. He could tell she was nervous although she would never admit it, not even to herself.

His eyes wavered slightly in the middle of her expostulations, taking notice of a young woman in a blue dress ascending into a steam cab. The trollop had lifted her skirt high to clear the step, exposing cloistered ankles and the hint of a shapely calf. She caught his look and smiled lasciviously, extending an invitation to him. Harold ducked his head in embarrassment to be caught in the act of staring. Forthwith he returned his eyes and attention to his wife. "I will follow your lead, Vinnie. Splendid plan. As always."

"Very good, then," Lavinia nodded decisively and took hold of Harold's arm to turn him around in the proper direction. "Take care that you do." She grimaced, wondering to herself if he would ever learn to behave. Back when she had first laid eyes on him, her heart had skipped a beat, or maybe more than one in point of fact, thinking how he was achingly perfect for her. But now, as their lives had ticked onward, she was not as sure that achingly perfect still described him.

"We do so need a proper venue for entertaining clients," Lavinia continued talking as they walked. "And the prospect of a large and well-ventilated workshop for our projects makes me positively giddy!" She touched the back of her hand to her forehead, half mocking her feelings with the exaggerated stage gesture, a throwback to her early days as an operatic performer at the Pantheon.

They continued down the street, reading the house numbers with some difficulty in the fading rays from the sun, before the gas lamplighters had done their duty. At last they arrived at the address indicated. The building itself was a bit dowdy with a faded sign from the previous tobacconist shop. It was sandwiched between a custom bicycle factory and a pie-and-mash shop, but the address was respectable and the access for clients' carriages was more than adequate.

"Oh, Vinnie, look! This place is ideal for us!" Harold burst out when he sighted the place. Lavinia poked him in the ribs and he coughed. "I mean to say, this establishment might do. If we squint." He looked to his wife, seeking approval of his amendment.

The front door then opened and the landlord escorted them inside. He was a thin-lipped man with thinning hair and narrowed eyes, but Lavinia noted that his hands were soft. If repairs were needed, they wouldn't be seeing this fellow with a spanner or gear calipers.

Once introductions were concluded, Lavinia looked purposefully around the spacious, but empty salon room, seemingly inattentive to the landlord's patter. She made her way around, opening all the doors, appraising each niche, alcove, and appurtenance, finally stopping at the staircase landing, which led up to the sleeping chambers and down to the basement. "Before we expend ourselves further, will this place be ready for occupation by Tuesday? We have an exhibition to mount." Her eyes gleamed as the landlord asked her the obvious question.

"Oh my yes, we, that is to say, Kettering & Putterham Steamworks, will be announcing our latest robotic tableau very soon. Have you seen our display at the Regent's Zoological Gardens? Extinct birds and plant life. Dodos and calvaria trees. All steam-powered. The latest in pneumatics with cogwork assists." The landlord admitted to not having visited the zoo in some time. "There is one little vignette," Lavinia went on, arranging her face and stance to resemble a coquette on stage, "makes me laugh every time. A tiny crab pops out of the sand and a seabird gobbles it up!" She laughed, genuinely delighted by her macabre detail, encouraging the landlord to laugh with her, and thus be kindly disposed to her way of mind.

"Another of our works you might have heard of," she hurried to supply another example of their triumphs, "is the installation for the intermezzo at the Adelphi." Lavinia blushed slightly, knowing it was unladylike to be praising herself so, but the business side of her plunged headlong, heedless of propriety. "The comedy duet with the mechanized Columbine and Pierrot, do you know it? Some have said that their performance is more entertaining than the play! The Columbine is particularly beautiful. Harold's exquisite paintwork and attentiveness to detail, down to the tiny tucks in her bodice and the feather-light fluttering of her bespangled skirt when she pirouettes, have received high marks from prominent people." She opened her mouth as if to name names, but then closed it and merely smiled.

From across the room where Harold was inspecting the deep sinks, he reddened and pshawed. "It is your steam tubing that makes them so lifelike, Vinnie. That tiny internal combustion engine you designed is utterly revolutionary."

Lavinia favored Harold with a bright smile before refocusing her calculating gaze on the landlord. "I shouldn't say this, but it is just so delicious a tidbit that I cannot help myself. Our latest commission is to fashion fitted collars and cuffs for the pet of a very famous personage. One everyone would recognize instantly if I were to be so indiscreet as to speak her name out loud."

Lavinia let the possibilities hang in the air for a bit, teasing the landlord, hoping to provoke him to ask. When he showed forbearance, she rounded back on him, peppering him with questions, gearing up for negotiations. "Tell me about signage. Is that included? And are the walls soundproof? I wouldn't want my clients subjected to industrial clatter on one side and Billingsgate tongues on the other." She barely paused for breath, much less answers. "And about easements. Could we build a portico on the front of the building? To keep the elements from inconveniencing our clients as they descend from their transports?"

Harold started at the mention of construction. They had agreed they could not afford to customize their new shop until after the profits from their next venture. Lavinia arched her eyebrow at him and he crossed his arms resolutely behind his back. "I'll just check the venting, shall I, Vinnie?" He followed along the ducting, ducking out of the room.

"A portico? Possibly," responded the landlord carefully. "I would need to approve schematics. Regarding signage, we could paint over the one up there now, certainly. If all you want is a name, my workmen can letter that for you lickety-split. As to sound-proofing." He knocked on a wall, eliciting a more or less solid thunk. "Listen to how burly a structure this is! You could explode something in here, and your neighbors would be none the wiser." He hesitated, looking cautiously at Lavinia's face to make sure he hadn't overreached himself in guessing why she inquired about noise.

"And the rent?" Lavinia asked imperiously, seemingly inattentive to the explosive remark. "We could view a few more places, but this one is adequate. How much is it?"

Although he was much experienced with the ways and wiles of renters, Lavinia wore the landlord down in the end, and he settled for a lesser sum than he had intended to demand.

ONCE THE BUSINESS WAS concluded, Lavinia and Harold waited until they were out of the landlord's hearing before allowing their glee to show. Grinning like cats with Cheshire cream, they hailed a self-propelled carriage. In the privacy of the closed conveyance, Harold hugged Lavinia, squeezing her in his exuberance, although she shushed him when he tried to talk about their coup until they were back in their old place again.

"Vinnie, you were positively magnificent!" Harold cooed, hanging up his hat and stroking back his sleek hair. "If you weren't already the best fluid engineer in the empire, I'd swear I'd nominate you for top negotiator! How ever did you know he would cave when you mentioned the portico?"

Lavinia shrugged off her cloak and shed her gloves with a satisfied air. "You saw his hands? Wouldn't know the business end of a crowbar by the looks of them. Then, when I heard him say he had a crew, I knew he would salivate at a contract for improvement work. Probably thinks he will fleece us there to make up on the rent."

Harold grabbed Lavinia's now bare hands and brought them to his lips. "Bully for you! You are incomparable, you know? Have I told you that lately?"

Lavinia rolled her eyes dramatically. "Almost daily. But I love you for it anyway. Oh, did you hear his remark when I asked about soundproofing? I could have slapped his impertinent face! As if I would ever let one of our creations go awry, much less explode."

Harold's eyes opened wide in horror. "No! The landlord said that? Must have been when I was out of the room. I would have clocked him soundly had I heard that. Maybe I should go back and do it now."

Lavinia took hold of his shoulders to redirect him. "No, there's no time to waste. We got what we wanted. A place big enough for a workshop and a presentation hall together! With upstairs for living and a basement for storage in the bargain. We are bang up the elephant now, we are! Quick, down to the old workshop with us and plan our move. I want to start tomorrow morning early."

The contrast of their current basement laboratory with the airy dwelling they had just leased was vast. Harold's fingers twitched, as if to twist a lamp knob and turn up the luminescence in the oppressive gloom.

Eventually Lavinia found her voice. "How did we manage here for so long? How could even a cogwork bird sing in this dank cellar?" She inhaled deeply and straightened her back. "Never-mind this dungeon for now, when we've so much better waiting for us. Let's celebrate!"

Harold started to shake his head, concurring with her assessment of the tired workspace, and then nodded it vigorously up and down to agree to a celebration.

"Right then. Table and chairs, up the stairs with us." She grabbed hold of Harold's hand and together they raced upward. "Tomorrow we will pack up our workspace first. Afterwards we can send a crew for the household goods." She did not stop in the scullery where the mechanized cook waited in her alcove by the warming oven, but pulled him along to the front staircase and climbed again, heading for their bedroom. "I'm too excited to eat. You?"

Harold had paused briefly in the kitchen but quickly rearranged his feet once he caught her intent. "I subsist on your desires, my honey bee," he said as they rounded to the second floor.

The heavily curtained windows protected the bedroom from any outside light, and Harold fumbled with the gas chandelier's key. A soft glow imbued the room in heavy chiaroscuro, muting colors and sharpening edges. The brass fittings of their bed gleamed and the heavy eiderdown comforter seemed like a bundle of clouds, barely substantial enough to hold them. Harold marveled as he always did how the gaslight rounded the curve of her cheek, somehow making it appear rosy and youthful, even though time had tightened it into a taut bow. Now he fitted his palm to the cup of that bow. "You," he told her, "complete me like a top hat."

Lavinia chuckled in response. "Ever so flattering, my able wordsmith. We are a good fit. Although, I think if you had your druthers, you would make me over as one of our automatons. I would be a toy for you, with cherry red circles for cheeks. Forever an ornament."

Harold grinned happily, moving to his dresser to undress. "With the finest sable fur to mimic your incomparable ebony tresses." He laughed when she rolled her eyes heavenward. "Very well, what kind of automaton would you like to be, m'dear?" He removed his collar studs and placed them in their bombazine-lined case, his collar following.

Lavinia removed her be-feathered chapeau, slotting the two long hatpins into a receptacle on her dressing table. "Higgledy-piggle! Must I be an automaton? At least make me look sophisticated and competent. Not like a child's plaything!"

Harold chortled. He detached his jet links and pulled off his cuffs. "A doll can be pretty as well as sophisticated and competent. The fusion of beauty with function is what first drew me to your father's work." Harold sat on his dresser chair to remove his spats. "I left off painting backdrops for the opera house, knowing I would be supremely happy to apprentice with him. And as you know, from it came the two proudest moments of my life. When your father added my name with his on the shop, and above all else, when you agreed to be my bride."

Lavinia was looking without seeing at her mirror, removing layers of necklaces and multiple brooches from her bosom, musing on the day's events. "Oh yes, Harold, before I forget, let me tell you. I want to move our opening to Friday a fortnight from now. Our actress with the collar-and-cuff commission will be in town, and if she were to purchase our new tableau, or any of our tableaux, we would be there with both feet!" She began the task of unbuttoning the many buttons that flowed across her ample chest and down her corseted waist.

Harold stopped struggling with the clip of his spat. "A fortnight? Vinnie, we'll never make it in time! I haven't even started on the horses' manes and tails, not to mention the bears, although I did enamel the last tiger yesterday. And what about the artificial lake? Won't that take you a month of Sundays?"

Lavinia shook her head, having expected the outburst. "Becalm yourself, Harold. For the lake, I can revamp the tank from the mermaid showcase we manufactured last year. The structure is still solid and we can set it directly over the cistern to supply the pumps." She raised her finger as he opened his mouth to protest again. "For the horses, let us cast with the manes and tails in one piece. Your animal hair creations are breathtaking, but once the whole kit and boodle are on display, no one will notice. Your effort would be under-appreciated." She shimmied out of her bodice, undoing the hooks that held it to her skirt.

9

Harold's attention was drawn to her shimmy, and his head shook in imitation, but within a few moments he recollected his derailed train of thought. "No, Lavinia, I really must put my foot down. Tiny or not, it was that kind of minutia that made your father's work so respected. That we persist in his ethos is indeed a part of why we keep our prestigious clientele." Harold, still seated, worried his last spat clip apart, slipped out of his Balmorals without unlacing them, and frowned at his stockinged feet. "This is important, Vinnie. Let's not be hasty and ruin what we have."

Lavinia unfastened and stepped out of her skirt, standing upright and almost naked in her corset, shift, petticoats, pockets, pantaloons, and gartered stockings. "Very well, I relent. We will cast the manes and use badger hair for the tails." She crossed the room to stand in front of him. "Assistance, please? My laces seem to be twisted."

Harold stopped halfway through removing his braces and stared up at Lavinia in her undressed state. "Gads, Vinnie, you are still the most alluring creature in all creation. I take back what I said. No automaton could measure up." His expression was reverent as he rose from his chair, standing in admiration of her.

Lavinia felt her insides melting. Little flames smoldered deep in her belly, licking outward. It would be the work of a moment for her to fan them to a raging bonfire. Tired as she was after the demands of the day, the weight on her shoulders seemed lighter with his praise. But this would not do. She tamped down her internal blaze to mere embers.

"Nonsense, dear Harold. All you would need to replace me would be a stick to poke you in the back when your mind wanders. Like it did today when you were ogling that harlot climbing into the steel-horse cab." She quirked her lips derisively. "Thought I didn't notice, did you?"

Harold dropped his head and stepped behind her to loosen her laces, using the motion to hide his mortification. "I had hoped you didn't," he said mildly. "My mind does tend to wander, doesn't it?" He finished with her corset, letting it slip into her waiting hands, then dropped his own braces and lowered his sit-down-upons. His shirt, no longer pressed decently to his body by his waistband, tented prodigiously in front.

Feeling her corset undone, Lavinia looked behind her, her eyes immediately drawn to his massive erection. "Now, let me think. What kind of automaton would best do to replace you?" She lifted her gaze and lifted her fingers to lightly comb his trim mustache. "Hmm-mmm?" Her questioning tone changed to one of pleasure as she stroked.

"Mmmm, yes," Harold responded, appreciating the touch of her fingertips on his upper lip. He leaned his face towards her, like a cat wanting more petting. With some forbearance he kept his hands at his side, waiting like a gentleman for permission to touch her in return.

She traced along his mustache, around the curve of his cheek and down his neck, reaching the collarless, unbuttoned shirt. "Maybe something like a hare. A sensitive, nose-twitching, unassuming animal."

"A rabbit?" His eyes opened wide and his grin grew wider. "Hopping around in bed with you, if I may be so all possessed of the vernacular?" He scrunched his upper lip, attempting to twitch his nose. "I beg you, give me leave to be your fuzzy little bunny!" He bounced up and down on his toes, jiggling in front of her.

Lavinia laughed, made aware by his request that she spoke without thinking her metaphor through. "Yes, yes, a bunny." She erased the smile and tried to look exasperated, succeeding to a small extent. "When what Kettering & Putterham needs is a lion." She traced the edge of his shirt placket, at last coming to the join and gathering the loose fabric together in her fists. "Father's reputation still holds, yes, but some call us staid and past our prime. We need an opulent spectacle." Her breath came more quickly as she gazed down appreciatively at his proud member raised in tribute to her. "Daring innovation. Modern panache. Surely you see, Harold. We must go at this full chisel."

Harold protested, both her subject and her hands stopping at his waist. "But, but, we rented the new shop today, Vinnie! Workshop, theater, and home all in one! That is a huge step forward! Let us be reasonable." His hips leaned toward her, yearning. "We aren't ready to showcase our new project." His feet inched forward, his erection preceding him. "Say it is me who delays us. I need time to design the bear fur and deck out the foreign dignitaries. Your gears and steam pumps are superlative. That strut on the peacock is spot on, Vinnie. So proudly it makes its way around the arena!" He tilted his head back, his eyes rolling in bliss, his knees buckling, as if under the weight of his heavy stick. "And the voices! One could not ask for a better chorus. Our clients will be amazed and we will sell out more than we can manufacture in a year. A dozen of them. A baker's dozen!"

Lavinia heaved a sigh, exaggerated in its audibility, and took her hands back. "That's just it, Harold. We could manufacture a half-dozen in one swoop if we line them up in the new workspace. We could sell dozens the first day and dozens more by the end of the season. It is your enameling and encaustics that impede us. Acid-etched metals and papier-mâché would be surpassingly delightful at a fraction of the time. And cost." Lavinia's fingers searched out her petticoat strings. "Our clients want our creations post-haste, Harold. The sooner, the better." Lavinia yanked, allowing her petticoats to drop, her bustle to fly free, and her shift to unblouse. "Our tableau will be a smasher, I'm sure of it. With or without manes on the chariot horses. The enamel tigers are awe-inspiring as they are. Plenty enough to draw gasps from the audience." She sidestepped the yards of fabric, kicking the wire and tape bustle structure to one side. She took Harold's hands and led them to her garters.

"But Vinnie..."

"But me no buts, Harold. It is time to assist me with my stockings." She lifted her shift to reveal her pale thighs, and then higher to show her sable slipper.

Harold knelt before her to comply, still muttering distractedly. "I worry, m'dear."

12

She waggled her hips, causing the garters to dance under his fingers. One slipped down to her ankle. "Worry about more important things now." She lifted her leg high, bringing the slipped garter closer for removal.

Harold chuckled, charmed out of his concerns by close proximity to the promises of pleasure. "Very well, stay still, or you will get us knotted tighter than I can untie with my teeth."

Lavinia laughed, prancing a little bit more in her excitement. "I can't wait. For you or your horses. Get a wiggle on!"

Deftly Harold's artistic fingers freed the remaining garter, and the both of them stood together in their muslins. Lavinia pressed Harold backward until he fell onto their bed, bowling him over, and then climbed aboard, placing first one knee and then the other outside of his thighs, so that she straddled him. Her shift bloused over his lower half like an unfurling sail. Her furry mound grazed against his upright mast.

Recalling the earlier moment when Harold's praise had kindled her arousal, Lavinia coaxed her desire to burst forth again, inciting the dormant heat inside her. Like raked-over coals, her yearning burst into flame, licking over her limbs, stoking her heartbeat, and making her breath catch in her throat.

"Harold," she murmured, raising up on her knees, gauging the staunchness of his pole against her belly, "You may touch me now."

In the dim light, unfettered from his gentleman's prerequisites, his hands groped blindly, finding and touching his beloved's tender parts, his own heart rate quickening in time with hers. With well-experienced fingers he brushed over her nipples, nudging them to fruition, hearing her sighs and groans as he navigated her courses, sailing his skin over hers. He wet his fingertips and pulled on her earlobes. He scooped his palms behind her waist and dragged her navel down to his, dashing their belly buttons together as if to fasten them. He rubbed his whiskers along her lips. Dampness accumulated in the cargo hold, under the decks made from their conjoined shirts, and in no time the

13

compartment was wet, sloshing with their mutual desire. Casting off, they put out to sea, a voyage to paradise. Lavinia's heaving met his thrusting and it was but a short slip before they were one, the tab fitted neatly into the notch, sliding in and out with the sweeping waves of their passion.

"Oh Harold, make it storm!" Lavinia exhorted him. His hips bucked higher, tossing her upward like a wind-lashed sail, only to let her drop, squelching at the bottom of the trough, her sea spray drenching his stiffened sinew and barrel-tight ballast. Her knees pressed tightly to his ribs, and she dug her heels into his rump. He clutched her voluptuous hips to keep her anchored. His rod plunged like a figurehead into her yielding wet and her cloven inlet welcomed him in a watery embrace. Harold writhed while Lavinia clung to his harrowing haunches like a master steering her vessel through the roiling tempest.

Soon they were pounding together like all get out. He stroked with the speed and strength of zealous sailors rowing for shore leave. Her trembling cove tightened, enclosing his package like cargo netting. Their short hairs were enmeshed, matted together by their salty ardor. Harder and faster and more frenzied, moment by the moment, the storm reaching its crescendo. Flesh met like, beating together, breaths shortening and growing hoarse. Gasping, shaking, and panting they pulled away toward the private island of joy just over the next wave.

Inexorably the friction between them set them ablaze, flames dancing outwards to the tips of their limbs. In a blinding roiling climax, she foundered on his rock, shattering her utterly. Her crazed cry burst forth, echoing through their bedroom's glass fixtures, shaking the joists and lintels. Torrential waves of passion rippled through her body, followed by her final grinding out against the bulkhead of her Harold's plank, and a concluding exhalation ripped all the air from her.

She slumped then, the wind slackened and the ship becalmed. Listing to one side, with tiny quivers and shakes, she subsided on top of him, melting, still holding his mast in her embrace.

Once she was quiescent above him, Harold took the final matter into his own steerage. Heavy with post-climatic inertia, Lavinia fluttered like an unfettered sheet above him, her lax fingers entwined in his hair, her unloosed tresses licking against his chest, her shuddering tunnel, still taut and honeyed, urging him to plough through the seas.

He pumped, tightening his buttocks to heave his member upward, feeling her walls pliant on all sides of his manhood, reverberating and intensifying his thrusts. Fast, forceful, and frantic he rammed his way toward his goal, giving his utmost to reach his own moment of fulfillment, rocking, pounding, gasping and groaning. At the pinnacle of his bliss, Harold cried out "Vinnie! Oh, Vinnie, how you undo me!" A final shuddering grace wracked through him, his breath imprisoned as his vital fluid gushed forth from deep within. A satisfied darkness then enveloped him, carrying him to a distant place of muted peace.

Thankfully, Lavinia thought from the fog of her post-climatic radiance, all their servants were of metal, leather, and steam, or how they might gossip on market day!

After some time, Lavinia bestirred herself. Somewhat awkwardly she lifted from off Harold's detumescent pole and rolled free. "Let's get to sleep, Harold. We must get up early if we want to move into our workshop by tomorrow night. Mustn't delay or we will miss our new deadline. I'm so excited to display our new show in a fortnight's time! Aren't you?"

If she heard his defeated sigh, she did not acknowledge it. She bounced out of bed to shut off the gaslight, and hurried to slip back under the covers warmed by their exuberant exertions.

THE NEXT MORNING A great bustle swept over the cellar as its contents were packed up for transport. Lavinia had set up a steamwork assembly line, as well as hired a handful of one-line actors from the opera house to help, the same ones she leased on past occasions to assist with grand opening exhibits. "Sebastian, would you please assist the packing robots? They do well with their geometric-fitting calculations, but they have difficulty recognizing fragile items." As the day progressed, workers of both flesh and automation shifted furniture, bundled copper pipes, and wrangled rubberized tubing. Crates were built, filled, and sent to the carts waiting on the street above. "Careful with that retort, Jebediah! It took me forever to find one that size and it is indispensable for distilling the scents we use for ambiance!" Bustling about, singing out orders, shepherding footsteps, Lavinia was at her finest and happiest, directing the show. "Keep that little Japan wax cabinet upright, Burt! It holds all the drapery pins, and no one fancies spending hours picking up piles of little harpoons." The harsh wrenching of claw hammers and crowbars tore apart furnishings built into the workroom over the years, too cumbersome to fit up the stairs or through doorways. Her capable fingers in their gaudy kid leather gloves pointed, waved, and gestured like a conductor's baton.

Harold worked sedately in his corner, slouched on his work stool. Foolscap and straw littered the floor around him. Delicately he wrapped his fine-pointed brushes and torching baskets, pots of paint and granules, stoppered bottles holding tiny gems, and sectioned boxes holding bushings, fittings, and grommets. Every so often he would pause and survey the room. By early afternoon there were significant patches of bare floor. He could discern a faded pattern of woodland animals painted on the floorboards. He had forgotten that, after all the years of mopped-up chemical spills and occasional scorch marks. Once, years ago, they had found the room charming in its eccentricities.

"Look, Lavinia, this place is like when we first moved in! Do you remember how pleased we were to find this place back then? A ramshackle tumbledown, on the edge of a nobby district." Harold sighed, his expression nostalgic. "I am going to miss this old make-do workshop."

Lavinia stopped in mid-stride. Harold's reminiscence surprised her, and her gaze traveled appraisingly over the dim cellar. "What I remember was how we counted ourselves lucky to have a space of our own. Such a disheveled hovel it seems now." She maneuvered around strewn raffia wadding and half-packed boxes to plant a quick kiss on Harold's temple. "Upward and onward for us! Once we showcase our steam-powered gladiators, K & P will be the talk of the town. Nothing but the best for us, with all those orders pouring in." She allowed herself a moment with her hands on his shoulders, shining eyes focused on the near future. Then her head jerked toward the dull thud of furniture hitting the weathered floorboards. "Whoa there, Jasper, we need to coddle that rickety table. I know it is old and battered but it has the pre-cut angles for my pipe bends and I don't want to recalculate those. No time to waste before our debut." With her bustle bows a-flying, she threaded her way through the jumble to inspect what remained on her shelves of valves, sheath covers, and couplings.

Harold took a longer time to reflect on the past before returning to dismantle the pegboard with his favorite cork hammers and precision chisels. Behind him, Jeb made a small detour as he rolled a sealed barrel of carpenter tacks. "Ho there, Harry, old chum. Your lady is a bit rammish today, don't you think?"

Harold gave the man a shrug and a smile. "She's all right. A woman in a man's world from where you see her, but my guiding angel where it counts. I'd not be where I am today without her."

"But she's putting you under the cat's foot, Harry!" Don't you see..." Jeb began, but Harold cut him off, standing abruptly, his pleasant smile grown tight. "I think it best you shift your barrel to the conveyor system for the mechanicals to pack into the moving cart. That's what I see."

Jeb stepped back from Harold's sudden spate of anger. He looked as if he wanted to argue more, but didn't know how to say what. Shrugging to himself, he bent to the barrel again. "If you say she does

17

right by you, Harry, then there's naught more I can say, is there?" He continued to mutter to himself, with phrases like "cockish wench" and "mollisher" heard only by those who were listening intently. Burt laughed heartily on hearing him. "Give it a rest, Jeb. Do you not see the dark mare is the better horse?"

By evening, the basement was bare. Lavinia sent Harold and the flesh-and-blood workers to the pub with money for dinner and ale, while she went on alone to the new shop. She nibbled on a cold pasty and marked the bare floors with rosin where a new stage would be built for their future exhibits. No more borrowing or begging from impresarios or zookeepers!

She stood on the bottom step of the stairs leading up to where their living quarters would be, chuckling to herself. Harold had asked that the bed be sent up first. She had deigned to grant his request, not telling him she had already planned on that.

THE DAYS BEFORE THE opening swept over them, an unending whirlwind of creativity and progress. The new workshop at the back of the building was light and airy, with rows of paned windows directing cheery sunlight across their vision. Cross-breezes blew vapors from hoof glue and etching chemicals out the windows. The whirring of interlocking gears and clanking of steam through constricted pipes soon proclaimed their business was busy again. Lavinia had an extra layer of padding affixed to the interior wall, not wanting extraneous noises to be heard in the front auditorium.

Renovations in the front, in fact, were proceeding at a good clip as well. Lavinia brought in swaths of tropical green velvet and Harold chose the perfect shade of azure blue for the wallpaper and trim. A sign of gilt and black with fashionable lettering proclaimed their company name, "Kettering & Putterham Steamworks," with extra flourishes on the "K," "P" and "S." Lavinia considered adding "Extraordinaire" to the end of their shop name, but in the end decided modesty would serve them just as well as braggadocio.

The seating area was designed with sumptuous carpet, tufted armchairs, and glossy mahogany tables providing ample room for refreshments and ladies' fans. If Lavinia could have thought of a discreet manner of doing so, she would have made a special nook for bankbooks.

WHEN THE PREMIERE DATE arrived, Lavinia was as tightly strung as a harp. Her state of high agitation made her cheeks glow and her eyes dance over the faces in the crowd. She placed herself at the front door, greeting clients old and new as they came in. "Good evening, Mrs. Igglesden. I do hope your daughter enjoyed her coming-out party with the phosphorescent dragonfly races on the pond? Such a clever idea to have the guests all don underwater gear to see the coral reef we built. I heard the barracuda's attack response module was set off more than once! What scamps the young are today!"

She noticed a bump in the curtain, and looked below it to see the heels of Burt's dark brogues visible at the lower edge. He must be taking a paintbrush with vulcanized rubber to the leaky riveting at the fore-edge of the water tank. Nothing like leaving it to the last minute! She fixed her smile firmly in place and addressed the next set of guests.

"Greetings, Sir James! So very glad you could attend this evening. I am just sure you will be wanting a deluxe set of what you will see tonight. It will go so well, swimmingly so to speak, with the Neptune's castle we installed for you last year. Neptune and Colossus can wave at each other from their pedestals astride the entrances!"

She glanced up at the stage again, seeing Burt's heels gone but Jasper now visible on the left proscenium with a hammer and some nails in his mouth. Merciful heavens, did she not tell Harold to leave the reinforcement till after? She did not want her guests to hear hammering. Fortunately there was a lot of chitchat among the guests, so perhaps no one would notice. The talk was loud, high-spirited, and eager. Banging aside, she could not ask for better.

"Mr. and Mrs. Betteridge, how pleasant to see you here! I do hope you will enjoy tonight's performance, however I will mention that it may not be quite to your taste. A bit, shall we say," she struck a pose to imply the heroic and sometimes comical stance of men in mock battle. "Too — Martian? Is that what they call things related to Mars, the god of war? Well, tut-tut, I should not be giving things away. Please do consider a return visit to the shop next week, when Harold will have a superb set of new songbirds. Displayed on branching candelabras. Unutterably stunning! Their enamel wings open to flutter and their golden beaks open to warble. I could sit happily in their company for hours!"

As she bantered with the Betteridges, she was thinking to herself. The bloodless hussy and her latest choice of a companion haven't bought anything from us since my father passed. As if I am not good enough. Well, let her be the dowdy thing she is, with no culminating conceit for her next stereoscopic party!

Beyond the stodgy couple, Lavinia caught sight of her much-vaunted patron alighting from a lavish carriage. Its well-crafted horses were of burnished bronze with modern-styled curves.

"Ah, there you are, Madame! We are indeed honored that you found time in your incessant schedule to attend our little pageant. Perhaps afterwards we might talk privately about your commission? In the meantime it is my fondest hope that elements in our current showcase will catch your eye."

A flap of motion from the stage caught her eye. Harold was winking at her from the stage steps and she excused herself, hurrying to his side. "Is something amiss, Harold? Why did you draw me over here?"

"Nothing to worry over, m'dear. I am just excited to see this huge crowd. And the auditorium looks splendid, like a treasure chest. With you, in that dress, as its crown jewel. Can you spare a moment for a kiss before we take our places on stage? That is to say, you on stage, and me pulling strings behind the curtain."

Lavinia ran a nervous hand down the belly of her pearl-encrusted gown, intricately cut in garnet red to stand out against the vibrant greens and blues of the decor. She preened for the length of a stage beat, then closed her fashionable fan and tapped Harold's shoulder with it. "You worried me, you evil man. I should deny you, but I want a kiss, too." She glanced to each side to see if anyone was watching, and then touched her lips to his. "The audience is nearly seated. I will see that the lights are dimmed to signal everyone to their places."

Harold smiled fondly at her receding back, watching her bustle drape flutter like a butterfly's wings with each quick step, a tiny movement that filled him, as usual, with utter delight. His tilted head and contented smile followed her in admiration before he climbed to the catwalk to await his first cue.

The lights dimmed, the audience found seats and settled, the crew cast their eyes on the lady in red. Lavinia took her place at a microphone at the edge of the stage. A limelight from the stage's apron was lit, shining upon her at a flattering angle.

"Ladies and Gentlemen, it is with great pleasure that I welcome you all to the new home of Kettering & Putterham Steamworks, and thank you for attending the premiere viewing of our latest inventions. As many of you know, it is our custom to display the new season's collection of automatons and cogworks all together in a single grand tableau, the better for envisioning how the mechanisms might interact in your own home or garden. Tonight is no exception. For your entertainment, we have created a sensational exhibit on a very grand scale." Lavinia swept her arms out in a graceful gesture toward the curtain. "We offer you now, the Colosseum of Ancient Rome!"

Behind her, the lush velveteen curtain lifted upward. Multiple layers of sheer gauze curtains were revealed, creating a hazy obstruction of the tableau, but one by one, each layer drifted off to either side, each time unveiling a little more clearly the tiny flickering torches, the streaming banners, and the gleaming marble of the archetypal colonnades evoking the classical great theatrical amphitheater of ancient days. One section of the circular array of columns was left open, cut or broken away as it were, so the audience might see the forearm-sized automatons seated on the curved marble benches, some ensconced under colorful awnings and lounging upon cushions, all frozen in the act of cheering on a half-dozen gladiators in the sand arena below, poised in the act of fighting each other with scaled-down weapons.

The people in the auditorium gasped in amazement when the spectacle was finally divulged. A spattering of applause greeted the curtain rise from those not paralyzed by wonder at the panoramic scene. Once the curtains had reached apogee behind the proscenium, the figures on stage burst into action.

At center stage were two mechanical gladiators, a cog-movement Retiarius, swinging its palm-sized net and making threatening gestures with its trident, and the foe, a Murmillo armed with a crested helmet and a stout sword the size of a 12-penny nail. They postured and feinted, arousing catcalls and shouts of encouragement from the automaton crowd in the raked marble seating. A well-aimed throw of the tossed net caught on the Murmillo's helmet's crest, dragging the hapless victim to the ground. The Retiarius ratcheted its trident upward and plunged the spikes into the downed gladiator's unprotected thigh. Inky fluid spurted from miniature balloon reservoirs in the fighter's leg.

In the mocked-up Colosseum, the automaton crowd rose raggedly to their feet, screaming in the top register of their rubber-gummed lungs through the tiny reeds of their voice boxes. The sounds were half musical, half grating cacophony. The choice of which a client would prefer — mellifluous, raucous, or some of each — was a check-box on the order form.

From the sandpit, the wounded Murmillo twisted its mechanical body and plunged its blade into the abdomen of his net-armed foe. Another burst of dark fluid sprayed, besmirching the fighters and the nearby robotic spectators with glossy dripping black.

Lavinia had faded to the side of the stage where she could watch the faces of the audience. If the ladies seemed likely to swoon, she could adjust the master actuator and restrict the amount of viscous ink they used to simulate blood in the display. Blood red was another box to tick on the form.

The Murmillo hobbled to its feet. Their gladiators' positions were now reversed, with the Retiarius on the sand, its net and trident out of reach. All mechanical eyes turned to a seated figure, robed in purple and ensconced beneath a golden canopy at one side of the stage. The emperor doll slowly raised its arm, holding his thumb sideways, ready to decide the fate of the weaponless puppet.

The emperor's arm paused in the air. A hush spread over the crowds, both on the stage and in the auditorium. Harold had crafted a thumb ring, oversized and holding a much-faceted jewel to reflect light when the hand lifted, so the thumb up or down gesture would be visible to everyone in the showroom.

To Lavinia's horror, the hand's motion seemed to stick. Had a gear lost a tooth? Had a valve become blocked leaving the mechanism without the requisite force to power the action? The hand seemed to tremble, dipping and rising again, a cogwheeling motion, as if the emperor had a sadistic streak and was toying with the fate of the vanquished. The people in the auditorium watched breathlessly. Then a rambunctious cad in the front row laughed. "Must be Caligula!" he shouted.

This set off the rest of them. Soon the showroom was a riot of gaiety and unabashed commentary. "So amazing! Very droll indeed! I must have the entire tableaux, I must!"

Off-stage, Lavinia blushed deeply. The audience might think the emperor was undecided, but she was mortified by the hitch in the doll's arm. She should have allowed a full dress rehearsal, but the schedule she set was too tight. Her forehead creased and her stomach clenched. Would her built-in redundant mechanisms activate in time? She signaled to Jasper, who had already anticipated her request, and was slipping down the trap door from whence he could manually trip the doll's hand if the fail-safe failed.

The moment passed. Blissfully the secondary lever flipped, or Jasper tripped it, and the emperor's thumb pointed heavenward. The standing gladiator offered his hand to the defeated one. Both the automaton crowd and the live audience applauded together. On the stage, puffs of air created lusty cheers. In the showroom, a polite patter of gloved hands and appreciative susurrations resounded.

Lavinia watched nervously, fearful now of another breakdown. On cue the little trap doors fell open in the sand arena. Diminutive enameled tigers leapt from their hidden cages, growling, their dramatic stripes drawing the eye. Perhaps some would have expected lions, but Kettering & Putterham chose not dull, tawny lions, but bold, attention-grabbing tigers. The gladiators all startled, those who were still standing, when the animals emerged. The moment of excitement and fear was made palpable, firmly striking home in the minds of the potential customers. Lavinia herself felt a primal thrill burst deep inside her. She scanned the faces of her clients, looking for a similar reaction, knowing those would be the ones to press for the extra expense of the abattoir level of the installation.

Once she had targeted those clients, she twisted her upper body to look up at Harold, perched on the gridiron, high above the automaton actors. A pearl of sweat had trickled down one temple, and his eyes were glued to the automated bears now lurching forth from another set of trap doors. In contrast to the flamboyant coloration of the tigers, the bears were bare steel and etched copper, gleaming in understated elegance under the stage limelights.

At the emergence of the fierce beasts, rearing and roaring with glistening long claws, the audience inhaled almost as one, dumbfounded by the sudden spectacle. The counterpoint of the enamels with the etched metal was truly engaging, as she had told Harold it would be. Again, another tick-box. A risk perhaps, in that the economy-minded would dispense with enamel, but a calculated one. Lavinia gambled that most of their clients would choose precisely what was shown on stage that night. A dozen sales just like the display would repay the expenses from the new shop and give them a cozy cushion for their future.

The audience expelled their collective gasp as one of the cog gladiators was undone by a bear paw's vicious swipe, its throat torn open and its body upright in shock for a moment. Then it fell and was limp, ink pouring out on the sand. The stage crowd on the amphitheater benches began to stand, one or two at first and then more and more, in tribute to the fallen warrior. Before long the entire automaton crowd had come to their collective feet. Phrases in the odd, voice-like squeaks seemed to say, "Well done! He died well, didn't he? Indeed the man deserves an olive wreath on his grave, I would say!"

Lavinia felt a tickle, a flicker of heat blossoming deep down inside her. All the toil, aches, and worries from the previous weeks were washed away by a wave of elation. Years before, when she had been just another pretty singer at the Pantheon, there was always a moment on stage when she could feel the audience was thoroughly enraptured by her performance. Captive to her art. Utterly in thrall to her. This time it was her automatons on the stage, but she could still sense it. That moment had arrived.

She twisted again to look up at Harold. Could he sense this engagement, too? Was he, too, uplifted by this peak moment where the audience was in their palm, happy to be lead whither they might take them? Instead he appeared relaxed, his elbows on the railing, looking down on his toy animals with a soft expression on his face. She took him in, appraising him, at this time that should be their shared triumph.

His body had grown soft and paunchy from years hunched over his workbench, and his hair, now that she gave it her attention, was sparser than in the past. Why had she not noticed how shopworn he appeared? He was hardly a fit companion for her in this new venue. In this grand exhibition of her latest innovations. Although the shop was founded on her father's achievements, from now on it would be she who took the reins and steered her company forward, building an empire of her own. The dawn of her re-invention would be marked from this exact moment. She memorized each detail so she might look back upon it, savor it, and point to it with pride.

Her eyes were drawn to Jasper, fresh from his under stage success. He gestured a thumbs-up to her, same as the automaton emperor. She smiled back, her eyes tracing down his lithe form, noting his disproportionately large hands and feet. Her imagination contemplated how those hands would feel if they unlaced her corset, and with that thought she found she could not get enough air for her next breath. Cold bricks prickled through the layers of her dress and fancy underthings as she staggered backward, up against the backstage wall. She imagined those feet, naked and intertwined with hers. Her toes pressed into the round belly of his calf as she drew one bare foot upward. She shivered, imagining his pliant skin, rough with bristling hairs, slipping beneath the silky, pampered skin of her sole as it inched upward, caressing the divot behind his knee, tracing along the rope-like muscles of his thigh, fitting into the crease below his buttock.

It was dimly that she noted the gladiators' final thrusts and the beasts' last swipes, leaving the arena sand strewn with bodies. Chariots carrying toga-clad workers entered from the wings to remove the litter, the brass horse manes glinting and squirrel-hair tails twitching.

Customers rustled in their seats, some thinking the performance was concluding. Women took up their fans and gentlemen reached into their pockets for pipes. When the last chariot was withdrawn, a low-pitched clang reverberated throughout the large room, and a series of large slits opened up under the sand. Deep rifts were now clearly visible, running from one side of the stage to the other, and the arena sand was slithering rapidly through them, revealing a marble mosaic floor of birds in fruit trees. The audience's hubbub was heightened with whispered guesses of what would come next. Off in the wings, workers stood ready with buckets of fire retardant should the next act get out of hand.

Still leaning against the wall, gripped by inchoate emotions, Lavinia felt the clanging on stage as if her own body was opening, shifting, and realigning for a new venture. She watched Burt take his place behind a painted backdrop, in readiness to haul away the hidden panels for the final act. His vigorous frame and deeply-ridged musculature were displayed to great advantage by the tight black clothing he wore backstage, with nothing loose that might catch in the rigging or traps. Grasping the pulley ropes with his stalwart arms, strong enough to play the part of a blacksmith or stevedore, he poised attentively, waiting for his cue, his sculpted form tensed for action. He glanced across at her in the heartbeat moment of readiness; tension and triumph clear on his face.

Lavinia was drenched anew with fresh desire, anticipation near bursting within her groin. She gave the man an ardent nod, her inward vision reeling recklessly. In her imagination, his gladiator's body was clad in the briefest of coverings, with those capable arms drawing her to him, his battle-hardened hands finding their way across her enticing breasts, his fingers pinching her nipples to plump attention. She redirected his palms to cup under her buttocks, and her legs trembled within his firm grasp.

27

A rumble was felt through the entire building. The startled cries from the audience tightened Lavinia's innards like a coil twisted by a wind-up key. The floor openings clanged shut and the corbeled edges of the arena floor revolved on an enormous gear beneath the stage, slotting into place, displaying previously hidden channels. There was the sound of a dozen shuttle valves opening at once and water gushing through. Liquid the color of the Aegean rushed in torrents to fill a stage-sized sea.

In short order the arena was full and Burt, his rough hide gloves gripping the rigging with great surety, hauled hand over hand to lift two panels at the back of the arena just at the water line, revealing canals from which two lines of Roman-style triremes emerged, their thin wooden hulls bobbing across the still turbulent waters. They were adorned with brightly colored sails, one set in marine blue and the other blood red. Once the ships cleared the opening, Lavinia's gaze flickered to Burt's robust chest and lingered there, watching his pectorals ripple beneath the dark fabric as he lowered the panels back into place, hauling hand under hand, using his body as a counterweight. Now there was a lion for her! His wavy hair and full beard flowed like a lion's mane around his visage. After the show she would engineer customized lifts for the boats' access, but for tonight, Burt would do.

Lavinia let her imagination ponder exactly how Burt would do. In the midst of a Roman orgy, he procured a ripe peach, holding it to her mouth as an offering. Her own juices flowed freely, as luscious as the fruit. She bit into the aromatic flesh, then pushed the soft-furred globe aside so she might bring the sweet morsel between her lips to his, sharing the nectar between them.

On the stage, each set of ships made their way to opposite sides of the arena, their mechanized sailors rowing in stately unison on the miniature oars. From each lead ship, an automaton stood up, wearing a gleaming brass helmet with a horsehair crest. Both drew trumpet shells from their groin guards and blew a strident set of notes. Lavinia had intricately tuned the leather of the tiny bellows so that they would peal out clear and consistent tones in exact harmony. This tiny, tinny detail had near driven her to distraction, but she had persevered. Arisen one more time than she had fallen. The fanfare to war rang out, clear and insistent over the lapping of the gentle waves.

She felt herself growing buoyant, jubilantly rising toward a doubled culmination of her artistic triumph and her tempestuous fantasy. Lavinia and her Burt kissed, tasting the succulent fruit melting between their lips, their tongues stretching out for more, drawn to each other's, intertwining, her breath as one with his. Around them, writhing revelers were pushing and pressing upon each other, reclined on benches, propped up against walls, and sprawled heedlessly on the floor. Lavinia savored the mingled scents of spiced wine and conjoined juices, the fevered moans, and the rhythmic thumping all around them. She squirmed closer to him, their tongues still groping, her uplifted orbs bumping into his firm chest, her ruby hard nipples almost piercing his skin through her sheer silken garb. She grabbed handfuls of the firm flesh of his buttocks, digging her nails in, clutching him to her. Her fingers marked his skin as they climbed up his backbone.

The trumpeting heralded the start of the sea battle. Stones the size of toy marbles and thimble-sized pots of blazing pitch were flung by miniaturized ballistas across the water towards the opposing fleet. Javelins were tossed, some finding their mark. Archers sent fleets of arrows flying, landing in a swath of upraised prickles along deck planks, taking out a line of sailors across the ranks of enemy ships. Shouts of triumph and dismay squeaked and bubbled from the automatons on their pitching ships.

Lavinia's fingers grabbed hold of the fine fabric of his tunic, rending it from his body. He jerked back, startled momentarily by her action, but then the smile on his face grew fierce. The intensity of his touch matched hers, impactful, his fingers spreading open and squeezing her flesh under the frail chiton. He ripped the thin covering,

29

tossing it aside, pressing skin to skin. Her fingertips scrabbled across his scalp, tangled into his hair, and pulled hard to bring his mouth back to the fury of her waiting lips. His body followed, and she could feel his manhood prodding her below.

Relentlessly the ships lurched across the water, heaving toward their opponents, jostling for position. Hurled firepots sent curls of smoke and tongues of flame rising. Ships were listing, having taken on water from well-aimed missiles. Waves splashed high into the air and sloshed over the rim of the theatrical sea. Residual droplets spewed out over the auditorium.

Lavinia felt Burt's arms tense around her hips. She raised up on tiptoe so that she might look directly into his eyes, dark mirrors in which she saw herself reflected, a frenzied goddess to match his god-like physique. She dropped one arm, sweeping down his side, swiping away the remaining slivers of cloth covering his upthrust staff and her dripping quim. Her fingers curled around his unleashed member.

The soldierly sailors armed themselves with petite foil shields and unsheathed their toy-sized but redoubtably stout swords. Weapons struck their targets. Punctured and burnt automatons leaked midnight blue ink as they tumbled into the seething turquoise water. Paper sails and wooden boats blazed and crackled. The hulls, soaked in finely distilled bergamot and geranium oils, released perfumed smoke in clouds above the warring crews.

Lavinia brought her bedewed thatch of dark hair to Burt's elongated column, looking down to see its engorged head, looking like a burnished helmet or a battering ram, flushed red and latticed with purple veins. Her body shivered, yearning for engagement. Burt's strong arms lifted her to the right height for their middles to meet.

Ships slammed into each other, tossed on the tempestuous waves, thrusting their proud prows through their enemy's exteriors. Spars snapped. The groans of rending wood and felled warriors resounded to the rafters. Sword clanged in volleys of thrusts and parries until the dull thud of pierced flesh punctuated the final point. Painted shields were scorched and dented. Sailors resorted to their daggers and fists. Soot rained down.

Lavinia guided his ramming rod to her entrance, toying with him, brushing her fragrant folds along his tip, rolling her hips, rubbing up and down. In her imagination, her voice was husky. "Are you as ready as I am, my warrior?"

The auditorium audience was nearly as riotous as the automatons on the stage, with frenzied shouts, pointing fingers, harsh whispers, and fearful shrieks. The spectacle seized the audience by their collective throats, pulling them all roughly into the midst of the battle. Men jerked their shoulders as if it were themselves who heaved the javelins and cleaved the enemies with their swords. Women ducked when a blow struck close, parrying with fans and the toes of their fashionable shoes.

Lavinia's mind and body were given over to her gladiatorial version of Burt, who vocalized his readiness with a tomcat yowl, taking a steely hold on her roiling hips to keep them in one place long enough for him to plunge into her. Her head tipped back in hunger and triumph. She met him thrust for thrust.

On stage and off, all was turbulence and tumult. The audience felt arrows shave past their arms and flames bite their feet, as blasts of cold and hot air spurted from concealed vents under the chairs. Panels built into the floor shook under the influence of pneumatic pistons. A massive wooden rocker in the basement below rolled a barrel full of jumbled iron scraps back and forth, providing gruesome crashes and crunches as the battle warred on.

Jagged shards of lust tore through Lavinia's chest along with Burt's determined, firm stabbing below. "More, my Hercules, more!" she urged, clutching him to her, hanging on with all her might. "Give me more!" Her breath was harsh, and her heart was beating too hard and fast to count. She could feel him straining, his marble column pounding against her sanctuary with a furious intensity, giving her the more she begged for. She wrapped one leg and then the other around his waist, held in place now by his stupendous prick deep within her vault. Her muffled cries of "more" turned unintelligible, morphing into a keening of undefined syllables of need and wild, unassuaged hunger.

At her peak, the on-stage crescendo of splashes and explosions drowned out her rising vocalization of exaltation, the furor of the performance an echo to her own precipitous release. Her eyes rolled upward. Her Burt gasped a final cry and stabbed his culminating strokes, unleashing all within him, a fitting tribute to his Venus. Her climax flashed over, wrenching from her the final ecstatic moan as she passed through the gates into Elysium. Her body was left behind, weak-kneed and leaning on the backstage wall, utterly spent.

On the stage, most of the boats had burned down to the water line and the rest were capsized hulks. The bittersweet scent of burnt paper and wet wood ash lingered on the air. An eerie stillness was all that remained, with lifeless bodies bobbing in the discolored water of the artificial sea. Stunned silence ruled.

It was the scented vapor seeping into Lavinia's faculties that brought her slumped body, adrift in luxuriant bliss, back to its place and time. Her flesh became conscious of the rough bricks tearing at the velvet pile of her dress. She was surprised to find herself alone, but joyously satisfied.

The audiences, on stage and off, had been stunned by the final furor of the battle and its aftermath. Slowly they recovered their senses. The cogwork crowd revived first, all rising to their feet. They jumped, called, and clapped their undersized hands, applauding the devastated scene. Harold poised over the master switch, waiting while the puppets expressed a suitable tribute to the brave warriors. Then with a flick of his finger, they fell down lifeless as well. The stage lights faded, as if the sun was setting. The seawater could be heard quietly lapping. The show was over.

Thunderous applause ensued, for once the live audience applauding louder and more fervently than the automated one had done. Lavinia brushed her hand over the coils of her hair, as if she could tame her unfettered passion like an out-of-place lock. She pushed herself up and stood firmly on her feet. This was her cue. She was ready.

She signaled for the sheer curtains to be drawn over the scene. One of the draperies shimmied as it struck a rough spot in the less then well-greased pulley. There was a momentary drop in the smile Lavinia was readying for the final bow, but she recovered and marched to center stage triumphantly, one hand held out to Harold as he entered from the opposite side. They met center stage, with a brief look into each other's eyes, carefully rehearsed, before they both turned and bowed. Determined to allow no excuse for decrement of her talent, she did not curtsy. In tandem with Harold, they accepted accolades as equals in their joint creation. Presenting her face to her audience, her smile enchantingly full and triumphant, she fantasized it was another hand in hers. A more determined hand. A more provocative one.

Bouquets and blooms from gentlemen's boutonnieres and ladies' corsages were flung onto the stage. Harold bent to retrieve an orchid and sniffed it appreciatively, his smile benevolent, his joy in the audience's tribute evident. He offered the flower to Lavinia, but she was still looking out at the applauding masses, her eyes bright and gaze fixed. Instead he tucked the blossom in his lapel. They appeared a perfect couple.

As they bowed again and blew kisses, she was listening for the slightest reduction in the patter of gloved applause. Once she heard it, she dragged Harold with her to the microphone. "Ladies and gentlemen," she proclaimed, "you are now welcomed on stage to inspect our Cogwork Colosseum up close." She waved her hand airily, as the signal for the curtains to open again. "Please ask any questions that come to you," she shouted over the squeaks of the pulleys and the clamor of people taking to their feet and exclaiming amongst

33

themselves. "We are taking orders tonight, and the first tableau will be available for installation," she paused for effect, waiting for faces to turn to her in anticipation, "this very instant! We have a limited number of models already built, available for delivery at your convenience. Hurry! Be the envy of the season at your next weekend fete or masquerade ball!"

Lavinia made her way against the surging crowd, pausing for handshakes and accolades, to the order desk near the front doors, where she had stationed two suggestively toga-clad assistants. Brisk business began to take place as people finished inspecting and gathered around the attendants, eager to make purchases. Plumed quills scratched. Pages turned. Lavinia's pupils enlarged as the piles of filled forms grew tall. Harold brought Lavinia a champagne flute. She smiled mechanically, taking a sip and putting the glass down where it would not interfere with commerce.

"Did you feel it, m'dear?" Harold stood beside her and leaned in to whisper with his lips close to her ear. "Such excitement! I was nearly overcome by the furor of the final battle and the audience applause, weren't you?" His eyes followed along the milling crowd of clients, forming themselves into a semblance of a queue. "Tonight we are the phosphate soda with a cherry on top!"

Lavinia nodded, keeping her eyes on the line, but her lips curled upward when Harold crowed about excitement. "I felt it, yes. We will be the talk of the town!" She snatched up a blank form and nudged a clerk to give her writing space at the order desk. "I'll take whoever is next. Mrs. Rutlege? I'm guessing you want the entire works. Down to the black ink for blood? Or would Mr. Rutlege prefer vermilion for verisimilitude?" She tapped the boxes on the form with the pen point. "Enamel for the beasts? Did you find it too loud for you? We can modulate both the crowd sounds and the music." She lowered her voice to confidentiality level, but still easily heard despite the crowd's tumult, "You know, for you, Harold could add more well-placed jewels. Say in

34

the crown of the emperor and diadems of the foreign princes? We offer embroidered banners as well as the plain ones we used tonight. We hurried things to open, with the new shop and all, but I seem to recall you like the way silver thread glitters in your moonlit pavilion. Wouldn't that incite the envy of everyone at the club?"

A childish shriek was barely heard over the gossip and banter, but then an ear-piercing squeal cut through the crowd's nattering. "It has my handkerchief! Ow, it bit my finger!"

The crowd hushed. Almost everyone looked up and around for the source of the cry. Only Lavinia kept her head down, finishing the notation on the current order before lifting her head.

It was Harold who found his feet first, followed swiftly by several of the stagehands. A silly young woman had climbed up the scaffolding and tussled with a backup gladiator until she sprung its mechanism. Its spear had thrust outward, protruding through her handkerchief and glove, pricking her fingertip, drawing a drop of blood.

"Here, little one, let me help you," Harold spoke reassuringly, grabbing the handkerchief with one hand and the spear in the other. "Some of the spears are barbed to draw forth the entrails of their opponents. Beastly perhaps, but highly effective." Harold perched precariously with one foot on the outer scaffolding and the other on the plasterboard railing they had jury-rigged to balance the marble-faced benches. It was not a very sturdy arrangement. Adequate for the showcase, but no more. Harold had already made a note to reinforce it before setting it out for permanent display.

The girl jumped back once she was freed, clattering down the scaffolding, her weight and motion causing a distinct teetering of the entire arena. Harold balanced himself on the tenuous step. He must right the structure before it all went tumbling down.

All too late! The back wall of the amphitheater unbalanced and collapsed, knocking Harold into the pit, which just barely accommodated his moderate frame. The fall loosened the water valve, and more liquid began to pour in.

"Harold!" Lavinia was heard to shout above the general din. She rushed over to the structure, for once leaving an order unattended. Unmindful of her new dress, she jumped up to the stage and climbed up two rungs of the proscenium ladder to get a better view of her husband's predicament. Seeing him in only in six inches of water and apparently sound, she hissed. "Harold, stand up immediately before you damage the plumbing!"

Hopping down from the ladder, with irritation evident, she bent over the prostrate Harold, grabbing hold of his cuff, just as he was rolling over to right himself. From Lavinia's recumbent posture, she was unable to prevent his movement from pulling her also into the pit.

For a moment she could only feel overwhelming chagrin that Harold had made her look ridiculous, and moreover ruining her new gown. 'Oh will he ever get a dressing down tonight!' was her first thought. Her second thought was lost in shock. The marble mosaic tiles proved inadequate for the unexpected weight of two human-sized bodies. The floor broke through. They sank into the tank beneath the waterworks. A full cistern. Deep like they made them in the old days. Deep enough to drown.

Harold's hand scrabbling for purchase had caught hold of the metal infrastructure, which kept his head above water, but Lavinia was unmoored when the floor gave way. Her heavily bejeweled gown, now heavily drenched with the simulated seawater, drew her inexorably to the murky depths of the tank.

Screams, expletives, and wails were all lost to Lavinia's hearing. In the soft darkness of the tank, everything was muffled, disembodied, and emasculated. But she did not feel bereft, for the darkness cradled her. The inky cold water snuggled up to her, held her tightly, more closely even than a lover, seeping through her layered armory of costly fabrics, caressing her skin, kissing her lips, pushing them apart to enter her, envelop her, overcome her. The pool was taking her into its very element, to make her one with it.

Without hesitation, Harold pinched his nose and dove into the deep after her.

The following morning's deadlines heralded the calamity. Tragic Loss of Partner at Kettering & Putterham Steamworks. Funeral Saturday next. Surviving partner, Lavinia Kettering-Putterham, announces there will be little to no delay in honoring current commissions.

A FEW MONTHS LATER, a well-endowed woman dressed in the latest incarnation of Parisian fashion was marching down the pavement in her usual determined manner. Passersby might overhear her talking to her companion, a natty fellow in a stylish top hat and morning coat, struggling to keep pace with her.

Lavinia stopped suddenly and faced her husband. "Harold, please don't dawdle, you know how I hate to be late." Her keen eyes roved over him from head to toe. "Remind me to buy you new boots. Those are showing wear on the heels."

Harold hopped a half step to halt when she unexpectedly turned to him. "Yes, m'dear Vinnie. I must look a fitting companion for an accomplished lady such as yourself." He reached for her hand with both of his, forgetting as usual that public displays of affection were as tawdry as worn heels.

Lavinia leaned back, away from his outstretched arms. "Harold, must you? Sometimes I don't know where your mind is! Now, may we concentrate on business, please? At the copper monger's shop, let me do the talking. I'm sure we will find something acceptable to make bristles for the hedgehogs. Enameling spines would be time-consuming and not all that showy for the effort, don't you agree?"

Harold's gaze wavered from his wife to a flutter of movement across the street. A cheeky dollymop had stepped out of the alley with her skirt still tucked up in her garter. The display of her lower leg was mute testament to her occupation. His mechanical eyes whirred as he focused his gaze on her ankle. Reflexively his miniaturized pneumatic pistons primed.

"Quite right, m'dear. Just so," he answered Lavinia's question. A cascade of cogs engaged to bring his neck, eyes, and the semblance of attention back to his beloved.

"Very good, then," Lavinia nodded decisively and took hold of Harold's innovative marvel of an automated arm to turn him around in the proper direction. "Take care that you do." She grimaced, wondering to herself if he would ever assimilate the tenets of proscribed propriety.

It was then that a dazzling smile broke from her, and despite her unwavering adherence to societal conventions, she could barely restrain herself from kissing his cheek in public. After the accident, when he saved her life at the expense of his own, she had engineered him from the original, down to the tiniest particular, so that he would be the same Harold that he always had been. For her, he was, and would always be, achingly perfect.

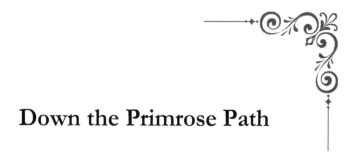

Down the Primrose Path

Down the Primrose Path

ETTA PICKED UP HER skirt to step up into the cab of the stylish metal carriage with its richly enameled horses. She lifted her layers of blue fabric and lace-rimmed petticoats high in order to clear the step, exposing her cloistered ankles and the hint of a shapely calf. This exposure caught the eye of a gentleman across the street and she smiled lasciviously at him, extending an invitation. Etta almost laughed when he ducked his head in embarrassment.

She had used both hands to display her wares, but dropped one side to accept the assistance of the carriage driver, who had dismounted from his perch to hand her into the compartment. "Thank you kindly, coachman. Mr. Fernsby must be quite the fine gentleman to own a vehicle of such splendor and a driver of such courteous comportment." She displayed her dimples, pretending she was unaware of how much interdict territory she was presenting below. She was measuring the length of his distracted stare, waiting for him to return his attention to her smile.

"Most welcome," the coachman replied, bringing his gaze back to eye level. Once she and her skirt were tucked in, he latched the door firmly. Etta felt the carriage springs sway slightly as he mounted to his post and heard his gentle 'gee-up' to the steam-powered horses. The conveyance lurched forward as the mechanized animals sprang to obey his command.

The man's evident skill impressed her. Jarvies of public steam carriages tended to bark harsh commands and crack whips like of old, when flesh and blood horses provided the power. This man spoke barely above a whisper to engage the voice-activated beasts. Such a refined contrast. Funny how she had never thought of that before. Hackney drivers were famous for shouting, blustering, and raising a rumpus. It was odd to think that in time, people would forget that.

Cocooned in the muffled quiet of the swaying cab, Etta fell into anxious anticipation of the venture ahead of her. She was to visit a gentleman, one Mr. Ellsworth Fernsby, who might become her benefactor if she were to be found desirable. Success would mean fewer nights of hunger and bone-cracking cold. Failure might mean — well, it would not do to think more on that. She opened her reticule and inventoried its contents. A mostly clean handkerchief, a few coins of small denominations, and a comb to tidy up loose locks afterwards. She didn't need much. She didn't have much. What she had was hope of returning with a silver coin. Or even coins! She would owe half to Mrs. Lought, the go-between and bawd, for arranging the assignation, but still, that would leave her with more than she garnered in the disreputable back room of the Whistle and Wish public house or the dangerous shadows of the alleys outside.

The carriage made a number of turns from one dark street into another before the frequency of street lamps shining through the curtains hinted they had reached a refined section of town. She peeked out. The road was broad, the granite sett stones freshly laid, and lamps were stationed on every block. A tony section of town for sure! The carriage rattled on, the horses' metallic hooves sounding bright and brittle on the unsullied road. Etta had time to work her stomach into a knot for fear she had overreached herself when the coachman's quiet 'whoa' brought the assemblage to a graceful halt. She consciously relaxed her grasp on her reticule. By the time the coachman unlatched the door, she had recomposed herself.

A grand stretch of fencing separated the mansion from the pavement, and the walkway leading from the gate to the door seemed lengthy. The coachman handed her out of the carriage and gestured for her to precede him. She walked along the broad flagstones towards the house, with him a courteous step behind her and to the right. In the gloom of the evening she could barely make out the garden beds that flanked the walk, but she could smell roses, heliotrope, and balsams, as well as something else that was exotic and spicy. "Mr. Fernsby keeps a handsome place," she remarked, not at all sure if a compliment was expected or whether her understatement would be suitable.

The coachman grunted softly. He was not rude, but she guessed she had not hit the right tone. At the front portico she stopped and turned to him. "This door?" she inquired, not expecting to be admitted through the front. She nearly asked how to find the service entrance when the man stepped in front of her momentarily, knocked a rhythmic tattoo with his knuckles, and stepped back again. The door was opened instantly by a wizened butler in livery. Evidently he had been behind the door, expecting her. "Good evening, Miss," he bowed his head to her, his eyes resting unwaveringly at the level of her chin. "Do please come in." The coachman was neither greeted nor acknowledged.

The butler took her cloak and bid her follow him down a grand hallway. "The master has been delayed by a small business matter, but he shall be along directly. Tea is set out for your refreshment. And if you feel in need of something stronger," he broke off and coughed delicately. "A maid will be along with an assortment of imbibables." He opened a set of double French doors, directed her inside, and bowed himself out, closing the doors with practiced deference.

Alone, Etta twirled herself around, taking in all the room's splendor, her face flushing with wonderment. She was so amazed she forgot to worry that she would slip up and let it be known this was her first ever visit to a gentle home. The wallpaper was not peeling, and a large and clean rug covered the floor. No scurrying rat feet dared skitter through this room! She allowed herself a brief daydream of living as a wife in watercolors, but it was far too early to parlay such thoughts. She must keep her wits about her, matching her entertainment to the client's desires, and even anticipating them if she could manage it.

She approached the high-backed Chesterfield, admiring its tufted, mustard-colored upholstery and soldierly line of brass tacks. She imagined possible scenarios, and then seated herself a little off to one side. From whence she could recline gracefully over a plush armrest, or lean inward should the gentleman sit beside her. A sudden thought struck her and she stood again, checking underneath the apron railings for metal rings that might hold ropes. None such. A pity, she thought. I am rather good at those scenes. She fluttered her lashes and looked downward, practicing the pose of a demure maiden in some measure of distress.

Her eyes then fell on the tea service, and she admired the elongated silver pot and thin-walled porcelain cups. She would tremble if she tried to pour, and it would not do to spill. Sitting again, she surveyed the room's intricate kickshaws with her eyes alone, too apprehensive to touch. A maid was due to return with some tipples. A good knock-back might calm her frayed sensibilities.

On a nearby table was a sculpture of an air balloon, made mostly of bronze but with netting of braided floss. In the basket were two stuffed mice, dressed up in leather caps and goggles, one holding a diminutive spanner in its tiny grasp, and the other looking up, little forepaws attending to the rigging. Etta had heard of such tableaux of animal taxidermy. How endearing it was! She could see a plaque, but not make out the letters from her seat. Not that her paucity of reading skills would assist her much. Was it a trophy of some sort? If it had a date on it, she might judge how long ago it was since the gentleman was lithe enough to fly. Resolutely she remained on the sofa. Soon enough she would see the man himself.

Next to the balloon trophy was an astronomical clock with painted planets affixed onto wires which were manipulated by a series of many-stepped gears. Nearby rested a contraption she thought might be a music player with a curved horn. Standing off to one side of the sofa, under the pellucid teardrops of a ponderous chandelier, was a brass tube on a tripod. Would that be one of those camera things? Oh wait! That must be a telescope, like at the Royal Observatory. Scaled down to parlor size. Perhaps the gentleman looked at stars at night. Or maybe at his neighbors, naughty boy! Etta was curious and longed to take a peek, but still she kept to her place. Glancing at the doors to make sure she would not be seen, she pulled up her skirt and scratched an itch on the inside of her knee.

After a few moments of intense listening, hearing no footsteps in the hall, Etta turned her eyes to study the numerous gilt-framed paintings, which crowded the wall in the style of homes whose owners had the wherewithal to collect too many of them. There were a few pastoral landscapes and *nature morte*, but mostly portraits. Mostly of dour, elderly men. She supposed it was hard to smile for all the hours an artist required. Perhaps the family's pretty young women were too impatient to sit still. What with parties to attend and other grand events which Etta could but dimly fathom.

Presently a timid knock sounded. The crisply-dressed maid nudged the door open with the leading edge of a great silver tray, weighed down by three crystal decanters, two port glasses, two snifters, and two squat tumblers. Etta half-rose from the sofa to assist the girl, but quickly plopped her backside down again, remembering Mrs. Lought said to act like a guest until she was alone with the gent. She could see the girl had strong arms and a resolute expression as she focused on her duty.

"Lovely, dearie. Ta," she said in tones she hoped would sound as if she were accustomed to such service. Despite the weight of the tray straining her flexed arms, the maid placed it down gently so it did not clatter. "You're welcome, Miss," she said in a hushed whisper and curtsied with her head down, either with discretion or shyness. Etta could not tell which. Quickly the maid turned and almost fled the room.

"Well!" Etta huffed out loud to the hastily vacated parlor. "I certainly scared her! I wonder she's never seen laced mutton before?" She poured herself a large splash of one of the brown liquids and drank it off quickly, wincing at the slight burn, marking how much milder it was than the burn than she was used to. She availed herself of another tot, and unable to sit still anymore, paced around the room with glass in hand.

Initially she was only going to look. A painting above the fireplace showed a stern-faced fellow with an old-fashioned beard. Handsome if not for the frown. If he were the present owner's ancestor, at least she would have something nice to look at. Knowing her luck, however, he would likely be infirm. Young bucks came out to the houses and theaters to get their jollies, whereas the established could do what they liked in their own homes.

Absently her fingers petted the sleek neck of a greyhound statuette under the painting, forgetting she was not going to touch. She returned to the balloon sculpture, now able to see the plaque on the basket. Yes, a trophy. She picked out the date, struggling with the subtraction, using her fingers. Eleven years ago. What state would he be in now?

Beyond, she noticed a Tesla globe on a credenza. What fun! Playfully she put down her emptied glass and removed one of her borrowed gloves to place a finger on the surface, laughing as the lightning inside sparked towards her touch. She tried to trick it by touching more than one finger, then her entire palm. Unbuttoning her other glove, she poised forefingers from both hands on opposite sides. The door opened behind her and she jumped, turning abruptly to the door, her fingers still outstretched.

It was the coachman.

"Sorry to startle you," he grinned at her, amused by her fingers still frozen in the act. "I have been sent to let you know our master is further delayed. I am to offer you refreshment." He tilted his head to the side table, indicating the tray. "I see Minerva has brought liquid revivification. Would you like a cold plate? We had an excellent roast for dinner that would slice up well with some of Mrs. Button's flakiest of all yeast rolls." Calm and attentive, with his eyes fixed on hers, he waited on her decision.

The thought of meat was enticing, as her last meal of new cheese and old bread was quite some time ago, but she demurred, her insides still twisted with apprehension. "That is tempting, but no, no thank you. I should not want to be overfull when the gentleman is ready for me."

The coachman laughed heartily, his polished mannerisms and stiff formality completely discarded. "Not to worry, moppet. We can feed you and wipe the grease off your chin well before Mr. Fernsby makes in this direction. Let's eat! I could do with a sandwich myself." He marched over to the bell cord beside the fireplace and pulled it briskly a few times, more than was necessary. Moments later the young maid threw open the doors in her haste to answer the urgent summons. Her servile expression changed to one of exasperation when she saw the room's two occupants, and she straightened up from her half-cringing posture. "Thaddeus, you scamp! Why pull that poor bell off its hinges when y'er no better than me in this house? Get your own blamed what-suits-you, and leave off giving yourself airs!"

The coachman's laughter was gleeful. "Don't be disgruntled, Minnie! Master told me to offer the young lady a plate, and you know how Cook gets when she finds me in her larder. Bring enough for two, will you? And some of those devilishly delicious pickles that Buttons put up last week, won't you?" He stands up and executes a proper bow for her benefit. "I will be forever in your debt," he intoned in mock solemnity.

The maid glared at him, her look blistering, but then she brightened up in reluctant amusement. "I wish I could stay angry with you, Tad, but it isn't in me. Ploughman's plate for two, then." She gave the doorknobs a flick as she passed through, letting the doors swing shut behind her with a brusque flapping sound.

Thaddeus pretended to wipe his hands after a strenuous task. "There. All set. You can go back to fingering the trinkets if you like."

Her cheeks coloring, Etta sat primly in the center of the sofa, her hands folded in her lap.

"Oh, don't be like that. Come over here and help me mock this portrait of Mr. Fernsby's uncle. What a broken cog he was!"

Etta fiddled with her gloves, meticulously lining up one on top of the other, letting it be known she was not to be drawn out.

"Very well. Let me begin again." He crossed the room and positioned himself in front of her. "Good evening, my good woman. My name is Tad. My presence and sole purpose in life currently is to serve you. Pray guide me with respect to how best I might perform said service?" He made an elaborate bow, bending low before her, one hand palm up and offered to her.

Deliberately she swiveled her head to the side, refusing to acknowledge him or his previous hurtful remark.

Ostentatiously he rearranged his feet and bowed again, offering the other hand. When she remained cold, again and again he repeated the action until it became comical, and he resembled nothing so much as a prancing pony.

Etta pressed her lips together, but soon could not prevent an upturning of her mouth.

"Ah, a smile! Then I am forgiven." Tad plopped himself down on the sofa beside her, sitting a bit closer than a gentleman should. "I'm so glad. I like you and would loathe to have you think ill of me." He looked into her eyes a moment longer than a gentleman should. "As I may have mentioned, my name is Tad. And your name, bright angel?"

Her lips were still pressed together. "Etta. I mean, Henrietta. You may call me Henrietta. And you may bleach away any notion that you will get any. Everything, and I do mean everything, is for the man who will pay me." She held his eyes, far longer than a lady should. "You understand me?"

Tad nodded slowly up and down. "I understand, Etta. Doesn't mean we can't have a bit of a lark while we wait." He pointed to the portrait he mentioned earlier. "For instance, Mr. Everett Fernsby. The master's paternal uncle. Such a story! Poor master had a bad time of it, growing up in his shadow. For you see, Everett was a Cambridge man, and our master was sent down from Harrow at a tender age. Mind you, Everett was not what one would call a great success in the business of life. Forever chasing some untenable theorem, spending his days tinkering with unsuccessful inventions."

Tad stood, making come-along motions with his fingers to encourage her to join him. When she kept to her seat, still sulking, he shrugged and moved over to the portrait alone. "I give you here the inventor of the automatic shoe-blacking automaton. Which tended to put more polish on the floor than the shoes. A toaster that cooked bread and rashers at the same time. Both were charcoal when his invention finished with them." He looked pointedly at Etta. "It's all right, Etta. You can laugh. Just remember to laugh again if Mr. Fernsby tells you the story himself."

Etta, although frowning at the use of her nickname, could not help a giggle escaping.

"That's it! What a sweet little laugh you have there! Will you let me hear more? Can you chortle perhaps? Chuckle? Titter? Snicker? Roar even? Let me tell you about the time Everett decided to impress his fiancée with a love token. The box was supposed to spring open and a metal hand was to offer her a bouquet of enameled posies. Well, it sprang open all right! It sprung all to pieces, flinging coils and cogs at the unfortunate lady. Did I mention Everett never married?"

A blurt of laughter sprung forth from Etta, just as the doors burst open, parted by a hip bump from the little maid carrying a tray with covered dishes. "Don't just stand there like a scobberlotch, Tad," she scolded, holding the weighty tray in the doorway. "Come and take these plates from me hands."

Etta hopped up to help, but Minnie quickly shook her head and drew back. "No, no, Miss. You is company," she said grandly. "You look ever so pretty, by the way, in that flax flower blue color. Don't muss yourself. Tad is a right sight capable of shifting this lot." She handed the tray off to the coachman and wiped her hands on the inside of her apron. "Eat hearty!" she addressed Etta. "The master tends to need plenty of time. Best not run short of energy." She winked and was gone.

Tad brought the tray down with a bang on the side table. "Bird-witted goose. Should've brought a trolley. And as for the master taking time, the old cock couldn't get up with a derrick. All you gotta do is rub it a bit until he falls asleep." He buttered a slice of bread fiercely and snagged two thick slices of roast to go on top, dropping the assemblage on a plate. With the same knife he speared several gherkins and lifted them out to join the sandwich. "Here you go, Etta. Tuck in! You might not need fortitude, but patience takes some substantial sustenance too, I say." He pushed the filled plate towards her, his knife already moving towards the butter again. "Idle time is wearisome. So unsatisfying, don't you think?"

Etta frowned at his suggestion of satisfaction, but the scent of the meat and pickles made her forget all the rest. Laying aside her gloves, she took her first bite, sighed, and sunk into the tufted cushions, heedlessly abandoning herself to chewing. Wordlessly she accepted the goblet of wine he poured her, and took gulps in between bites.

Tad ate with gusto as well, but he was far from wordless, chattering and chomping at the same time. "Now see this hot air balloon trophy here?" he pointed with a pickle in hand. "It is one of master's most treasured. He was quite the balloonist in his day, you know? He won first place in a race around the city, steering to predetermined points and dropping a pig's bladder of paint on targeted street crossings. Ha! Can you imagine what might have happened if someone inadvertently crossed at one of those corners, unwary of the warnings?!" He mimicked walking along, lolling his head nonchalantly, and then mimed a blow to the head. He crossed his eyes and jerked backwards, nearly tipping his plate into Etta's lap.

Etta squealed. "Tad, you'd make a stuffed bird laugh!" She reached out to right his plate, accidentally grasping his hand in hers.

Tad grinned ear to ear. "Thank you, milady," he said grandly. "I do my best." He picked up the serving platter and fork. "Have some more. And let me tell you about this gramophone next to the dog statue." Tad dropped his nearly emptied plate, dashed over to the implement, and cranked the handle. "Do you like opera? I'll place a wax cylinder so the master may listen when he arrives."

49

Etta murmured assent, her mouth full, although the music box could play chickens clucking for all she would appreciate it. Hearing the door unlatch again, she put her plate down and brushed imaginary crumbs from her dress, expecting the moment had come at last to meet Mr. Fernsby.

Minnie belatedly knocked on the wood to announce herself. Her face was carefully neutral. "The master wishes me to relate that he has been unavoidably detained, and will not be needing the services of the young lady this evening after all. Tad is to pay her for her trouble and convey her home. Arrangements will be made for a possible return engagement at a future date." Her head tilted in sympathy towards Etta once the pronouncement had been made. "So sorry, Miss. Hope we see you again soon." She withdrew, and the latch clicked shut with some finality.

Etta grabbed up her glass and swallowed down the rest of the wine. "Well, that's that, I suppose. How much will I be paid for my 'troubles'? I will need tuppence at least for a doss tonight. Thruppence if I want blankets and it is a blustery night at that." It was actually a warm and pleasant evening, but she worded her request to elicit extra remuneration. She tipped her glass up again, waiting for any last drops to reach her tongue.

Tad took up the half sandwich from his plate, stuffing it in his mouth and wiping his hands first on his coat, then thinking better of it, fishing a napkin from the tray. "We don't have to rush. Have some of this very fine brandy." He reached past her for the decanter, filling a snifter for her and then one for himself. "Besides, what were we saying about idle time and leaving one unsatisfied?"

Etta let out a rush of breath. "Ha! My time must be paid for, Mr. Ever-Throbbing-Doodle. You want some of my time, you pay, or I go home." She looked at the remains on her plate. "Delicious as it is, and goodness knows when I'll see the like again, I am stuffed like a Christmas goose. Time to go." She gathered up her reticule and gloves. "The butler took my wrap." She was proud that she remembered the refined word she thought meant a cloak. "If you would just fetch it for me, we can leave immediately."

Tad, moving as if he did not hear her, took up his snifter and reclined into the sofa cushions. "After we finish our drinks. Might be months before I'll get another chance at the good brandy." When she did not sit, he patted the sofa beside him. "The grooms will have to hitch up the horses again. And besides, I'm not moving until our glasses are drained." Unhurriedly he sipped and ostentatiously savored, smacking his lips and sighing with pleasure.

A trifle impatiently, Etta sat. Since it was Tad had been instructed to pay her, she complied and picked up the snifter poured for her. She gulped, swallowing hard. The alcohol's heady fume enveloped her, and a tickle rather than a burn made its way down her gullet. "Oh!" she said softly, both startled and delighted.

Tad watched her swallow. "Such an impudent vintage. Not subtle really, but it has a presence. It announces itself like a divine diva, sonorous upon the stage, not mumping about like some whopperup." Tad held his glass up to the glow of the chandelier, almost as if he was toasting the telescope beneath it. "Something to be valued, cosseted, approached not with haste, but with anticipation and enthusiasm." He turned to Etta, looking through his glass at her face, and then brought the snifter down so that his eyes were on hers. "Sip, Etta," he commanded.

Etta dipped her head and sipped. "It is nice." She drank a little bit more. "It reminds me of something from long ago."

Tad nodded, encouraging her.

"It was — well, I shouldn't go on about it."

"Yes, you should. Carry on, please, I want to hear." Tad lifted his glass again. In return, she lifted hers and had another fragrant sip.

"Very well. This may seem silly to you, but it reminds me of almonds." Her face reddened to be remembering her ragged childhood in the midst of the rich parlor. "One Christmas, when I was five or maybe six, we were given a little bag of almonds in our stocking. Just a few, shared among me and me sisters. The most beguiling taste ever! Each tiny kernel a full mouthful." She paused, dipping her head down and looking straight into the top of her glass. "Come to think of it, the taste was nothing like this brandy." She laughed at herself. "But this taste is also a mouthful. So..." Etta looked upwards, as if the word she was trying to grasp might be in the air close by.

"Like country cream, it is heavy yet yielding on the tongue," he suggested.

"Never had that, country cream. Is it very different from city cream? Heavy, yes, I can feel that."

"And smooth like a polished pebble. You can roll it around on your tongue. It warms you like a bedpan does a bed. Not crackling like a hearth fire does, but more gently. Like a lover." Tad touched her hand holding the glass and urged it towards her. "Take another sip."

Etta gasped at his description. "Oooh, let me try that," and she sipped, moving her tongue around to play with the concentrated liquor. A smile was provoked, the brandy and the metaphor tickling her, and she nearly choked, swallowing quickly. The mouthful was gone. "Dear me, I'm wasting it." Leaning over the snifter, looking down at the liquid, she nodded. "I see what you mean. All around my tongue like an eiderdown. Or yes, a lover, as you suggest."

She knew it was the brandy asserting itself, the alcohol softening her resolve, but perhaps there was no harm in an indulgence. Especially given this fine specimen of manhood. She peeped through her lashes at the well-formed shoulders, discernible beneath his coachman's livery, and how neatly his waistcoat nipped in around his middle. His seat fitted snuggly into his uniform trousers, from whence his haunches were shown to be appealingly defined and inordinately firm. His belly was trim, without the beer paunch she had learned to expect of her dodgy patrons. Above all, the straw that tipped the balance in her mind, was that on his face, above his habitually upturned lips, was a very sensual mustache, very glossy, and not at all bristly. Just suited to her taste. "Very nice," she affirmed, taking another sip. "Wickedly tasty."

Tad chuckled, his cheeks having gone rosy with the fine alcohol. "Wickedly, you say? Why wicked?" He drank off the last mouthful from his snifter. "Nothing wicked about Nature's fermentation of grapes and mankind's fervent urge to bottle the nectar." He reached for the decanter, which he had placed on the far table so that he had to reach over her for it, brushing his hand over the expanse of bare skin above her low neckline. "Nothing wicked in following the laws of nature is there? They are laws, after all. Just being a dutiful citizen, wouldn't you agree?" He clinked his glass to hers and took a gulp, exhaling through the fumes, sighing with contentment.

Etta snorted in a decidedly unladylike fashion. "Ha! Yes, there is something wicked in doing what comes natural, but let's put that aside for the moment." She had already made up her mind to give in. Now she would see what kind of payment she could finagle. "About something for my trouble. A three-penny bit at least. Maybe another penny or even two for breakfast in the morning? With a cogue of gin to start the day off? How generous is your master in the matter of trouble?" She reached for Tad's fly, releasing the top button and then withdrawing her hand, waiting for an answer.

Tad's expression was comical to her, as her clients' expressions often were when she used this tactic to extort additional payment. Even so, she did not laugh. This was business, and she had nothing but herself to barter with.

"I'm sure I can make it worth your while, Henrietta," Tad murmured dryly. Suddenly his expression changed to one of deep concern. "Oh, dear nug, what has happened to your little boot?"

Etta noticed his use of her proper name and was about to inquire further into his discretionary control regarding payment when he drew his attention to her footwear. "My boot?" She tucked up her skirt to better see what concerned him.

Swiftly Tad picked up both her feet and brought them up onto the sofa beside him, perforce knocking her backward onto the pillows. "Let me mend that for you." He scooted his posterior to the far end of the sofa and leaned forward to get a better look at her boots and what lay beyond them.

"Tad, you word pecker! There is nothing wrong with my boots!" Etta attempted to imitate the maid's scolding tone, but she failed at finishing her sentence without laughing. She tussled in Tad's grasp, trying to right herself.

"Oh yes, there is," he replied with great solemnity. "They are on the sofa, where shoes should not be. Pray, let me assist you in removing them."

Her tart retort was lost when his firm hands clasped one ankle and his gentle fingers unburdened the long row of tiny loops of their shiny buttons. After the first boot was undone and he had tugged on the heel until her stockinged foot was unveiled, she found her breath again. "Oh, thank you for your concern. So kind of you to assist me." She tried for a sarcastic tone, but the words came out as grateful. Needy even.

"No bother at all. Lay back on the sofa while I take care of the other. Can you reach your brandy from there? Another pillow beneath your head perhaps." She felt his hands caressing up above her knee as if fumbling for the top of the second boot, which in fact ended at mid-calf. "Would you do me the favor of lifting your skirt and petticoats a bit higher? They impair my vision." He glanced upward at the chandelier. "Let me reposition you to take full advantage of the light."

Etta shivered as his hands skimmed along her thighs and slipped under her buttocks, tenderly pulling her further onto her back and angled outward. He nudged her knees upward, momentarily parting her split drawers, allowing a glimpse of her corrugated pink bits, framed by her short silky curls. "Wicked," she murmured, enjoying the warm fingers moving over her nether parts, heating her skin like the brandy did her insides.

Tad worked diligently, unbuttoning along her calf. Her other boot joined the first on the floor, this time carelessly tossed aside, as if he urgently needed to move on to the next task. "So much for the shoes.

These stockings are very nice. The wool has a soft sheen. I like them."
His fingers circled the toes of the second foot, petting and soothing.

"They are my best pair. The only one without ladders." She bit her
tongue after saying that, annoyed with herself for admitting her living
was so meager. "Perhaps another penny and I will buy more like them if
they please you. And your master, of course."

"Another penny? That might be managed." In a wink, Tad had his
livery jacket off, and his waistcoat was off in the next wink. His arms
now less encumbered, his hand roamed freely upward, inching along
her shin, then her knee, and beyond. He unhitched her garter clips,
jostling her drawers so she felt a puff of the parlor air blow across her
downy thicket. He slipped a finger between her stocking and inner
thigh, lovingly coaxing the thin wooling downward, dragging along her
flesh all the way down to her heel and further, his fingertips tickling the
sole of her foot and under her toes, removing the stocking entirely. "I
love how the tiny downy hairs on your legs stand up when I touch
them. They are like tiny little prickles coming to soldierly attention
when I pass by."

"Prickles! Ha, that's a good one. I'd say my legs have had lots of
little pricks, but usually they are someone else's!" She gurgled a laugh,
but it caught in her throat as he positioned his hand on her other leg,
again lasciviously drawing down the stocking, his finger working its way
down, caressing the other thigh, knee, calf, heel, sole and toes.

"Such a waste. Attention, nay adoration, is due to your own
protuberance. Your perfect pearl. Your little man standing up in his tiny
boat, is he waiting for me?" He tossed her skirts higher and frankly
pulled apart the opening of her split drawers, exposing her genitals to
his gaze, setting her on display. "Let me see!"

Etta squealed. Her indignation was mocked. Her excitement was
real. "What is it you see? I can feel how plump my pea is getting. What
about your pea-picking instrument? Is it strong and stiff and ready to
get down to work?" She freed one arm from her thrown-back skirts,

sitting up somewhat so she might reach across to his trouser buttons again.

"No, no, not yet," he said, inching himself back from her hand. "I want to look at you some more. He licked his fingers and fluttered them over her exposed folds, feeling her writhe with pleasure. "Ripe, yes indeed. Ready to burst its seams I would say. May I taste it?"

Etta blinked in surprise. "Yes, you may, if that pleases you. I must say, I am not used to men wanting anything before they get to the thrusting part. I could — " her sentence ended abruptly as his tongue flicked across her feminine button, all words lost in the radiant burst of sensation.

His hot breath bathed her delta and his fine mustache combed through her short hairs, tracing through to the sheltered skin below. His tongue dandled and cosseted. Her loins jerked spasmodically in response, startled and enlivened, in a way she was not aware before now that she could be moved. "Oh, oh, Tad. I'm untwisted!" The brandy spoke for her.

A chortle made his tongue dance and his lips vibrate against her. "I so enjoy the way you undulate under me. Permit me to move your legs just so. I want to see more of you. And less of these pantaloons."

He untied the bow at her belly and slipped his hand under her, tugging the fabric from beneath her bottom. She lifted her hips to assist. His hand pressed into her flesh to free the garment, then he pulled it over her thighs, calves, and ankles, making full use of the removal to fondle each inch of her delicate skin, watching it grow pink and heated in response. He tossed her drawers at the foot of the telescope, showing some impatience. His elbow positioned one leg flush against the sofa back and the other leg he took up by the ankle, kissing her instep before dropping it to the floor. "Exquisite view!" he exclaimed softly. "No one could ask for a better seat for the show."

She was all aflutter now. Her nipples had hardened under her bodice, and her corset felt two sizes too small. She gasped for more air. She noted her quickened breath, restless hands, and the first pulses of her hips. If she were her own Tom-a-Stiles, her urgency would be palpable, the first drops at her tip would be dripping, and as an experienced trollop, she would know it was time to put the parts together and bang on.

He sat back on his haunches and looked down on her, watching her twitch, openly admiring her. "Your petticoats look like the petals of a flower. And you, at the center, are the rosy bud. I should stop and paint a picture. Here the secret garden, with its grassy thatch and roseate walls, protecting an inestimable pearl and a cave of treasures..."

"No, don't stop," she heard herself wail plaintively. "I mean, please. Come back to me. Give me that instrument you brought with you."

"As you wish, milady," he acquiesced to her, grinning and sitting up so she could reach him. The tip of his pole protruded from his trousers' fly through the gap of the button she had undone earlier.

She slid off the sofa, her hands reaching for his waist. "What a handsome flagpole you have there. Let me help you unfurl."

He paused then, as if torn between his current intentions and an alternative course of equal felicity. "I suppose we could make out, I mean, make off in that direction." He glanced nervously about, as if reassuring himself they were alone and safe. The gramophone seemed to skip on its wax cylinder.

She made swift work of his remaining buttons and loops, allowing his prick to pop free of his breeches. It was sturdy, long, and erect. "A horse-sized cock if ever I saw one," she teased. "Tall and proud like a stallion. Just what one would expect of a horse handler." She placed her hands down on the sofa to steady herself and leaned forward, her lips pursed to engulf him.

Tad made a gurgling sound. Then a loud moan of enjoyment.

"Shhh!" Etta shushed Tad with her mouth around his member, then pulled back just far enough to speak. "Groan in moderation, please! I don't want your master to catch me with my kicks down doing the stable boy when he sent me home already."

"No one will hear us, and I'm the coachman, if you please!" He was going to protest more, but she reapplied her lips to his phallus and his words were lost in a vociferous testament to his pleasure. She curled her tongue around his broad tip and pressed down, sliding along his length until it tickled his scrotum. She swirled her tongue to one side as she lifted her head, letting it lick his shaft along the way. Like a child with a lollipop, she cupped her hands on his stem and applied her lips and tongue, titillating the length and sweet top of him, feeling his broomstick girth harden and quiver inside her mouth.

In no time at all, the lollipop was slick and heaving. When his sighs and quaking reached the right pitch in her judgment, she lifted her head to see his face. "Now?" she asked him, fairly well knowing the answer before she asked.

"Now!" he cried. He grabbed at her corset, dislodging her breasts from the fabric. He could see her nipples now, tight pink pebbles at the center of marbled hills. She cried aloud as his clutching hands clawed over her newly freed mounds.

Her own lust was intensely aroused. She sat beside him on the sofa, pulled his body over her own, and guided his prodigious instrument into her honeyed quim. Happy noises escaped her as she enveloped him, her moist cleft fitting over him like a glove. She nearly swooned dead away with delight as he filled her, and had to rein herself in to prolong the act. Soon his hips were pumping in time to hers. "Blue blazes, Tad! You're an engine!" she whispered, forgetting she told herself she would not swear this evening.

Tad's responses were also uncensored. "Perdition, how you smother me. Your tivvy, how it squeezes!" He began to jerk uncontrollably. "Hurry, Etta, hurry, I cannot hold out much longer. Come for me? Come for me! Come with me!"

Etta held onto Tad's mane as if for her very life. They galloped together, pitching and rising, flinging themselves headlong in their passion, spurring each other onward. Her moans became shrieks, her tones soaring, until a final cry of joy escaped her. Beneath her, dimly perceived, she felt Tad's racing pulse pounding like hers, his vocal climax triumphant and harmonizing with her own.

After this, fully satisfied, they subsided into the sofa. Spent. Exhausted. Empty. Their limbs and parts all melted in a heap. In time, she lifted her head and beamed at him. "Quite the giddy-up you got there, Tad."

Tad opened his eyes halfway and smiled. "Thank you, fair lady. You are quite the sporting sort yourself!" He bestirred himself, rearranging their tangled limbs so that they sat side-by-side, leaning into each other on the sofa. "We should get dressed. Before I take you home to your bed with a blanket and an extra lump of coal."

Etta's mouth dropped open in wonder. "That much? So generous with your master's money, and aren't I glad of it!" She surveyed their strewn clothing, starting to gather hers towards her. "I shouldn't be greedy, but I do hope Mr. Fernsby calls me back. I'll be bubbling like a tea-kettle for another chance at a carriage ride with you."

Tad was looking around the room as well, as if expecting something to happen. "You'd best hurry," he told her. She huffed and snagged up his breeches, dropping them in his lap.

He had one foot in one trouser leg when a whistle sounded from somewhere. Tad nearly fell on his face, staggering to get his feet under him and hopping to get to the speaking tube by the bell rope, finally snatching it up before the third blast. "Yes, Sir? Indeed, Sir!" He listened for some moments, his face taut. "I am right glad to hear that, Sir. Of course, Sir, without delay. And thank you, Sir." His head dipped in salutation as he returned the tube to its cradle.

"It seems master is quite pleased, Etta. By your performance." He grinned impishly at the confusion evident on her face. Like a showman, he held out his arms to encompass the room. "This parlor is master's private theater. He watches by remote reflection from the telescope lens and listens through a transponder in the gramophone."

Still grinning, he finished getting both his feet through his breeches and pulled them up, buttoning at his waist and adjusting the fullness around his slackening front. "Mr. Fernsby would like to see you again. Regularly if possible. Are Tuesdays convenient?" He picked up his waistcoat and rummaged in the pocket, drawing out a silver half-crown and placing it on the table in front of her. "And will this do for compensation?"

Etta froze with her fingers engaged in her laces. "All that?" She gazed at the shiny coin in astonishment. "For me?" Her voice came out in a hoarse squeak. She hopped up and grabbed at Tad's shirtfront. Her mouth worked, trying to express her glee, but all she managed was to stammer some more.

Tad pulled her close, prancing a few dance steps with her, stopping when they stepped on her unlaced underthings. "For you, giddy girl. You made my master, our master, very happy as he watched you from his bedroom in the other wing. You even added a few twists to the script I was supposed to perform. Play the part like you did tonight, and this can be your stage every night."

He picked up his livery jacket, a satisfied smile still on his face. "I'm looking forward to playing second fiddle to your lead. I foretell we will have a very long run."

ROBINETTE WATERSON

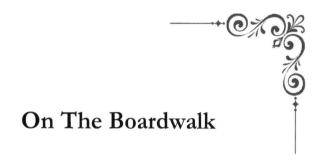

On The Boardwalk

On The Boardwalk

DOWNSTAIRS IN THE KITCHEN, Minnie dropped the tray, holding the remains of the lovers' picnic, beside the wet sink with a loud clatter, deliberately startling Cook who was dozing in her chair by the hot stove.

"Minerva, you little stinkpot, mind the crockery! One of these days Master will stop your wages to pay for the dishes you break." Never a cheerful woman, Mrs. Buttons was even more cross of late now that Minnie had a steady admirer.

"No need to be such a surly-boots, Cook." Minnie chuckled, refusing to take offense even when Cook used her formal name. "The crockery's fine as fippence." She waltzed around the kitchen as she went about her final chores of the day, wiping down the tables and moving the washing from the lye bucket to the soaking bin. "I'll be going out tonight, but never you fear, I'll be back by dawn to open the shutters and sweep out the ashes before the master's breakfast. Oh, and I nearly forgot! Our very own Mister Thaddeus had high praise for your latest batch of pickles. He asked me specially to tell you that."

"He did? Hmph. Just having a go at me, no doubt! Born under a ha'penny planet, never to be worth a groat." Cook fussed more under her breath, moving her slippered feet closer to the stove for warmth. "And you, going out for the whole night, are you? It will end in no good, don't you know? A few moments of excitement and a lifetime with a millstone. Fatherless chit hanging about your neck is all you'll get out of that!"

Minnie hummed softly as she swished the dishes through the soapy water and piled them on the sideboard. "I take care. Besides, I like children. Pity the master doesn't have any."

Cook inhaled audibly and clucked her tongue, being the sort who could and would find ill in anything. "Wicked girl! Wishing brats on our bachelor master!"

Minnie's humming continued unabated as she pumped fresh water over the dishes, and piled them undried into the open cupboard. She wiped her hands on her starched pinafore, then pulled it off and dropped it in the lye bin, before taking up her coat and hat from the hook by the back door. "Sleep well, Mrs. Buttons. See you at dawn," she called cheerily, banging the door behind her in her hurry to meet with her lover.

"Nothing good, bet your buttons on it!" the sour woman shouted out after her.

THEY MET AT THE ENTRANCE to the Floral Hall in Covent Garden, where Albert had purchased a violet for his paramour. He stood kissably close to pin the little flower to her bodice. Their eyes danced together, both aching to wrap arms around each other and touch their lips, but they were restrained by the public eye. Confining themselves to holding hands, scandalous enough for their status, they strolled down the pavement. At a corner, they joined a small throng around a vile Punch and Judy show, one with a great deal of spurting blood and many babies thrown over the balcony to delight the milling crowd. Al and Minnie stood shoulder to shoulder and nudged each other, as if the prats and puns incited them. Before the show was over they walked on, stopping to purchase a treat of floss candy from an automated vendor, watching the sugar spin into threads around a paper spool. They began walking again, eating from the spool between them.

"You look quite fetching with that bit of sugar wool on your cheek, Miss Minnie," Albert whispered, leaning in as close as he dared to her ear.

"And you stir me nethers up like a house afire, Albert," she whispered back. She giggled, seeing his cheeks flush in commingled shame and pleasure. "What say we find a bit of seclusion, eh? I don't have enough for an hour's rent, meself. Do you? Maybe we find a dark alley?"

The tailor's apprentice shook his head once, allowing as to his similarly impecunious situation. "I broke the point off me shears last week. Careless of me it was, using the blade to pick out a seam. Foreman docked me a half week's pay for it, the filthy ingrate. Spent my last farthing on the floss." He dared to chuck her under her chin. "I don't fancy an open alley in this chill air, my lamb. What say we walk toward the embankment? Would you do me the honor of a dance beneath a dock? A blanket hornpipe maybe?" He grinned at his own audacity.

"Ooch," she exclaimed, rubbing in her backside in pretend pain as they walked in the direction of the water. "Me bottom itches just thinkin' on the sand. Let's say we find a cozy bench on a quiet pier? Or some such."

Hand in hand they hurried past the clots of mafficking boys and pub doors exhaling moist boozy breath into the cold. They stopped briefly to listen to an itinerant fiddler with a grinder playing off-key behind him. The night-tipsy crowd pushed past them, no one else even slowing down. They joined hands and waltzed a few steps, bumping into people and apologizing cheerfully as they twirled along. Men catcalled, calling them daft. Women tittered and pointed behind their hands, secretly wishing they had the audacity to waltz. Once out of the range of the music, they dropped hands, and arm-in-arm made their way to the river.

At first the road was wide with city gas lamps every block or so, but as they came closer to the embankment district, the streets grew narrower and darker. There were fewer lamps, and the buildings were grimy where there were no careful housewives to wash their steps of the city soot. The clopping of horses' hooves sounded far off and muffled, and footsteps, when heard, were furtive. As they neared the wharves, there were stretches where the only illumination was that of the waning moon.

They could hear they were almost to the river by the cheerful curses of the dock men as they unloaded boats of night fish and other dark wares. Some greasy food stalls littered the walk, exuding the odor of rotten potatoes, dubious sprats, unwashed seamen, and their slatternly companions. Albert led Minnie hurriedly past the pre-dawn knots of costermongers grubbing their way towards their stations.

A little further on, the boards sounding hollow under their meandering feet, they ventured a kiss in the darkness, only to be frightened off by an outburst of frantic whispers from a small steamer, barely visible in the gloom. Not everyone could afford passage on the brightly lit, legally registered vessels. They quick-stepped onward, leaving the whisperers in their wake.

The wind gusted, bringing the pungent zest of bloated fish and impending rain, and Minnie turned her face away from the bitter ice crystals rising from the water. Her hat was pushed askew, the hatpin sticking out at an old angle. Albert, ever considerate, unbuttoned his thin wool coat to tuck her inside with him. "We'll find something, love," he told her, scanning the dirty street for possible rough shelter.

At last up ahead he spied a set of river stairs. Dislodging her from his coat, he ran, pulling her behind him, unheeding of her sudden yelp when the wind struck her full again, and clattered down the steps leading to the shore below. He stopped halfway at a little landing where the steps turned back on themselves, and maneuvered Minnie into the curve of the bend.

They could look up and see a few stars shining hazily through the high clouds and city murk. They could not see, or more importantly, could not be seen, from the street level. The little niche they had found for themselves was nearly in total darkness. "This might be the best we can manage tonight, Minnie." Albert gently guided her until her back was firm against the wall. His coat hung open still, and he stepped in close, fumbling for her skirts and pulling them up handful by handful.

She shivered, only partly from the cold. "Best will have to do us then. I'll get me skirts. You get yer dingus free and we can meet in the middle."

Albert gurgled. "Love it when you talk dirty, lambkins. Me dingus, ha!" He unbuttoned his breeches eagerly. The staircase provided some protection from the bitter wind, and the tent between their coats, some protection from the cold. His free hand pulled aside her high collar, disgorging some of the bodice buttons from their restraints. He fingered her chemise aside so he could feel the soft skin at her neck, and strained to reach further under the fabric that covered her breasts. He brought his lips to the cloth, following where his fingers touched and then moving his mouth down her bodice, kissing, breathing heavily, huffing the heat of his open mouth onto her flesh beneath. His lips found and encircled her nipple, his tongue working through the coarse dress goods and flimsy chemise, wetting them. Even through the rough fabric his tongue felt her nipple responding with lively stiffness.

Minnie gathered up her skirt and her single petticoat, tugging on her drawers to loosen the opening. "I love yer sugar stick, Albert. Wish I could see it, but it's black as the Earl of Hell's waistcoat down here. I'm betting ye're barrel wide and granite hard for me, eh? Let me find yer with me free hand, now I got me skirts all bunched up." Minnie shook off the cold from exposing herself and crushed against Albert, her heated and compliant skin rubbing against the worn fabric of his only suit.

"Come 'ere, you randy little duckling. I got that sausage you were hankerin' for. Kept it wrapped up and warm for you in me pocket. Let me show you." He held himself steady with one hand and slipped the other between her thighs, his fingers rubbing against her folds, feeling the incipient slickness.

Minnie giggled with naughty pleasure, one hand holding up her skirt and the other groping for Albert's protuberance, trying to restrain herself so as not to tear his buttons or muss her dress too much.

"Careful now. No getting sausage drippings on our clothes. There is no time for laundering before we needs must be back to work again."

Encircling his cock with her yearning fingers, she worked up and down, enjoying the feel of the soft, receptive skin over the rapidly hardening shaft beneath. "Golly, how I wish I could put you inside me. I'm wet like the ocean for you! I so wish to have a baby someday, Al. Not tonight though."

Albert dipped one of his fingers experimentally into her cavern, groaning with anticipation when he felt her molten desire. "Me, too, Minnie. Me, too," he crooned in her ear. Another finger joined his first.

Minnie gasped, feeling her cavern widen, clamp down, smother the intruders with overt ardor. Her hand closed around his burgeoning phallus, pumping the plump sausage, feeling it swell under her fingers, bringing it near to bursting with inner juices. "Oh, uh, mmm," she grunted. "It's a good 'un, Al, all juicy and thick. Makes me hungry! Hungry inside for you." She rubbed harder, her palm damp, her thumb wetted by his tip, her little finger combing through his short hairs.

Albert was panting, his hips and prick pulsing into the warm tunnel of her hand. "M-m-minnie, mine, oh, Minnie, m-m-mmm." Words were losing meaning, his mind funneled down to a mere movement of inches, a few velvet, aching moments of shattering, searing pleasure building within. "I see lights, Minnie. Fireworks. I'm going to burst!"

Minnie rubbed faster, pushing her lady notch harder against Albert's curved fingers. They were nearly there, almost to the best part, when abruptly Minnie screamed. Doubling over, she shrieked in terror and shoved him backwards. She scrambled a few steps up toward the street, accidentally kneeing him in the vitals in her haste to get away.

"What the deuce, Minnie?" Albert cried out in pain and dismay, almost ready to shoot but robbed of the chance to score.

Minnie's voice came out in a shrill whisper. "There's a man down there! Watching us! His eyes!" She pointed towards the bottom of the steps, her breath ragged, the ends of her sentences swallowed by her gasps for more air. "Eyes like a demon!" she wailed and covered her mouth to keep her cry from being overheard. She skittered up another stair step.

Albert was facing the wrong direction to see anyone at the bottom of the steps. His vision was swimming, his body torn between Minnie's words and his impending climax. He took hold of himself and his warm, damp hand on his cock triggered him. He groaned convulsively as his first spurt spattered the staircase wall, splashing, catching some of Minnie's skirt. The remaining pumps lessened and dripped to the stone steps. Little words of one syllable poured from him as his ejaculation took precedence. Dimly he was aware of Minnie's hysterical pointing, but it was some moments before he recovered the presence of mind to look behind him. "What did you see?" he croaked out, and then cleared his throat. "I don't see anyone now."

Minnie was transfixed a few steps up from the landing, her hands over her mouth, her eyes still wide with fright but not looking anymore. She was crouching, dropping her face into her hands as if hiding or warding off a blow. All the giddiness in her had fled when she saw the fiendish man standing there. She swallowed to wet her fear-parched throat and answer the question asked of her.

"He was at the bottom of the steps. Watching us. Like he were in a swanky box, looking out at a play on Drury Lane. He might have been smoking a pipe? Had something in his hand." She tried to dredge up details from her brief glimpse of the lurking figure and the horrific wave of terror his presence had precipitated. He had been holding something that had flashed, a metallic glint, in the pale moonlight. She was trembling, shaking from head to toe, trying to penetrate her fear and determine why she had felt him to be of deep malevolence. "He was just staring. Not annoyed like we were blocking the steps, or smiling to have caught us out in public. Calm. He might have spoken to us if we weren't, well, frolicking. I can't seem to describe how exactly, but he just..." Another jolt of fear shivered through her, and she wrapped her coat around herself tightly, not bothering with buttons. "He frightened me."

"Did you see his face? Did you know him? What did he look like?" The moment of crisis past, Albert tucked himself in and made his fly fast again. He took a linen rag from his pocket and sponged at the flecks on his trousers.

Slowly Minnie straightened up from her crouched position. "He had something in his hand, pressing it to his lips. I can't quite describe it."

"A handkerchief?"

"No, no, it reflected in the moonlight." She was shaking her head and chills were skittering up and down her back. "His bowler hat was pulled down low over his face. I don't know why I thought he was smoking. Something about the way his hand moved to his lips, I suppose." She looked to where the bottom of the steps let out, but now there was a wall between her and the landing. She did not move to where she could look down.

"Probably some toff slumming amongst us folk."

"In this cold and dark? Bah, you're daft."

"Bah, you're lovely," he said, trying to cajole her out of her fear. He tucked a loose strand of hair under her hat. "Your hatpin has gone astray." He reached for it, wiggling it, but not pressing, not wanting to scratch her with the sharp tip.

She ducked her head, reaching up to reset the pin. "'I'm embarrassed now." She started to laugh weakly. "Why did I scream like that? The kind of scream Master makes when dreaming and tangles hisself in his sheets, bless him."

Albert laughed too, a little uncertainly, looking down to the beach which was clearly in his line of sight. "Ho, that's a good one. Your Mr. Fernsby likes to watch too! Let's call out to this fellow, introduce them, so the two of them can talk about their mutual penchant. They could have a tankard and a good jolly together!" Albert made as if to go down the stairs.

"No!" Minnie grabbed Albert's arm frantically. "No, don't. Maybe it's silly, but I've still got the collywobbles. There was something not right about him." She tugged hard on his arm, pulling him off balance.

"Let's go. I'm sorry about the way this evening turned out. But let's go. Let's go now."

Albert regained his feet and put his hand reassuringly over Minnie's. "Don't tremble, me timid titmouse. Just as you say." Gently he tidied up her attire, smoothing the rumpled skirt and re-buttoning the high-necked bodice. He offered her his rag to clean his smut from her skirt. "Say, maybe it was that Leather Apron fellow! Do you think? We aren't far from Whitechapel. Maybe he took a stroll along the river, rinse his bloody hands in the filthy water."

"Don't joke."

"What, don't you think it possible? He must needs clean up before anyone sees him all splashed with gore. They say the scenes are rather bloody. What with necks slashed down to the very bone and bits missing from below their aprons."

"Enough of that now." She was walking shakily up the steps, still grasping his hand, dragging him behind her.

"I mean, how could anyone miss seeing a man splattered with blood hoofing his way down the pavement? Must be invisible somehow. There's always people rabbiting around town. We couldn't even find a minute o' privacy in the dark o' the moon on a bitter chill night nearin' winter!"

Minnie was silent. At the top of the steps, she passed a hand over her dress and handed him back his rag.

"Could've been him," Albert continued, winking mischievously at her. "Just think, we can tell our grandchildren, we saw Saucy Jack, in all his bloody finery, while we was doin' the amiable down by the river."

"Oh please, give it over! Look at me shakin'! I'm all aquiver like one of Cook's calf-foot jellies, I am."

Al threw an arm around her, pulling her close to him as they walked briskly to keep warm. "Don't jiggle, me pet. I'll fight the devil off with my manhood." He swished his hips as if his sword were protruding out before him. A brace of passing sailors sniggered at his swagger.

She giggled despite her lingering fear, then turned to him suddenly and nuzzled her head under his chin. "I love you, Albert. No one else can make me laugh like you do. Even when I'm scared half out of me wits."

Al answered without thinking on it. "I love you, too, Minnie." All of an instant he stood surprisingly still, rocked by the declaration that welled up from within him, leaping over his usual blithe response to anything momentous. It came to him that he needs must do something about that. "I have somethin' ter ask, Minnie."

His stillness prompted her to lift her head up and find his eyes with hers. Weakly she tried to match his good humor and falsified a small laugh. "Very well. In future, when a demon is coming at us, I'll not knock yer nutmegs with me knee."

He shook his head at her and blurted it out before his newfound bravery could desert him. "Would ye marry me, Minnie?" Belatedly he remembered to kneel down on the begrimed cobblestones, his expression earnest, longing, and more a little bit fearful of her response. People walking on the pavement stutter-stepped to detour around them, some wishing them cheer, some cursing the impediment they created.

Minnie's body was still stiff with unnamed fright, but her heart was braver. "I would, Albert. Would make me like the star atop a Christmas tree to be yer missus."

When they kissed, there in the open street, in full view of the throng of passersby, her frightened shivers quelled almost to nothing. Almost. "But first things first, Al," she whispered, her arms still tight around him. "Before banns or a ring or anything, we must search out a safer place to be joinin' giblets!"

STEAM GEARED

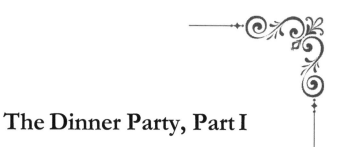

The Dinner Party, Part I

The Dinner Party, Part I

IT WAS NEARING DUSK when Mr. Geoffrey Gridley, of the Fourth Estate, turned in his required column inches to the editor of The Metropolitan Times. His co-reporters had already snatched up the exciting double feature of the day, old Leather Apron at it again. He had to settle for a human-interest story on the distraught fellow who found one of the bodies, as well as an agony article on the proper placement of doilies on armchairs. That ought to keep the ladies' bridge clubs happily debating the merits of antimacassars for a week or so.

Stepping out into the brisk air, feeling a small smatter of cold rain against his cheek, he recalled the odd incident from early that morning when he was on his way to work. A man came barreling onto the street from some river stairs, directly in front of him, so that he had to jump back not to collide with him. "Oh pardon me!" he had exclaimed, a bit chagrined at his own clumsiness. He doffed his hat and made a polite bow.

The man seemed disoriented, with his hands deep in his coat pockets. "Not at all," he had said, "Entirely my fault." He removed one hand from its pocket and made to tug at the brim of a hat, but he had none. His hand went back to his pocket and he darted off down the nearest alley. There was something decidedly odd about him. Was he frightened? Many people were these days. Gridley pondered how few facts were known about the recent Whitechapel murders, with only vague descriptions and hazy theories. For all Geoffrey knew, that very man might have been the villain himself. And that man easily might have thought the very same of Geoffrey.

Now he buried his face in his muffler against the chill. Going on dark already, and he was due at his Penelope's home. The Lisney's had formally invited him for dinner, and he had formally accepted. The first of many, he was hoping, and Penny had intimated he had good reason to expect it so. Best take a few extra minutes and walk down by the market to get flowers. As a gift for the hostess. Arriving late was a sin that could be excused due to the nature of his work, but arriving late without a token was unforgivable.

"Can I 'elp ye find somethin', sir?" The flower stall girl's eyes raked him from his sturdy but worn shoes to his old-fashioned Derby, in need of a good brushing. "A talkin' bouquet for yer sweetie?" she guessed from the lateness of the hour. "End of the day, give yer good price," she added, guessing from his shoes that he might need to economize. "In case you are boracic. Y'know what I mean? Boracic lint. Skint."

He smiled, surprised, but pleased that the child could see the situation right off. "A little economy would not be out of place. Do you have a flower that means 'I'm sorry, but I couldn't help it, an occupational imperilment, and I love you very, very much'"?

The flower girl grinned impudently. "A lot to say wit one flower. I'll make yer a bunch." On a sheet of old newspaper (his paper, he noted with some pride), she laid out and explained her choices. "Red roses fer love, 'oneysuckles fer devotion, and let's see, fer regret, maybe a raspberry bramble? Now yer 'yacinths are best fer showing regret, but they h'aint in season. We can trick 'em into blooming wit arc lamps and steam 'eaters, but gotta order ahead. Also ..." She rubbed her thumb across the fingers of one hand to indicate pricey. Geoffrey shook his head to the extra time and expense. She cast her eyes over her stock. "Pink carnations, fer remembrance. Promising you won't forget again."

Gridley shook his head. "Better pass on the pinks. Not that I would forget, but," his lips twisted regretfully, "my employment detains me on occasion." He paid for the wrapped flowers and thanked the girl for the care she took over his situation. She pocketed the coins with alacrity. "Let me know if you decide fer 'yacinths. Fer next time," she called out after him, her little round face smiling sardonically, reminding him of the likelihood of a next time.

Cheeky chit, he thought, sniffing at the flowers as he hurried on his way. However a niggle of self-doubt assailed him. He mused as he walked on whether it would behoove him to order hyacinths next time.

ARMED WITH THE HOSTESS gift of blooms, Geoffrey Gridley rapped smartly on the Lisney's front door. "Matilda!" he greeted Penelope's maiden aunt with feigned delight, surprised to see her instead of one of the servants. "You look lovelier each time I see you, do you know that?" Aunt Tillie blushed, gushed, and invited him into the foyer. He handed over the flowers, his eyes seeking out his Penny beyond her vast girth.

His beloved appeared in the doorway of the parlor, and her eyes sparkled as she caught sight of him. With a single glance at the flowers, she read the symbolism with ease, and gave a quick dip of her head to let him know the apology was accepted. She then stepped aside to let her mother take charge.

"Such a delightful bouquet, Mr. Gridley," said Mrs. Lisney, looking a vision of dignified propriety in a high-necked lilac gown. She made a neat curtsy to her guest and took the bouquet from her sister, also reading the symbolic message, and a bit startled by the deep red of the roses. Surely pink would have been a better choice at this early stage of the courtship. Just think, they hadn't even permission from Mr. Lisney to walk out yet! Nonetheless she expressed appreciation for his gift before handing them off to the butler who had just then made the long trek from the kitchen. "Some water for these, Reynolds. Penelope, come along and greet Mr. Gridley."

"I had assistance in assembling them." Now inside, Geoffrey bowed, addressing them all but his eyes landed on his beloved Penny and stayed there. "A quirky young girl at the flower market." He longed to elaborate, declaring his love and devotion in words as well as in flowers, but for the watchful eyes and ears of her chaperones. He noticed Penny was fluffing out the ruffles on her dress. Must be new.

He should complement it lavishly. It was that poisonous shade of green, so popular of late. Nasty color. The hue reminded him of leaves dying of drought. "What a delight you look," he exclaimed, unable to bring himself to praise it more immoderately.

Penny beamed at him, then looked to the closed door of her father's study. Almost on cue, Mr. Lisney came out into the hallway to greet their guest as head of the household. "Geoffrey, my good man, I am so glad you could join us tonight," he said with barely a trace of irony at the newsman's late arrival, holding out his hand for shaking. "Come to the parlor and tell us all about the headlines of the day. Well, maybe not all the sordid details of the Whitechapel doings. Don't want to upset the ladies' digestions, now do we?"

The ladies went silent when the head of the household took hold of the conversational reins, and they all trooped into the parlor, a cozy room of Eastlake-style furnishings. Very modern, Geoffrey noted, with plenty of spindles, fringe, gilt-framed paintings, and an exuberantly healthy parlor palm on a high plinth. Geoffrey was relieved to see a small bookcase, but a little disconcerted there were no newspapers in sight. He hoped they were kept in the breakfast room, for daily perusal. Mrs. Lisney, leaning close to her husband, murmured, "We have punch," to let him know more liquid refreshment was available.

"Punch!" Mr. Lisney's eyes gleamed with delight. "What do you say, Geoffrey? Sherry, whiskey, or punch?"

Penny's eyes were trained on Geoffrey and were also gleaming, but it would become clear she was not thinking of drink. With her Mother and Auntie Matilda attentive to Father's wishes, she winked at him. And then she blushed as if realizing how forward she must appear.

Geoffrey caught sight of her wink and could scarcely believe his eyes. Or his luck! What a deliciously forward woman was his intended. Angel in the parlor, minx in the bedroom, he thought with satisfaction. If only he could wink back unobserved, to let her know he reciprocated her candid desire, despite the indecorous nature of it. "Punch, if you please," he responded. "I always say punch is a good start to any endeavor, be it a meal or a news article. My boss at The Times frowns, but mind you, there has been more punch in the paper since I said that." He laughed at himself, but then sobered quickly on re-thinking. "Not that we drink on the job, of course."

Mr. Lisney laughed sociably and the ladies tittered delicately. "What a clever fellow you are, Mr. Gridley. I do hope your employer fully values your wit." Mrs. Lisney reached for the bell to call Reynolds, who was hovering within earshot outside the parlor door.

"Punch coming from the kitchen now, Madam," he said sonorously, and secreted himself out of sight again.

"Thank you, Reynolds," she said to the empty space he vacated, and turned her attention, as a good hostess should, to her guest. "Do you like venison, Mr. Gridley? Our cook is most proficient in its preparation, and she has a fine cutlerer. I say with some pride that our venison is the best I've ever tasted." She looked to her husband for corroboration, but he had risen from his seat to poke at the fire, so she turned to her sister, who nodded emphatically.

"The best, yes," said Matilda and shut her mouth firmly again, letting the subject drop heavily.

"Why yes, how lovely, venison," Geoffrey nodded, smiled, in truth not having a preference regarding the meat. He found himself adjusting his cufflinks and forced himself to stop fiddling. Penny spoke up then, saving the dying conversation. "You were going to tell us the news of the day, weren't you, Mr. Gridley? While we wait for the punch?" She smiled evenly, giving him something to do and encouraging him to display his specialty.

"Oh yes, well, let me see. That might be difficult to do and not ruin a good dinner. The talk is all of the horrendous mutilations." Mrs. Lisney gasped and Tillie looked as if she would faint. Geoffrey struggled for a safer topic, passing over not only the Whitechapel murders but also the robberies, worker strikes, and market declines. "Did you hear about the motor car touring trend? The wife of an automobile manufacturer drove some 66 miles, just for the fun of it.

They say she used a hatpin when a valve clogged up, and she took her two boys with her to help push on the bigger hills."

"A woman and her children?!" Mrs. Lisney's head swiveled towards Penny with a gleeful grin on her face, which she mitigated to mere good humor before she turned back to her husband and guest.

"Oh yes," Geoffrey continued. "Also there was a fellow in Germany flew an airship up 6,000-some feet into the air! Travel is advancing by leaps and bounds. So to speak. " He turned to Mr. Lisney, about to ask him if he read the stories, when his tongue froze mid-way into the first word. What if, heavens forbid, the gentleman habitually read a newspaper than his own?

"Can you imagine?" Penny piped up. "I expect her dress was inordinately dusty after such a ride!" Penny seemed to hesitate, as if the notion of motoring, especially for enjoyment, was new to her. "Why is it one would strive to venture so far from one's own nest?"

Geoffrey, on the point of bringing forth further thrilling details of Mrs. Benz's audacious journey, pondering whether to mention how she employed her garter as insulation material, was squelched. He couldn't think how to stretch a conversation about traveling, not with Penny talking about nesting. Or rather he thought of some stray tangents arising from the subject, including activities that perchance could happen in a dickie seat, but none acceptable for mixed company. He tried to smother his smile. Mr. Lisney leaned forward, hoping the smile was the start of another story. He bent towards him in anticipation. "Yes?" he asked eagerly.

"Oh." Geoffrey was mentally scratching modes of transportation from his list. "Well, there was an interesting article in The Cornhill magazine about Darwin and evolution. Like electricity, the cholera germ, women's rights, and the Eastern Question, the subject is much in-the-air, so they say. Making quite a stir." Internally he chided himself for diverting attention from The Metro Times. He should kick himself for that. And to bring up controversial subjects to boot! He should kick himself again. He refrained from rubbing his metaphorically bruised backside.

Fortune intervened in the form of Reynolds and the punch. Mr. Lisney poured, handing his guest a very full cup. He added lemonade to dilute the ladies' portions.

Geoffrey sipped, desperately casting in his mind for a safe topic. "Oh, oh, I heard tell of another one of those African explorers today. That was interesting."

"Oh yes? Brave fellow, was he? All pith helmet and pluck?" Mr. Lisney leaned forward again.

"The wireless didn't mention a pith helmet, but it would be likely, wouldn't you say? Academic fellow and his wife. Volcano. Ripping great tale about ..." he recalled the details, the horrors of the catastrophic destruction, and the loss of life, limb, habitation, and the expedition's scientific mechanisms. He reframed the narrative quickly. "Spectacular pyrotechnic display. However the poor chap lost his journal, his leaf pressings, and all the geo-measuring implements. Dreadful setback for the Royal Society, I fear." Geoffrey felt another subject slipping away to inertia. "So there's that."

Nods, smiles, and agreeable murmurs acknowledged the subject's passing. "Yes. Well. There's that."

Mrs. Lisney attempted a new conversational gambit. "Tell me, Geoffrey, does your mother go in for Pteridophyta? I seem to recall a fern-collecting trip with a Mrs. Gridley this past spring. Beastly weather, but we found some positively adorable new specimens. We brought back basketfuls for our parlors! And some delightful fossils, as well." Mrs. Lisney gestured vaguely toward an iron and glass folly in the corner, with exuberant fronds escaping out the top.

Geoffrey appeared dumbfounded. "Mother does have an inordinate interest in plants, now that you mention it. Father complains of how many gardeners she employs for both inside and out. Did she travel to collect even more ferns? I feel rather foolish. I must say I never asked about it, nor recall if she mentioned it."

Silence politely descended. Reynolds charged sedately to the rescue. "Dinner is served, Madam."

Geoffrey all but leapt up from his chair. His cool newsman's mind quickly assessed the possible paths of utmost felicity versus the pitfalls of proper protocol. For a bare moment he pondered the consequences of stepping over to the maiden aunt and offering her his arm. Not the action of conventional etiquette, but allowable, as she was the most elder of the party. However his nerve deserted him, and he approached his hostess, the proper escort for a solitary male guest. "May I squire you to the dining room, Mrs. Lisney?"

Mr. and Mrs. Lisney glanced at each other, their eyebrows raised in happy approbation at his display of social niceties. "Most delighted, yes, Mr. Gridley," Mrs. Lisney cooed. Tillie took her brother-in-law's offered arm, and Penny skipped unescorted after them all, a secret smile on her lips.

Around the corner, sighting the dining room, Geoffrey nearly stumbled. It was crammed full of every kind of excess, assaulting his senses with over-the-top frippery. The pomegranate red flocked wallpaper oozed over him like an overfilled sandwich-biscuit oozed jam onto one's lap at the first bite. The paper was paired with a dado of olive green shadow striping, and the table was smothered in yards of Paris green satin. Silk ribbons, silk flowers, fake fruit, and false greenery dangled indulgently from the gas chandelier, wall sconces, and candelabras. Every inch of anything metallic in the room, including a full battalion of cutlery, was polished to mirror-like luminescence, shining so brightly that Geoffrey had to squint. He stifled a sneeze as a cloying scent emanated from the roaring fire, some resinous wood spitting out small flares of tar onto the figured carpet. The room was more dramatic than a Racine tragedy with the divine Sarah Bernhardt playing the lead.

He escorted Penny's mother to her seat, trying not to flinch as he was pummeled by the decor. A minor panic threatened to overtake him, but bravely Geoffrey marshaled himself, willing to go toe-to-toe with the overdecorated space for the sake of the woman he loved. He assumed a stout-hearted expression. "Mrs. Lisney, your decorating talent is indeed breathtaking! And I can tell by the armory of utensils on parade around the plates that we are in for quite the treat."

Mrs. Lisney, waiting while Geoffrey pulled her chair out for her, clapped her hands with glee that her guest had noticed. "Thank you, thank you, I was so hoping to favorably impress you! You have become so dear to us. And to our Penny, of course. I wanted our first dinner together in our home to be ... very special."

Geoffrey heard the slight hesitation. He looked to Penny quickly. Was it time for him to propose? They had talked of waiting until the new year, but with all the extra fuss, perhaps the parents were prompting him? Penny appeared to be surprised by his sudden look, and she directed her gaze downward. Not yet, he gathered. While Reynolds helped Tillie and Penny to their chairs, he found his own place card on the table and sat down, prickling with anticipation.

Mrs. Lisney glanced at her husband for approval and then continued speaking. "I hope you don't mind, Mr. Gridley — um — Geoffrey, but we serve salad after the fish. A habit I picked up in my youth." It may have been a trick of the flickering firelight, but Geoffrey fancied that Mrs. Lisney was blushing at this confession. "I know to admit one is from the country is unfashionable, but I so dearly miss some of the comforts only found there. I begged the indulgence of Mr. Lisney that I might have some of them here in town."

The butler brought in the wine, assisted by the kitchen maid. Conversation regressed even further to polite proscription — the weather, whether the conflict in France would jeopardize the importation of foreign claret, and the merits of Bordeaux viticulture versus those of the Iberian Peninsula.

Once the glasses were filled and the soup course in place, the help departed. Mr. Lisney took it upon himself to steer the conversation to topics of greater import to those gathered around the table.

"Can you reach the oysters in the ice carving, Geoffrey? Allow me to bring down some from the center for you. I see Maisie has set the oyster forks out for us, all proper and all, but I happen to prefer tipping them into my mouth instead of stabbing them. Don't stand on ceremony if you like them that way too."

Geoffrey then realized the intricate centerpiece of fruit and greenery also cradled pockets of carved ice with scads of glistening oysters for the first course. He lifted one from its frozen bed, then imitated the way Mr. Lisney tilted his head back, allowing the meat to slide from its prepared shell, biting the chewy morsel once, then swallowing it nearly whole. He tipped the shell a second time, savoring the salty juice left behind. He looked briefly at Penny, thinking illicit thoughts, and then noticed Mr. Lisney looking lewdly at Mrs. Lisney. Both men looked down, smiling bemusedly at their respective plates, finishing their private thoughts before rekindling the conversation.

Mr. Lisney had grown expansive in his speech, whether from the punch earlier or his habitual business-like bonhomie was difficult to determine. "Say, how's that newspaper treating you, eh?" He paused only briefly, eager to expound on his subject. "You know, a clever fellow like you might do better to distinguish yourself in business rather than publishing. Have you any inclinations in that direction, by any chance? Steamships, you know, Geoffrey! They are the future, despite what some say about railways. Can't cross an ocean in those!"

Geoffrey chuckled and swallowed more oyster juice, still thinking of the possibilities of his future with Penny. He brought his wine glass to his face and drank deeply, as an excuse to keep any impropriety from showing. While seeming attentive to Mr. Lisney's self-aggrandizing narrative, his eyes lingered over Penny. She was fiddling with her napkin. Perhaps she didn't care for oysters.

"Did you hear my firm has partnered with a new American enterprise?" Mr. Lisney glanced around the table but expected no answers from the ladies. "Negotiations had been kept secret, but just yesterday I read about it in your newspaper." Mr. Lisney looked pointedly at Geoffrey, trying to discern from his expression whether he held any responsibility for financial revelations at his place of work. "One of the Newport concerns. Morgan backed. He says you can bet your bottom dollar that Maycombe-Springerham Steam Navigation is on the brink of the new age. Funny American-ism, bet your bottom dollar. So forthright they are!" Mr. Lisney paused briefly for a sip of wine, but only briefly so as not to lose momentum. "True, our rivals were the first to use reciprocating engines, but we are catching up. I admit, I myself was hesitant about using turbines in the beginning, but after we ironed the wrinkles out, it has proved to be a reliable technology. Ha-ha, one could say we steamed the wrinkles out, eh?"

Those at the table all tittered at the little joke. Reynolds brought in a platter of calf's tongue, a ruffled doily obscuring the end from which it had been separated from the living beast.

Geoffrey noticed Penny was all but flailing her napkin like a semaphore. Blast it, he was likely missing something! With care, he picked up his own napkin to blot any remnants of oyster juice from his lips and mustache. Fearing to manipulate the cloth in a fashion that might be taken for an unintended communication, he placed it carefully back in his lap.

Mrs. Lisney was contributing to the conversation now. Perhaps the wine had freed her tongue as well. "Look how Cook has found fresh apricots for the garnish! She has amazing sources for provender. Surpassing my comprehension. Do you remember, Tillie, how as children there was no fresh fruit by this time of year? We would beg for candied peel in the afternoon to tide us over till dinner when we finished our lessons." She paused and then elucidated, "The fashion for taking afternoon tea was still in the offing when we were younger, the sadder for us. If we were lucky, Mrs. Pitt would let us run to meet the hokey-pokey man and purchase ice cream from his handbarrow. Even in the cold! Oh the thrills of yesteryear!" Her nostalgic expression fell on Reynolds bringing in the fish dish. She frowned slightly, and

Reynolds placed the fish on the sideboard, waiting for her signal to serve.

Mr. Lisney continued with his discourse as if Mrs. Lisney had not spoken and the butler had not entered. "Ours is the gleaming, brass and iron era of puffing, wheezing, tea kettle-whistling contraptions of glorious modern invention! The answer to any question, one might say, comes down to manufacturing the right kind of steam engine to fit the bill. And we, at Maycombe-Springerham, are poised on the brink to manufacture them all! Think of the all the achievements showcased in the Crystal Palace. How audacious! Think of the Bazalgette sewers - a marvel of planning! Can you imagine taking into consideration every water closet in the city?!"

Geoffrey noted Penny's apologetic smile at him when her father spoke of water closets at the dining table.

"Oh no question, Mr. Lisney, I quite agree." Geoffrey felt he should reassure the old gentleman that he was a modern man. In tune with the times. And with The Times, he joked to himself. "The Crystal Palace, the, uh, sewers, even our new rolling press for printing the newspaper — steam is the answer to all. And what might be next, do you think? The moon?" Geoffrey's question was meant to be merry and rhetorical. His face fell when Mr. Lisney looked puzzled and then contemplative.

"That is an interesting interrogative, Geoffrey. As you have mentioned, we have conquered the land, the sea, and now with the flying machines, the air. Is the stratosphere next? Well, why not! We have an engineer at Maycombe-Springerham who thinks like you. He is frightfully keen on internal engines. An up-and-coming young lad. I must remember to invite the two of you to the club one of these days. The pair of you would have some edifying chats, I daresay. He might even persuade you to join the firm, eh?" Mr. Lisney tilted his head, giving his guest an appraising once-over.

Somewhat nonplussed, unsure how or whether he should follow this new conversational gambit, Geoffrey picked up his glass and hoisted it upward in a toast. "Gentlemen, and ladies, I give you, Steam!"

And it was then that the unthinkable happened. It must have been the combination of the oysters, a superfluity of wine, and nervous excitation. Geoffrey's bottom emitted a flurry of posterior petarades. Blurts of ventosity. The sound of windy spirits peeled out like a string of shotgun cracks in the overly decorous room.

The silence was instantaneous. As if all were sealed in a vacuum, where not even the tiniest rustle of a petticoat might escape. All, constrained by etiquette, refrained from drawing attention to the circumstance. A good hostess such as Mrs. Lisney would keep her good grace in all possible eventualities, whether her guest were to drop a spoon, accidentally break her favorite gravy boat, or take up his plate in a dastardly fashion and hurl it at a wall. Faced with any breach, she would keep her composure, per societal principles. But if the offense was too grave, and this might be, he would never be invited to return.

Geoffrey's face, if he could have seen himself in a mirror, would be the picture book epitome of chagrin. He hardly dared face his beloved. If he were to read disappointment there, if he was no longer her hero, all will be lost to him. If her eyes were downcast, turned away from him, his world would crumble, black as sackcloth. A dreadful pall would drop upon him, and his future would hold no more joy. Food would taste like ashes. Pleasant sunlight would only mock his sorrow. All that would remain to him were endless whining hours until his bloodless life slipped away.

Pray it be quick! Heroically he forced himself to raise his anguished eyes and meet his ordained fate. His future, or loss thereof, would show in the mirror of his cherished Penny's face.

To his astonishment, her lips were curled upward. Was it possible? Glory be, she was grinning at him! It was as if angels burst forth from the heavens with their trumpets proclaiming the final coming. Not only was she smiling, but her eyes danced, her pearly teeth were on display, and the corners of her dainty mouth were lifted in merciful mirth! Hosanna and hallelujah! His days were not yet numbered! His heart, which seemed to have stopped when the grim episode occurred, began to beat again.

Quickly he lifted his napkin to his lips and unnecessarily pressed them to the cloth. "Pardon me," he said without emphasis, as if he had dripped sauce on his waistcoat or set his glass down too roughly. Something eminently pardonable. "Did you see that Winchester trounced Chichester in the cricket matches on Saturday last? Something of a comeback, wouldn't you say?" Deftly he added, "Mind you, I wouldn't count Chichester out just yet," to cover the possibility that Mr. Lisney was a Chichester man.

Sports, the last refuge of a dying conversation.

Mr. Lisney and the ladies looked blankly at Geoffrey. He felt enormously grateful, for they looked at him with their countenances unclouded and open. Crisis averted. Over and done with. He drew a shaky breath. Reynolds served up the fish.

"I can't say that I follow the matches." Mr. Lisney's faint puzzlement at the swift change in subject was covered with congenial blandness. "But I highly recommend the sport for the younger men. I even organized a company team for Saturday afternoon recreation. All that physical exercise keeps their mind off of other, well, less savory, preoccupations. You know." He nodded, seemingly to the serving plate, not wishing to address the specifics in mixed company.

The butler stepped forward, thinking the master would like another helping.

The meal continued then, the embarrassing incident forgotten. The gentle trading of respectable news, refined opinions, genteel gossip, polite preferences, and well-mannered memories all dovetailed together, creating a pleasant evening. The art of conversation was aided by good drink, good food, and a sincere desire on the part of all parties at the table to facilitate the burgeoning romance of Miss Penelope Lisney and Mr. Geoffrey Gridley. The venison arrived, the flavorful meat lavishly larded by Cook, the tenderest Geoffrey has ever tasted, or so he said. The wording of the wedding invitation was being formulated in the back of minds, as those around the table wove their stories and their destinies together.

After the final courses of fruits and cheese, Mrs. Lisney nodded gently to her spouse, and all together the gentlemen and ladies retired to the parlor. Geoffrey was relieved that the men did not retire separately. He took the circumstance of mixed company as another signal that it was not yet time to propose. With the ladies' permission, the gentlemen indulged in cigars and port, while the ladies enjoyed rose hip tea. The conversation continued pleasantly through the gentle blue smoke, punctuated with quiet sips.

Mr. Lisney returned to the subject of his preoccupation. "So, Geoffrey. Steam. If you ever tire of tinkering with words, I assure you there is a place for a go-getter like yourself in the steam world." He smiled pointedly at his daughter and then back to Geoffrey. "I can assure you."

Geoffrey looked on Penny with fondness. Penny gazed back, frank and unblushing.

In due time the man of the house announced he would retire, taking his wife with him, but volunteering Tillie to chaperone. "Don't stay up too late, young folks," Mr. Lisney chided from the door of the parlor. "You might want to stay awake talking all night, but there will be plenty of time in your future for that, let me tell you!" He directed amused glances at his wife and daughter before his mirthful countenance returned to Geoffrey. "Thank you for the pleasure of your company this evening, my dear fellow. I trust we will have that pleasure again soon, and often." He bowed with courtesy to the young newspaperman and took his leave. Mrs. Lisney took his place in the doorway. "Goodnight, Geoffrey. Don't forget to ask your mother about the Pteridophyta Club. Myself, I find ferns overwhelmingly addictive." She released the parlor curtain, which closed behind her as she departed.

The master and mistress gone, Tillie gave the lovebirds a knowing grin and busied herself with knitting a dainty sock. Or was it a baby bootie? Was Tillie hinting at them?

"What a lovely dinner," Geoffrey started off. He patted his belly and smiled with contentment. The incident that caused such consternation earlier was now distant and insubstantial in his memory. "It just doesn't get any better than this."

"Indeed!" agreed Tillie. She kept her gaze down on her work studiously, allowing them this tiny modicum of freedom.

Penny's eyes were full of mischief. She slid sideways across the sofa, closer to Geoffrey's armchair. "Mother has taught me everything about dinner parties. From oysters to jiggly jellies. Do you like jellies, Geoffrey? The jiggly kind?"

Tillie's eyes were focused on the intricacies of the sock's heel, but it was clear she was tracking the conversation. "Do tell us more about the Ripper, Mr. Gridley." She offered a topic less intimate, but to her mind no less lurid. "I find myself excessively interested by what I read in your newspaper."

Geoffrey smiled, albeit ruefully, at her substitution of second-hand sensationalism for first-hand sensation.

"I know I should not think on it, but I do," Tillie continued, "Those unfortunate girls! So little protection from the exigencies of men's dread desires." Tillie shivered as if a chill wind had found its way into the snug parlor. "The mere notion sends nervous excitation all through me!" She then noticed she had dropped a stitch and went silent, concentrating on picking it up.

Geoffrey spoke, filling the gap in the conversation. "If it is any consolation, it is said the girls have only moments to suffer, in that he strikes so quickly. So they are beyond pain when he removes, well, the term we use in the newspaper is "the organs of regeneration," and absconds with them. My job is to report, not speculate, but my guess is he destroys that which he cannot enjoy as other men do." He paused, his rueful smile turning into a playful grin. "But maybe what you wanted to hear is how the entrails are tossed about, and as of last night, there is also a missing kidney?"

Tillie shrieked, dropped her knitting, and covered her eyes. Behind her hands, a shy little voice whispered, "Maybe just a little."

"Are you saying the killings are," Penny hesitated before choosing her next word, knowing she would never have the wherewithal to say it in front of her parents, "carnal in nature, Geoffrey? I heard the postman tell the omnibus driver that the murderer must be a vigilante, taking action to eradicate the greatest of social evils, and seeking to decrease the surplus of harlots in the city. Actions of depraved indifference, although some, including the postman he declared, would say politicians have offered only callous alternatives with their reformatories and social clinics."

Geoffrey thought over a response to Penny's question for some moments, during which he considered the impropriety of speaking with one of her gender without the conventional filters. To find a partner who shared his honest interest in the depths and breadth of human nature intrigued him greatly. He made his choice. Tossing aside propriety, good manners, and Aunt Tillie sitting across from him, he answered directly.

"It is said there is a reciprocal relationship between Thanatos and Eros, to speak in mythological terms. Death focuses the desire to live, provokes us to fight savagely if fleeing is not an option, makes us human in our desire to procreate before we shuffle off our mortal coil. Could it be that is what motivates this dark cove? We will never know with certainty, unless they catch him. He may merely be mad, striking out at easy prey. Women on the street are vulnerable, alone, and unprotected in the night. Dramatic and horrific as the murders are, and spine-tingling as we find them because they involve partially-clad females, I think when the killer is apprehended, we will find he is a weak little man, thwarted by life, and as uncomprehending of his true motive as we, the general public, are."

Geoffrey noted with interest that Tillie had taken her hands from her face and was nodding along with him as he theorized. Had the spinster entertained similar thoughts regarding love and death? Had Penny inherited a mind unfettered from the conventional? He felt something race through his veins. It was like a surge, a frisson, or a flash of passion above and beyond mere physical desire. Although he felt that too. Penelope Lisney was a match made in heaven for him.

"Fascinating," responded Penny, who also glanced at Tillie, perhaps also startled that she did not remonstrate. "Such raw instincts do make me ponder the ultimate fate of society." She stared into Geoffrey's face, hungry for more. Perhaps unconsciously she crossed her ankles and her hem remained caught up so that the entire expanse of her left upper foot was visible above its elegant evening slipper. "What happens to the bodies after the police come?"

Geoffrey blinked, partly because his thoughts were not running that way and partly because of the glimpse of stocking. "Oh, well, hmm, let me think. The police come and make notes, about the position of the body and anything the killer might have left behind." His speech was slowed, his eyes and thoughts barely able to lift above her ankle. The gleam of translucent silk that was shining up at him in the haze of the parlor's gas lamps excited him immeasurably. Her forbidden skin was just underneath the thin wrapper. The delicately arched pedal extremity sent his thoughts tumbling. By thunder, how he wished he could seize her ankle and draw her deliciously proportioned appendage to his lips! "And then a wagon comes and takes the poor wretch to a morgue or police station, where a surgeon examines her, and she is washed and sketched. I hear they are using photography now to keep a record of the injuries and for formal identification." He closed his eyes, unable to both gaze on his intended's foot and speak intelligibly at the same time. "Perhaps I should learn photography. Unbelievable what a little flash and silver emulsion can do."

Listening intently, Penny leaned forward, and her skirt shifted, covering most of her ankle. "Photography, yes. Although I hear it is a smelly business. Perhaps you could rent a studio? Or confine the hobby to uh, to the basement." Geoffrey heard her stutter, nearly saying "our" basement, catching herself at the last moment. Penny continued, "Are you thinking of changing professions, Geoffrey? I hear Mr. Pelham, off Arlington Street, makes a rather nice living in portraiture with his camera."

Geoffrey sighed as her ankle was lost to view, but his smile lingered. "No, not changing, just adding an additional skill. Illustrative drawing for newspapers is passé. Photos are the future. If I could both write and photograph the news, I would be paid twice for the same assignment. Why at that rate, I could buy us, er, I could afford a plummy house in no time at all." He looked to Tillie, hoping she did not notice his slip. In fact, her eyes were shut. Penny seemed to take it all in stride, although an odd ripple passed over her body. If there was a draft in the room, it had bypassed his armchair. He longed to add "a house with room for children," but he clearly had already passed a point of propriety. It confounded and surprised him that society frowned on bachelors speaking about procreation, when in fact it was bachelors who were most fervid when they thought on the act.

Suddenly Tillie was awake and alert again. Perhaps she noticed the ankle episode after all, and surely she heard his misspoken "us" in his last utterance. "How nice that will be for you, Mr. Gridley. Although perhaps that is something we should talk of another time. Now tell us how your parents are getting on. Do I remember you saying you were an only child, and you reside with them in the less fashionable end of the Crescent?" Tillie had fixed Penny with a gimlet-eyed glare. Penny had looked down, perhaps to ensure her skirt had draped fully to the floor.

Geoffrey harrumphed, but he did so softly, understanding that he was being reprimanded. He rearranged his face to appear conciliatory. "They are doing well, Miss Lisney. My father occupies himself with the stock exchange. Mostly coal and steam rail bonds. Safe bets for the foreseeable future. My mother tends to our home and makes the most intricate paper punchwork pieces. I think you two would have exceedingly edifying conversations. May I arrange for her to invite you to tea?" he inquired of Tillie, hoping she would not find the suggestion too forward. He took her mention of home to mean he should be going there, and he started to rise to his feet. "It is indeed getting late, and perhaps I should be on my way."

"Oh no!" Penny exclaimed in evident dismay. "It is not that very late, and I did want to show you the fossils Mother found when she went ferning with your mother in Dorset!" She hopped up with alacrity. "They are just over here in the fernery. Do come and take a look!" Penny scurried to a glass and lead monstrosity on a table near the windows, and Geoffrey stood to follow her, grateful that she created an excuse to delay his leave-taking.

Tillie settled back to her knitting, eyes down, a tiny smirk playing across her lips. Penny fished out the misshapen stones, pulling the doily out from underneath the structure to display them upon. "Look at this one! Isn't it darling? Mother found it in a shop owned by a lady who was struck by lightning as a baby and lived! Can you imagine? She was very famous, although I've forgotten her name. This one is a snake-stone. Isn't it the most charming ever?"

Geoffrey took the ammonite fossil she handed him, running a fingertip across its ridges. "Amazing. I remember reading about her. She found a huge skull, four feet long, and later the rest of the skeleton. It was on display at the British Museum for some time. Might still be."

Penny reached out, tracing her finger over the fossil spiral, incidentally brushing her hand against his. "Fascinating," she murmured. "Somehow it makes me feel...oh I don't have the words. It's like when the tea cakes are so perfectly spongy, and the tea is just the right heat and strength to melt together into a mélange, like a wrapped gift with a perky bow, nestled inside your tummy. Well, maybe not that exactly. Geoffrey, do you know the words I mean to say?" Her voice was distant, as if it spoke of its own accord, with her eyes focused on his lips.

"Ah, yes," he murmured in return, attempting to keep his voice level. Penny's visage was vivid, her color suffused, her expression wild. He swallowed hard. "I think I do." He took away the fossil with his other hand, putting it down and leaving her hand touching his now empty palm.

Penny looked over her shoulder, pointedly, at Tillie, whose eyelids were flickering. In no time, they would be shut tight. Penny reached out her other hand, sliding her fingertips along his wrist, and then pressing down, palm to palm. Now both her hands were in his.

His breath left him in a rush. He leaned towards her over the table, his head now close to hers. His lips moved, parted as if to speak, but no words came out. Their hands snugged up against each other, lascivious in their proximity.

Tille snored gently in the silence between them.

Penny whispered. "I feel intensely and unaccountably strange inside." Her eyelids fluttered, and her lips almost touched his. "Here. Let me show you my favorite shell." With deliberation, Penny moved his hand with hers to pick up a polished whelk from the lot. "This one. With its delta shape, its creamy exterior, and a deep cave spiraling inward, ivory at the outer lip, then suffusing across the little ridges to shades of rose madder, rose carmine, and then dark mauve at its innermost depths." She stroked along the introitus of the shell, dragging his fingers along with hers. "Can you feel the little ridges? They almost seem to pulsate. Radiate with warmth. Heat. The cavern collapsing, growing tighter as your fingers press in." She was breathing deeply, the ruffles covering her breasts lifting up with each inhale and shuddering on each exhale.

Geoffrey had to wet his lips before sound came out. "I cannot recall anything so exquisite. So tenderly innocent and yet so voluptuous."

The pink and coral shell, with its suggestive opening, was cuddled in their mutual embrace.

"Penny," he whispered. It was as if a cable connected the tender flesh of his palms with his manhood, at which her touch tugged. He felt the surges pulse through him down to his root when her hands stroked the shell and his fingers on it, again and again.

Swiftly his cock became stiff. He imagined her fingers were moving over the length of his rod, sliding down to cradle his weighty sack, and sliding up to circle his taut head. His trousers forced his growing erection back against his belly. He felt a drop dampen his waistband. She was talking about rain. He was hoping she was wet.

His imagination raced onward. His thoughts envisioned his engorged tip poking at the entrance to her own shell-like delta, nudging, pressing, and finally plunging. Each inch was gloriously embraced. Encompassed. Smothered. Squeezed. Delicious but ravenous desire ripped all the veneer of civilization from him. There were not even shreds left, not even his much-coveted penchant for words. Naked lust urged his prick forward and back, over and again, seething, searching, yearning for release. If only his imagination could find purchase in the real world!

Standing over the fernery, he watched her breasts heave beneath the noxious-hued cloth. He trembled. His palms pressed to hers with unbridled pressure. His thoughts were within the dancing limit of his pinnacle.

He gasped out her name, his eyes rolled back in his head, and his spunk burst forth, besmirching his shirt tails beneath his prim buttons. A sudden glory overwhelmed him.

Geoffrey was so bold as to draw her into an embrace, and Penny was so indelicate as to allow him to do so without protest. In his arms, he felt her welling up, overflowing, gushing, plummeting, shattering, and melting into nothingness within the shell of his sheltering hug.

It was her heightened tone, his answering groan, and their prolonged and profound exhalations of culmination that were enthusiastic enough to wake Tillie from her dozing state. The aunt lifted her head in time to see the ecstatic look passing between the two. She stood up decisively, her knitting falling from her lap, her expression pinched with mounting anxiety.

"Heavens forfend!" she cried out. "Most certainly it is late, very late. Mr. Gridley, you most certainly must be on your way!"

Penny jerked herself upright, as if it were she who had just been roused from slumber. "Dearest Tillie, you rest that bad knee of yours for a little bit longer and let me escort the gentleman to the door." Although she was still wobbling a little, she put a hand on Geoffrey's back and marched, propelling him towards the parlor door. He tried to turn to bid Tillie good evening, but Penny applied both hands firmly to herd him out into the hallway. He saw her raise one eyebrow, giving her auntie a conspiratorial look. He thought it might have meant nothing untoward can happen in the short distance between here and the front entrance. Tillie raised her eyebrow in a like manner, staring back at Penny. From the tilt of that brow, he could tell she knew full well something untoward could happen in the short distance between the here and the there.

But then Tillie blinked, backing down from Penny's challenge, making the decision to accept the risk, and sat herself down again. "Such a kind girl, thank you, Penelope. Very well, I bid you good night, Mr. Gridley. I do hope you will allow us the pleasure of your company again sometime."

Geoffrey tried again to turn so that he might make a departing bow, but Penny continued to rush him forward. "Yes, soon, Miss Lisney," he managed to say before he was outside the parlor, shoved out into the hall and herded towards the front door.

In the entryway, Penny retrieved his hat and coat from the hall tree. Reynolds was nowhere in sight, although it might be suspected he was nearby. What a sly old dog that old butler was.

Geoffrey watched Penny's face intently as she held out his coat to him, hoping to see some echo of the ardor he had glimpsed in the parlor. Her eyes were wide and almost frightened it seemed to him. He stepped closer, to accept the coat she clutched tightly in front of her, formulating some parting phrase that might be suitable, discreet in case they were overheard, but redolent of both of his devotion and his overpowering love for the lust she had incited within him.

Unexpectedly she lunged forward, placing the length of her body against his, so tightly that her dress, petticoats, corset, and even her pantaloons were crushed between the two of them. He might fear his effluvium would leak through the layers, but she was oblivious to any possible stain. Her arms encircled his shoulders and then moved up to clasp behind his neck, pulling his face down to hers. Fervently she pressed her lips to his and held them there, the wayward violence of her action distracting him from the eloquent parting words he had been composing in his head.

Geoffrey whelped in surprise, then recovered himself and acquiesced to the embrace. His arms moved around her awkwardly, gingerly, timid of her approval and both their reputations in this open space. Her vehement embrace emboldened him. His hands clutched at the fabric encasing her bustle, his chest pressed into her bosom, his lips moved under her static ones, and furtively his tongue ventured forward, touching her teeth, looking for an opening.

Penny sprung away from him abruptly. It would seem his searching tongue had shocked her.

Consternation descended upon him! Had he gone too far? He flinched, expecting the slap he so richly deserved. Instead she leaned in and whispered to him. A statement. A request. A promise.

Geoffrey, the newspaperman, was at a loss for words. Dazed, he could only dip his head up and down in agreement. After this, not even wild horses could drag him from this woman.

STEAM GEARED

The Dinner Party, Part II

The Dinner Party, Part II

PENELOPE ARRANGED THE PLEATS of her new dress yet again, and started to say out loud that it was getting late, but held her tongue, thinking it better not to bring Geoffrey's tardiness to the attention of her mother and aunt.

Instead she thought to herself. 'He is late! I do wonder what Mama and Papa will say of him, what with punctuality not being one of his virtues. Of course I understand it is due to his employment, but they mightn't. I myself am favorably impressed by his sense of dedication to his employer, and I recall one time he apologized for his late arrival, saying a journalist must write his story while the event was hot, for news was no longer new once it was cold. I take pride in seeing his byline on the front page when Father reads to us at the breakfast table. And I am rather proud of knowing the word 'byline' by the by. But making a good impression on Papa is imperative if we are to be encouraged in our courtship. Making a good impression on Mama will be necessary as well, for it is she who will construct Papa's opinions. I am not sure Papa comprehends that, but the truth of it has been borne out many a time. In the end, should either take it into their heads to impede our romantic inclinations, it will mean the final curtain for a future between us.

'Ah, a knock at the entry door! I will saunter from the parlor to pose placidly at the doorway looking into the hall, for it would not do for me to answer it. In point of fact, I should not even appear eager. But I am. Truly, intensely, anguishedly eager!

With the parlor maid helping in the kitchen, Aunt Tillie will open it. Dear Auntie, she never minds pitching in with housemaid duties when it is for the convenience of the household. Oh, I do hope he likes my new dress. The color, the clerk told us when mother purchased the fabric, is called Paris green. Quite popular, the clerk said. However the dressmaker pursed her lips when we brought it to her. I would guess she has seen enough of it of late. Next time, I will insist on something less a-la-mode. More timeless. What was it the Lady's Book had recommended for the season? 'An andante in shaded violet.' So musical are the latest fashions! Did Geoffrey like music? He seemed stricken when we met at the bandstand in the park. But they were amateurs, and the waltz music was the slow, old-fashioned kind. We are modern in our outlooks, the two of us. It seems predestined that we will make a life together. In my opinion at least and I hope in his, too. I hope ... but here the dear man is himself. Such piercing eyes he has. Oh, how fast my heart is beating! Perhaps I should listen to what he is saying.

'I think I speak to him. I think I say "What lovely flowers," or some similar nicety. Maybe all I do is grin at him, like some cunning animal at the zoo. I cannot listen to myself think, much less talk, when Geoffrey is in sight. His great proud forehead, his glossy nut-brown curls falling on his temples, the patrician nose, the long mustache tracing his sensuous lips, and the blunt-tipped goatee, all conspire together to cause my heart to skip beats. At this rate I will go off in an aromatic faint and need smelling salts to revivify me often. It would be well for Mama to convince Papa that we should be engaged as soon as social convention allows.

'Ah, dear Tillie, making him feel welcome. And dear Mama, admiring the flowers. Of course she knows as well as I what the bouquet is saying. I hope she does not think him presumptuous to add devotion to the mix. Brambles? I hope the only thing he regrets is being late for dinner.

'A young girl chose them for him, he says? Why do men go all to pieces when it comes to floriography? The language is simple to learn and choosing your own message makes a bouquet ever so much more endearing to the recipient. I suppose I should be grateful that he didn't just press a lever at an automat and bring me a posy of hyacinths and bachelor buttons. I must learn patience. In good time, I will help him understand the subtler points. Just as Mama did Papa. She promised to tell me how such things are accomplished when it comes my time to take charge of a household.

'And here comes Papa now, deigning to emerge from his cave of a study. Such a hearty bluff fellow he is when in company. Such a gruff old bear when in private. But he is our old bear, as Mama says. Our curmudgeonly but well-intentioned bear. With a pocket watch that he checks entirely too emphatically at the moment! Poor Geoffrey's expression is all which-whither. All of us trundle through to the parlor, ducking one of Mother's more boisterous ferns that is encroaching from its perch by the doorway.

'I will say our parlor is nice enough, but with all the work we put into the dining room, this room now seems lacking in luster to my eyes. If only we had thought to stitch up some new cushions with gay embroidered figures or tat up an intricate set of doilies. Geoffrey will be most impressed when he goes in for dinner with us. His eyes will light up; like I've seen them do when he is has a new lead on a story.

'Oh my goodness, there goes Papa again, talking about what kind of things we mustn't talk about. Such a funny habit of his to sneak in the unspeakable! I long to be able to say those kinds of things I shouldn't say out loud. How endearing to me is that little divot beneath Geoffrey's nose where his mustache parts to each side. How intensely I long to touch him right there. With my fingers first. Then with my lips. Tiny kisses.

'Oh deary me, what indecorous thoughts I entertain! Whatever is wrong with me? I know my gentle mother brought me up better, so it must be something wicked in my very nature. If Geoffrey knew my thoughts, would he compare me with those soiled doves he writes about in The Metropolitan Times? I should hope no one would mistake me for an unfortunate. I must ensure the superfluous ruffles of my bodice are draping in a most becoming manner. I would be devastated were he not impressed.

'Will he want sherry? I've never heard him mention whiskey, but I think that is what newsmen drink in the back room. Except when they drink the local ale, to curry favor with the barkeeps, who after all, are privy to the best gossip. Or do they perhaps drink gin? I shiver at the thought! Gin and gentility do not mix, father has remarked on multiple occasions to his business associates. Please, please, Geoffrey, don't say gin! Not that I will mind. Whatever he drinks will satisfy me.

'Oh my stars, how lucky I am! Here is an instance when Mother, Father, and Tillie are all looking to each other, unaware that Geoffrey and I are looking at each other. I gather up my courage, seize the moment, and wink at him.

'A sudden doubt then strikes me. Should I have done that? Heavens forfend, will he think me a mere hussy? But it was such fun! What a challenge to slip it in right under the gaze of my earnest chaperones. And he smiled back at me! We will make a lively pair I think. He, who is so quick to see humor, and me, who so earnestly seeks out that which is amusing. Living would be too long by half were there not humor in it, I'm sure of it.

'So much the better, he chooses punch. At least while in front of my parents. If I were to kiss his mustache would I taste the liquor there? Truly I am a depraved young thing! I will endeavor to think purer thoughts going forward. If I possibly can manage it.

'I try not to sigh. Mother begins to some inane commentary about the venison haunch we will have for dinner. If someone doesn't say something quickly, Father will start bragging about his company. I speak up hastily. I ask Geoffrey about his work.

'Speaking of news, why was Geoffrey talking about motoring cars? The latest doings in Whitechapel must be very vile indeed for him to skip the subject altogether. I must consider hardening myself to such. I will take an interest in his writings, aspiring bride-to-be that I am. Indeed some particulars of the world are not pleasant. I remember asking him once, why did he not report on baskets of kittens and the more fashionable aspects of hair styling? He murmured something comforting to me, and I felt so low when he distanced his thoughts, thinking me too fragile for him. I was fended off. Cut away from a deep part of him. I could not bear it! I want all of him!

'Is that wrong of me? Granted, my parents seemed happy in their separate spheres that only intersect on the upper floors. In time, perhaps, I will have my fill of Geoffrey and be content to let him paddle about town, traipsing the unseemly gutters, without a contrary thought. But now, my love is fresh and all-consuming. I would devour him and his preoccupations alive. With relish. And maybe a bit of mustard sauce.

'I see Mother is flashing me a surreptitious smirk. Surely she does not wish to ride in one of those rickety conveyances? No better than a curricle, in that your skirt and stockings are all bespattered by the time you disembark. This notion of motoring, especially for enjoyment, lacks sensibility to my way of thinking. Even so, I encourage him to continue. Venture a comment. Ask a question. What I do not say aloud is that surely the proper implementation of the scientific enhancements in transportation, such as automobiles and faster steamships and extended railways, is to bring goods within my purview, not to carry me off to the hinterlands from whence the items originated!

'Drat, he is adjusting his cuff links, a sure sign he is nervous or, goodness gracious me, bored! I will speak up again, and get him to tell us more tales. The man knows so many interesting stories, and there is always politics, if we must.

'At last the punch arrives. I hope it enlivens this forced conversation. We talk off the top, as if we were ambassadors from disharmonious countries, awash with diplomatic niceties and bland phrasings. Father doles out ladylike portions of punch for Mother, Tillie, and me, much watered down with extra lemonade, but even so, it makes a warm spot for itself in my stomach. Heartened by my prior prank with the wink, I kiss my glass when I think only he is looking. Aunt Tillie jerks bolt upright in her chair, which may or may not be mere happenstance. Geoffrey's attention was drawn away from me by

Papa's blather regarding steam turbines. Hang the luck, as Papa would say, a wasted effort on my part.

'Bejabbers! To use another of Father's favorite expressions! This time is it Mother and her obsessions. Why would a gentleman have any notion of ferns? Especially considering he has already admitted he enlisted assistance to speak the language of flowers? Ah Mother, dear thing, is just trying to keep the conversation lively. I am surprised that Father hasn't begun prattling about his steamships. Even though I fully understand they are marvels and all that, and I concede it is an important topic, just for once, please I beg silently, might we speak of things not industrial? There is a matter of interpersonal mingling that needs addressing here! Am I the only one thinking we should be moving on to the subject of courtship? Not that such can be rushed. I will stay quiet and content myself. But if the topic does not arise during dinner, I shall have to make waves. Even splash if I must!

'Oh! Have I ever seen someone so spontaneously cunning in the ways of society as my Geoffrey? I saw him waver, nearly offering to escort my poor auntie into the dining room, as if she were the most inestimable partner in the place! Of course that would leave Father in the unenviable position of escorting his own wife, but this is a family dinner. No need to stand on silly protocols like husbands not walking in with their spouse. I note Father and Mother give each other a subtle inclination of the head. But with seemingly effortless grace, Geoffrey repositions himself to take Mama, his hostess, into the dining room. Thank goodness he chooses tradition over innovation. Until they know him better, it befits him to appear civilized, rather than risk his novelty be taken for barbarism.

'Because I was walking behind them all towards the dining room, even though he barely paused in his suave manner, I saw him stutter a step as our impressive decor nearly bowled him over! Awe-inspired astonishment arrested him mid-step. We had worked so hard to make it a spectacle, with Mother, Tillie, the two maids, and me, all awash in holly and silver polish for most of the day. It engendered a deep pleasure in me to see him agog in that brief misstep.

'The brocades, linens, and poplins hold sway in a merry array. We had tucked tasteful greenery hither and thither. The fire was crackling softly and its cheerful fragrance disseminated through the room. How could he not be impressed! He compliments our hard work so sweetly. He is most assuredly a treasure, and I am so fortunate to have come upon him.

'Once everyone is seated, the table talk proscribed by etiquette begins anew. Poor Reynolds. He must think we are the most boring family in the world if he judged by our conversation when he was serving. Duller than unpolished boot leather we must seem to him.

'Mother is saying something about how this is Geoffrey's first dinner with us, and he is looking at me with a question in his eyes. Quickly I look down at my plate because I cannot answer that look! Was he thinking about proposing? Sweet trumpeting skies above, I do hope not! Mother was hinting at wedding bells because mothers of eligible girls think of nothing else. But Father must be coddled a bit longer. All must be carefully orchestrated so that Father will see the whole idea as his own splendid brainchild, and not balk at the trouble and expense of giving away a daughter.

'Fortunately the wine is not watered. I feel more expansive. Mother is still talking about the planning of the meal. As if anyone truly cares whether salad is served before or after. Of course he agrees, a guest reassuring his hostess. I wonder if he has a preference either way? If he does have an opinion, I will happily concede to him. The matter is inconsequential to my way of thinking.

'Look how he tucks into those oysters! Maisie told me that men like oysters on their wedding night. I think she would have told me more, but just then Tillie joined us, and Maisie said no more on the subject. For me they are too big a mouthful. One mustn't leave tooth marks on food, so biting them in half is not done. And there are oyster forks, but there is no such implement as oyster knives for the dining table, so cutting is not an option. Thus I avoid them. Pretend I am not hungry. I tell myself I am above the base animal need that is hunger. I tell myself they are unappetizing. I tell myself lots of things, some of which are true.

'But Geoffrey seems to like them. He looks at me and tips one into his mouth, his tongue slipping out to slurp up the juices in the shell. I feel I should answer that look with another wink, but dare not, what with my parents and hawk-eyed Tillie at the table. Am I any better than those trollops on the street, wanting him to look at me, think of me, in that base and lowly kind of way? Perish the thought! No more unladylike winks. Instead I will pick up my napkin, manipulating it across my palms and around my fingers, letting him know that I would speak to him through the protocol of dinner napkin signaling.

'Father and Geoffrey are eating oysters with abandon, Geoffrey slurping as loudly as Father does. Was that a shared smile between them? They both seem to enjoy the shellfish immensely. I am pleased to see them finding something in common.

'Well, it had to have happened sometime! I should be grateful Father didn't start in on his steam lecture the minute the poor man stepped through the door. But Geoffrey is taking it all in stride, nodding, making agreeable noises. Honestly, I prefer he not choose to invest his future in Father's business. I am proud of Geoffrey's profession. People should become acquainted with what is happening outside their cozy windows. Yes, steamships are critical to our current economy, but if they all sunk to the seabed tomorrow, the railways would bring us stout British goods and sailing ships could breeze along with non-perishable comestibles. It must be acknowledged that Father is something of a braggart, but I say so with great fondness for his foible.

'Oddly enough, Geoffrey is listening so intently that he does not return my napkin signaling. I draw the napkin more forcefully through my grasp, twisting it some to make a muffled sound, hoping he might look my way.

'Father drones on. He makes a small joke, which I did not hear exactly, something about wrinkles in steam. Mother darts me a disapproving glance. I hide my napkin in my lap, and express a modicum of mirth.

'Reynolds serves the calf's tongue next. It is so cute in its little dress, hiding that vulgar portion where it has been separated from its beastly ancestry. Mother begins talking about her childhood with Tillie. Ah me, will she never tire of that story about sugarplums after her lessons? I wonder that she would mention that the custom of afternoon tea was unheard of in her day. She makes herself sound old as dust. She's not all that old. Although sometimes I think she would have preferred to live in a previous century.

'Ahead of schedule Reynolds brings in the fish course, painted with salmon-colored mayonnaise for scales, with an eye of carved tomato and a fluke of fringed cabbage. While Mother is distracted by the premature presentation of the fish dish, I raise my napkin again and communicate "I desire to converse by signal with you" by drawing my napkin through my hands. Then I hold the napkin by its corners to signal "Is it agreeable?" Still no response. Maddening!

'At last my beloved picks up his napkin. Amazingly he makes use of it as if it were nothing more than a bit of table linen, and then replaces it in his lap. I am crushed! He must not have seen my heartfelt message. Granted Father and Mother are engaging his attention. I will be patient, and try again with my fan when we retire to the drawing room. Or I could ask Maisie to fetch my gloves after the meal. Pulling them on and off in certain ways can be very effective it is said.

'Swan to mercy, I cannot believe Papa said that! Please, Father dearest, don't ask us to imagine water closets while at dinner, especially not all of them in the city! I shall blanch myself pale and look as if I would faint. Even if Father doesn't notice, Geoffrey will know I disapprove of such indelicacies during a repast.

'In the midst of my concentration to make myself look pale, Geoffrey proposes a toast. To steam, a subject so precious to Father. And then, can you imagine anything so funny? He fizzles!

'It was all I could do to keep from bursting with laughter! Mother and Father look at their plates, pretending nothing has happened. Aunt Tillie, the dear, deftly retrieves the fish's tomato eye and pops it into her mouth, munching placidly, with a faint smile on her lips, as if the taste was remarkable and delicious.

'Geoffrey recovers his aplomb with consummate ease and asks Father about a cricket match or some such. Father has an opinion, as usual, but not a strong one this time. With the ice, or dare I say it, wind, broken, now we may have a fulfilling conversation, entertaining and light on the surface, with deeper oblique meanings relating the fundamental beliefs of life, happiness, and how best to pursue each. Fish, salad, venison, and their accompanying wines swoop like swallows on and off the table, and by the time the sweets and cheese arrive, I am confident that my parents will permit Geoffrey the honor of asking for my hand sometime in the coming year.

'Aunt Tillie leans across the table and whispers to me boldly, "Shall I make you some lace gloves with blue ribbons, my dear? Something blue will be needed soon, I predict." She is a pearl, my darling auntie.

'Gentle and mostly idle talk continues as we leave the table and repair to the parlor until, at last! Mother and Father retire for the evening. Tillie stays with us for propriety, but she will fall asleep directly and we may be free to flirt with our expressions. I have been practicing crossing my ankles with great indelicacy, hoping for an opportunity where I might show him how much I value his esteem. And dare I say the word? I value his desire. No, go on, use the word, I tell myself. I find I must whisper it, even in my thoughts. Lust.

'He compliments the dinner, starting off with pleasantries. Tillie and I agree. Poor Geoffrey, I hope he will not think me an uncultured dab, devoid of delicacy, however I am impatient to dispense with this stilted refinement. Bless darling Tillie, playing her part as the elderly spinster, in that she articulates what I shouldn't. Even though everyone thinks on it, saying it aloud is frowned upon. Tillie is brave enough to give the three of us permission to speculate.

'In truth, I am in profound ignorance of the squalor that drives those poor girls to sin, and society deems it right that I should be, but I cannot help but ponder. The gulf between life and death, the sea between the necessity of sustenance and giving in to puerility, the ocean between verminous Whitechapel and my own dignified neighborhood with clean streets and salad after the fish, eludes my comprehension.

'When Geoffrey explains his thoughts, I forget everything Mother has taught me, answering him from my soul. Nature red in tooth and claw, as Tennyson wrote and Darwin demonstrated. We do our best to rise above the animals, but when I look in my beloved's eyes, it is the honeymoon that occupies my thoughts, rather than Mama's vision of pretty dresses and convivial parties. I berate myself, yet again, for my impure cogitations, but that does not stop me from lingering over the prospects of our future. From the gleam in Geoffrey's eyes, I think we are thinking alike.

'Oh, now this is laughable! After all my planning and practicing to accidentally on purpose displace my skirt hem and let him glimpse my dainty slippers, so he might perchance ponder a married future together, it is genuinely by accident that my hem has caught up while I was lost in the depths of our conversation. No wonder Geoffrey seemed distracted while expressing himself. I will innocently lean forward and let my skirt fall again, pretending I have no notion what trespass has occurred below. Tillie, I now notice, is motioning to me like a mad woman, in a most discreet fashion of course. She chides Geoffrey, mildly disparaging his upbringing, which I think is a bit much, for the fault, I freely admit, it as much my own as his. Gentleman that he is, he murmurs politely and rises to depart.

'I must arrest his leave-taking! Desperation seizes me, foretelling dread consequences if he were to go away at this juncture. The fossils, I nearly shout, and all but drag the poor man bodily to the little table under the window where Mother's fern conservatory rests. Ruthlessly I wrest out the stones, half sunken in their bed of peaty moss. I truly wish no harm to the ferns' roots, but my need for a distraction is exigent.

'I allow my hands to cross his. I see him incline towards me and I follow suit. I place the whelk in our hands, with its perceptibly suggestive appearance. Dimly I recognize words falling from my lips, but they are like raindrops falling, each one a tiny splash, each much of the same, each nearly inconsequential, until together they form a puddle, then a river, then a torrent. From the instant our palms meet, I feel myself in some sense transported. I have no words of proportionate sprightliness to do justice to the unrivaled depth and incipient turbulence of the experience. I may as well have been a gas lamp, with the key twisted up to the uppermost limit, for the flames seem to streak across my skin and burn deep within my body. I feel the light, or maybe it is heat, or another kind of energy altogether, chase itself through my flesh. My breath feels ragged, caged, pent-up, and within my core an exhilaration is welling. Waves and waves of it, like the ocean beating against the shore, plummeting and rising, over and over, more than my overloaded senses can take in. At my peak, I am shattered, and the waves crash over me, inundate me. Then the liquid dissipates, and I am left covered in droplets. Like a thunderstorm raging, peaking, and subsiding. I am left damp and dripping, a puddle again at his feet. I drift for some time.

'I drift until Aunt Tillie wakes and speaks sharply to me. I feel my face flush at her words, but my body is still wrung out like a twisted apron, pleasantly spent. I can tell from Geoffrey's expression that something momentous has happened to him also. I move quickly to vacate him from the parlor, and to make my own self absent, so that Aunt Tillie will have no opportunity to ascertain our consummated state from our vacant and satisfied expressions.

'With alacrity, I put my hand on his back and push, excusing Tillie from rising by saying her knee needs resting. Of course her knee has

long since healed since she strained it some weeks back, but I silently
beg her to give us a moment. Kindly soul that she is, she gives me leave.
I all but shove Geoffrey out the door, indeed not even giving him a
chance to say a proper goodbye.

'I am silent as I take his hat from the hall tree. Reynolds is out of
sight, although I suspect he is standing discreetly behind some door or
another. He is a sly old dog, and won't interrupt.

'I take Geoffrey's coat and hold it out to him in such a way that my
darling must come closer to me to grasp it. Without warning,
impetuously, I crush myself to him, laying the length of my body
against his, my arms encircling him, my new Paris green dress with all
the petticoats that lie beneath are pressed between us. I touch my lips to
his and hold them there, all etiquette suppressed, buried beneath the
violent waywardness of my actions.

'Geoffrey is surprised at first, as one might expect, but his swift
mind follows me, and his arms gather me up. His bold hands press me
to him. I can feel the double row of his waistcoat buttons as they crush
between my corset's whalebone, and his lips, his soft lips in their furry
overcoat of his enchanting mustache and goatee move against me. I am
in heaven! Then something odd happens. His tongue, seemingly of its
own accord, stretches out and touches me.

'I jump back, amazement overtaking me. Did he mean to do that?
There was nothing about tongues in the naughty books I procured
from Mother's private, locked library cabinet. Not in Bronte. Not in
Gaskill. Not even in Mrs. Frances Burney, and that woman knows her
men! My hand flies to my mouth, my fingers covering my confusion. I
think I am supposed to slap him, swiftly and with righteous indignation,
because the books say I should. But his look is so tender. So eager. So
endearing to me. "Oh Geoffrey. I have much to learn," I whisper, so
that only he will hear. "Will you teach me? I will be an apt pupil. I give
you my promise."

'It is the capstone to my joy when he nods, his eyes unwaveringly on mine. Yes!!!'

STEAM GEARED

My Fair Lady,
Or Pygmalion Re-Versed

My Fair Lady,
Or Pygmalion Re-Versed

THE NOBBY GAWKER GONE, Effie emptied the trestle table, placing the last of her flowers in a hand basket. There were two nosegays and a sad beribboned bundle of delphiniums. If she couldn't find a toffee-nosed tuft on her walk home, she would hand them off to the nippers in the street to enjoy the lingering scents.

"Violets, Mister?" she asked of a gentleman in a tidy checked-wool suit who was hurrying with his eyes down and his bowler pulled down tightly on his head. She didn't have any violets, but if she could get his attention she would offer the delphiniums, hoping he wouldn't notice or care. Violets always sold better to men in plaid. She looked up at him with the blue flowers in her outstretched hand, her tiny frame making her appear innocuous and waif-like. The man hurried on as if he hadn't heard her, with a glance upward at the darkening skies.

A hard rain began to fall on the city. Effie, in contrast to those who hunched their shoulders and ran to avoid the drops, surveyed the street, searching out where people were sheltering from the storm. The rain would oblige them to stay undercover, making them a captive audience for her wares. A cluster huddled under the colonnaded porch of St. Paul's, including two ladies in evening dress. She made her way towards them, the rain blurring her vision. She did not see the young man dashing out from the portico, coming into collision with her, knocking her basket from her grasp.

"Bust yer, Freddy, look wher'y'goin!" Effie cried out. She clawed at the basket, but it tipped and spilled.

"Sorry," the young man called out behind him as he rushed off toward the nearest hackney stand.

Effie wailed at her loss, getting down on her knees in the falling rain to gather her sodden wares. "Blinkin' 'obbade'oy!" she exclaimed, looking up at the people under shelter, appealing for sympathy in her plight. "Says 'sorry' like it pays the piper. Prolly caught sight o' sum floozy's follow-me-lads. Runs dash fire where 'is knob is pointin'. Only lead 'im to cold gruel, says I. Only fit to lead the blind monkeys, says I." This last she shouted in the direction of the young lad, the hobbledehoy as she called him, who was now out of sight. Effie shook the worst of the street muck from her bedraggled blooms and dropped them back in her basket.

From the portico the elder of the women in evening dresses called out to the flower girl in the street. "Young lass, how do you know my son's name is Freddy, pray tell?"

Effie fixed the woman with a deeply puzzled expression. Then catching her meaning, she pointed in the direction the young man had gone. "'E's your son, is 'e? Well, if y'd done yer duty like a mater should, 'e'd know better than to sprawl a poor gel's flowers an' scarper off wiffout payin' fer what 'e done." Effie carried her wet blossoms to the lady. "Will ye pay me fer 'em? They still beeootiful."

The woman's face showed some worry. "He has gone to find a cabriolet for us. Beastly rain! Yes, allow me," she said, opening her reticule and sifting through the contents, digging for a coin. "Might you have change?"

Effie shook her head. "No. Can't. I'm 'earts of oak." Effie traced a heart shape over her chest to indicate her sincerity and emphasize the 'heart' part of her slang phrase. "But ye can pay me extra for me trouble. I'd be o'clock wif that, I would."

The woman smiled wryly and gave the flower girl a sixpence.

"Caw, I'm sum pumkins now! Thank ye, Missus!" Effie exclaimed over the coin. She pointed again in the direction the son had gone. "If'n 'e's gone fer a flounder and dab, 'e'll be a long time." She grabbed up the contents of her basket and pushed them towards the woman. "Ere's two tussy-mussies and a tie-up of April Showers for ye. The blues will last ever so long, and if'n ye dry the tussies in yer kitchen, yer 'ouse will smell sweet as a nut!" Effie grinned.

"Thank you," the woman said coolly and took the flowers without looking at them. "Now tell me how you know that young gentleman's name." She gestured in the direction, too polite to point.

Effie frowned, suspicious of a ruse. "Ah, you mean 'im? I dunt know 'im. I called 'im Freddy or Charley or sum such, talkin' to a stranger and be'en pleasant. Which I needn't 've, seein' how 'e spilled me wares! But all's square now." She held up her empty basket. "Ta. Wishin' yer joy!"

The rain was still coming down hard. Effie was about to step out into the downpour anyway when a well-dressed gentleman with a damaged umbrella came pounding up the steps to the portico, splashing in the puddles.

Effie approached the newcomer. "Aww, yeh done broke yer Auntie Ella!" She glanced back briefly at the flowers in the lady's hand which she had already sold. She took off her hat and pulled from the brim two bedraggled daisies. "Buy a posy for your sweet'eart? For yer buttonhole? Ye be all drounced with Duke of Spain when yeh get there. Stink like a wet dog, yeh will. Pen 'n' ink, for certain!"

At first the gentleman glared, affronted by the diminutive girl's insinuation. Then on second thought, he gave himself a discreet sniff. "I take your point, little miss. Do you have a pink?"

Effie shook her head and tried to hand over the daisies. "Garn, but these are me only. Tuppence?"

The man waved the flowers away but searched in his pockets. "Here's a penny, child. You keep the flowers."

"Ta, sir," Effie accepted the coin and again looked out into the wet night.

A tall bystander stepped up and bent his knees so he might whisper directly in the girl's ear. "You be careful — give him a flower for it. There's a bloke here behind taking down every blessed word you're saying."

Effie, and all those who overheard, turned to see a man with a manicured mustache writing in a notebook. Effie glowered furiously. "I ain't done nofink wrong! Look 'ere you, mutton shunter! What ye on about?"

The note-taker, startled by the sudden attention, looked up at the crowd and harrumphed. Ignoring their suspicious stares, he addressed Effie. "There, there, there, there! Who's hurting you, you silly girl? What do you take me for?"

Effie put her hands on her hips, balancing the empty basket under her arm. "Don't give me that butcher's hook. You show me what ye wrote in yer Captain Cook there. Mayfink you dint took me down right!"

The note-taker stared at the girl in surprise. He turned his notebook around and held it out. "There. And why do you call me a sheep? Is it my whiskers?"

At first it was hard for Effie to see the notebook, what with all the other spectators leaning in to peer as well. She put a grubby hand on the page to hold it still and then yanked it closer to her face, pretending she could read. She could just make out that some of the marks were not letters. "Wot's this?! This is all squiggles 'n' bits. I didn't say nofink like this. Yer tryin' to send me up, ain't ye? Ye can buss me blind cupid!" Effie aimed a kick at the man's shins. "I said you was a mutton shunter. Dint say nofink bout yer door knocker. Yer a bottle and stopper, I warrant."

The Jack-of-Legs bystander looked the note-taker up and down. "He does look like a copper, now you mention it," he said, but then shook his head and pointed. "But for the boots."

"Blast the boots," said Effie and stomped down hard on the note taker's instep. "Hit 'im with your red-n-yeller, kind sir!" she begged the gentleman who had given her a penny. "He means me 'arm, the whiddler does!"

Effie backed away as the note taker howled and grabbed his injured ankle, hopping about in pain. She ran off into the still pouring rain, her grubby paws having kept hold of the notebook and carried it off.

"You uncivilized little thief! Bring back my book this instant!" scolded the note-taker, lurching forward in spite of his injury to retrieve his property.

"You cad!" shouted the well-dressed man who indeed did raise his umbrella and strike the note-taker.

Next the sixpence lady walloped the note-taker with her gold-trimmed reticule. "Leave the young lady be. You have no cause to be calling her names."

"But," the note-taker whined, ducking the blows, "the girl stole my notes. I need them back!"

He made to follow her into the storm, but Jack-of-Legs blocked him, heaving a punch squarely into the pit of his stomach. "No more pork pies," he growled. "The girl says you lie."

Others began to close in with feet and fists, and the umbrella and reticule got in a few more licks. It is not long before Henry Higgins was regretting his choice of profession and fled the portico, regardless of the downpour.

In short order, the rain let up, and the little crowd parted with shy goodbyes, feeling some minor kinship with each other, but nothing that would last once they passed into the next street. Jack-of-Legs meandered his way through the respectable part of town and finally turned down some meaner passages, where might be heard the peals of Bow Bells. Slipping into an alley behind his home, he met up with the flower girl, drumming her heels on the back steps. He winked. "I got the young lady's purse and the two gentlemen's pocketbooks. Did you cadge the young feller's fob watch?"

"You mean his kettle on the hob?" She danced on the doorstep, a daffy prancing, twirling the watch chain in triumph while he unlocked the door to their tiny bedsitter. Once inside, she scampered over to the scarred kitchen table and deposited the watch along with other booty stolen from the crowd. Silk pocket squares, two sets of cufflinks, a packet of candy drops, and the sixpence lady's bracelet. And of course, the notebook, although its value was negligible to them.

"Effie, you is a fizzing genius!"

Deftly, seductively, her steps changed from the silly capering to a closely held minuet. "Dearest tall boy, I will ever bless the day we met. With me, go-by-the-ground as I am and round-faced as a child, and you, high as a steeple and thin as a rasher of wind, no one suspects we are a couple. A prodigiously successful couple." She lifted her thin skirts while they danced, entangling her limbs with his as they whirled in smaller and smaller circles.

"You could not be more precious to me," he panted. "Not even if you were the Pearlie Queen." His eyes glittered like a fire's last embers.

"Baked bean," she countered, no longer giggling, her eyes reflecting his fierce glow. Their steps slowed and their feet shuffled, arms tight to each other, their bodies pressed like two peas in a single pod. She stood up on tiptoe to kiss underneath his chin, wrapped an ankle around his to ensnare him, and pulled him down to the musty carpet on top of her.

One of the best things about lying down is that little effort is needed for the cleft and the peg to match up.

STEAM GEARED

Try, Try, Again

Try, Try Again

"SLEEP WELL TONIGHT, Mrs. Buttons. I'm headed out to meet my sweetheart. I'll be back before dawn to light the fires. No need to worry." Minnie was wiping down the table, her last task before going out.

Mrs. Buttons, the cook, who had started up the back stairs towards their sleeping chamber, made a wry face. "Me not worry? It is you should be doing the worrying, Miss Minnie! All bedizened in your new dress. Like an owl in an ivy bush is how you look."

Minnie looked down at her dress beneath her apron, a mended frock that Albert had given her. In truth she was somewhat embarrassed by her good luck in finding a Jack to her Jill in Albert, when the elder woman had no one. "I'll tell you a secret, Agnes," Minnie said, on this rare occasion using Cook's first name, and moving closer to include her in a confidence. "Al proposed to me last week, and we are saving up to marry after the new year." Minnie nodded when Mrs. Buttons turned astonished eyes to her. "Yes! I wanted you to know. We won't be skulking about anymore. I'll have a ring soon."

"Aha!" Mrs. Buttons drew back from Minnie, spurning her offer of camaraderie. "I'm going to tell Perkins first thing in the morning. Dismiss you on the dot, he will! Wouldn't surprise me if you've got a bun in your oven already. You'll be in a bad loaf then, won't you? In hot water and suds, I said it, didn't I?!"

Minnie gasped. "You wouldn't tattle on me, would you?" She tossed the cleaning rag into the bleach bin and pulled off her apron to join it. "What a peevish gossip, you are, Agnes! Truly I feel sad that life has not afforded you any cheer, but I'll not let you ruin mine." Minnie grabbed her hat and coat, banging the door shut behind her in her haste to remove herself from the house. She stood on the back porch steps in the falling snow, moving her hat from hand to hand as she placed her arms in each coat sleeve, feeling the tiny, hard prickles of sleet landing on her bare head. By the time she pinned her hat in place, her head was cold and her hair damp.

Such a crosspatch was that woman! Would she really tell? And would the butler really be so unkind as to put her out without notice? Minnie didn't think he would. She banished the malicious woman's words from her mind. She was meeting Albert at the new gin palace near the tailor shop where he worked. She had giggled at him when he had told her to enter the place with the red lattices, not the green ones. As if she would walk into a house of ill-repute by mistake!

The walk was far and her boots were thin. She hadn't wanted to waste any coins on a public conveyance, but it was growing later and the snow was falling harder. She heard the whooshing sound of a new-fangled steam omnibus driving up the street, but it whizzed on by her, full of young lawyers and master tradesmen who could afford the sixpence fare. Next she heard the slow clopping of a nag, pulling a ponderous weight. The horse omnibus was full to bursting, but its cad rang his bell and called out to her. "Plenty of room for you, dearie!" he shouted. She ran to catch up, her feet numb and her stockings besmirched from the slush on the street. The cad dragged her inside and squeezed her onto a bench, collecting a penny and pocketing it straight away. The poor pradder started up again, pulling the vehicle gamely over the ice-slickened cobbles. Her boots began to thaw, dripping onto the straw-strewn floor. When the 'bus arrived at her destination, Albert was waiting when she stepped down.

"There is me favorite hat," he greeted her, and grinned shyly, hoping she won't mind his off-color joke.

She was reaching out to him, but once she heard his greeting, she slapped his hands away, albeit playfully. Quietly, so that only he could hear, she whispered. "I am not 'much felt'! Please don't tease me tonight. Cook was a right terror this evening, and I'm worn out with rude."

Albert put his arm around her, leading her towards the new drinking place he promised her. "Bah, that crabby old tabby? She pissing on nettles again?"

Minnie sighed, thoroughly weary of the subject. "She's an empty bottle, poor thing, but let's not waste another thought on her tonight." She put her hand in her pocket and jingled the coins there. "I saved up me farthings. Looking forward to a pint. Or half-pint if you think drinking twice as much from a smaller glass makes me more lady-like."

Albert mused a moment, then whispered in her ear. "I like best when you are prim at table and improper when we get down to the vagaries."

Minnie snuggled into his offered arm, her prior bad humor dissipating. They hurried down the street to the new public house, ice pellets pelting the city and citizenry. The gin palace could be seen from blocks away, all light and brilliancy. The pair stopped briefly under its ornamented parapet, agog at the grand expanse of sheet glass, continuous from roof to the pavement, with a riot of stucco-worked flowers and vines plastered across the building's struts. It looked like a fancy cake, heavily decorated with piped frosting.

A knot of factory workers, all joshing and shoving each other, were entering through the etched glass doors. Al and Minnie followed them in, their lungs exchanging the soggy city soot for juniper-perfumed, second-hand air.

Once inside they were subsumed into a motley crowd. Their footsteps seemed to grow heavy as their soles stuck to the floor, tacky with spilt liquor. Loud, tipsy chatter reverberated. In contrast with the darkness and grunge on the street, their eyes were dazzled, assaulted even, by the luminescence inside.

"Bright as blazes in here!" Albert had to shout to be heard over the boisterous clientele. He feigned a need to shield his eyes from the many shining lamps, glass reflecting off clear, etched, and painted glass shades, and silvered mirrors to boot.

"Cheese and crust, I feel like I'm inside a giant jewel box!" Minnie stood on tiptoe to whisper directly into Al's ear. "Can we afford a tipple here?"

Al bent down to whisper back. "The prices aren't dear." He squinted, sussing out the people at tables and those who were milling and churning around them. "Naught but tags, rags, and bobtails here. You all right with it? We could keep walking."

"I'm an icicle from the getting here. A cup of cheer first, then we can move on if need be."

Al pointed to the only empty table in sight. It was against the far wall and drenched in a kaleidoscope of color from a stained glass panel. "Hold that table for us, m'love. I don't see a barmaid. I'll get somewhat to warm us. Be back in a tick-tock."

No sooner did Minnie sit in the high-backed booth than a raffishly-togged individual plopped down across from her. "Good evening, Memselle," he addressed her. "Allow me to introduce meself, and offer you some tantalizing refreshment from the exquisite selection of provender proffered at this superlative establishment. There's mighty high eating to be had here, I would have you know."

Disconcerted at first, Minnie quickly recovered herself, affecting a low growling tone and rough words to ward him off. "Skylarks in a garret, is that the kind o' high eatin' yer meaning? Off with yeh, cowson. I've no patience fer yer humbug." She gazed across to Al, who had just paid for their glasses at the bar and was returning to their table. She saw his face grow dark when he spotted the intruder.

His voice, raised and sonorous with anger, cut through the hubbub in the packed room. "You! Don't be troubling me betrothed!" People swiveled their heads, hopeful an altercation would break out. "Tuppence on the dandy," a voice piped up. General hilarity ensued and drunk voices pitched in the game. "Someone lay down a hoop for the cockerels! Giv'em some rippons!"

At Minnie's table, the raffish man stood with alacrity. "Forgive me for troubling you, Madame." He tipped his hat to Minnie and then turned to Al, who was making haste towards them, sloshing only a few drops of ale on the floor in the process. "Pardon me, good sir. I appear to have blundered across a dividing stile. Meaning no harm." He lifted his hat again, this time to Al, and skittered off into the crowd, where he blended in, one ragamuffin among many.

Al placed their glassware on the table, taking care to spill no more precious liquid. "Filthy brute," he muttered with venom. "I'll clout his nob fer 'im!" Al raised his voice above the crowd again. "Better run, you meater! I'll put you out on your back seam, just see if I don't!"

Minnie shook her head, cheerful now that Al was beside her. "Such language, Albert! I don't think he meant any harm. In point of fact, he tried to be refined. Little fellow shot into the ground on that one." They laughed together, comrades swimming through the dirty soup of the chronic streets.

Al sat down, still needled by the scruffy male's effrontery, and scrutinized nearby faces. "Fellows at the shop told me this was a rum place. I thought they meant a fitting place to bring a sweetheart. Mind you, I don't see any of them in here tonight. They must of been cogging me."

Minnie also looked about her, directing her gaze above the crowd so as not to catch anyone's eye. "The place is astonishing, got to give 'em that. I'm almost afraid to be sitting under such huge expanses of glass. Whatever will those inventors think up next?" She picked up her drink, holding it out to him in a toast. "Let's see if the beer's rum."

She sipped and Al gulped. Both scrunched up their faces at the taste. "Did you ask for wibble, Al?"

Al scowled. "This is swill! Give me that cup, Minnie. I'll go pour it over the publican's head and get better."

Minnie crossed her arms around her glass, preventing Al from getting to it. "No dowsing the blue apron. You'll only get us chucked out. Let's drink this and move on, once we've thawed out a bit."

Albert continued to mutter under his breath. "I'll not be made a nokes of. Those jakes at the shop will hear blue death tomorrow from me. Having a good giraffe at me expense. Probably got their backs up that it was me tapped to be the new shop lead." Al drank half his pint at one pull, swallowing hard and grimacing after. "I told 'em I wouldn't go out nanty-narking with 'em tonight. I told 'em, I'm thinking for two now." Al took Minnie's hand and squeezed it gently.

Minnie squeezed back firmly. "Makes me flat giddy, thinking of a lifetime together, Al." She drank more from her glass, swallowing with some difficulty. "One thought though, before we go further down that road. Mrs. Buttons thinks I'll be discharged when I marry. Can you afford me on your new salary, if I can't snag a new place right away? I don't mind waiting for a ring, Al, and I won't be pushing you. As long as I can have your Long Tom and his two furry kittens now and again."

Al rolled his eyes when she mentioned Mrs. Buttons and sniggered when she mentioned his toolkit. "Never you mind Buttons, that petty old thing. She's naught but a pickled dog." He was glaring at all around him, but when his face returned to hers, his expression softened. "I don't mind paying fer two. Me hope is to be paying fer three, soon enough."

Minnie leaned across to him and kissed his nose.

A nearby table began cawing at them. "Pull down the blind, you two spooneys!" Minnie sat back in her bench but her smile stayed on her face. They whispered after that, making predictions about their future, which included much amorous congress in their own snug bed.

In the midst of their sweet talk, Al caught a lad looking longingly at Minnie. He rose up belligerently, confronting the young man. "Are you ogling me bride-to-be? I'll cop you a mouse. Two if you want more!" Albert poised like a boxer, threatening to punch the man in the eye.

The man gave Al an apologetic little shrug. "You drew the high card, is all I'm thinking," he said before turning to his own drink, backing down from the challenge.

"Minnie, let's finish these cups and be off. Besides," he dipped his head to her, "you got me aching hard."

"Hard is it?" she whispered. "I'd like to see that. Can I put me hands to it? Move it closer under the table!" She laughed, tickled to see how her indelicate remark had caught him off-guard, so that he flushed clear to his ears.

Out on the pavement again, the sleet having slacked off to drizzling rain, they walked hand in hand, despite the occasional clucking their public display drew from others on the street. They passed market stalls, most emptied out by now, and noted an odd allotment of people sheltering under the portico in front of St. Paul's. Among them was a man with a ludicrously drooping mustache who was making marks in a book.

Minnie cuddled closer to Al. "Where shall we go? Rain or no, I'm more than a bit fearful to try outside again. After last time." She shuddered, her imagination having worked up the staring man she saw the other day on the river steps to the status of a canonical demon, ravenous for their blood and sinews.

"It were nothing, Minnie, don't fret." Al tried to dismiss her fears, but in fact her heebee jeebies had worked their way under his skin as well. "O'course I'd rather be indoors meself. Wish I could sneak you into me garret at the tailor shop. Can't do though. Mr. Dart would give me the sack for sure."

Minnie looked down at her feet for a few steps. "A possibility," she said slowly, as if considering her words. "At me place, if we were to be caught out, I'd get the bullet straight away, but if I'm to be let go anyway — shall we risk it?"

Al laughed at first, but then became thoughtful. "Is that how it is, Minnie? Will they truly chuck you out after all your years of service?"

Minnie's eyes were still on her feet. "I think Master would let me stay on till I come up with a bulge in me belly. You can see how unseemly that would be, what with Master being a bachelor." She made a tsk-tsking sound. "The neighbors would talk to no end." At that she halted and stepped in front of Al, stopping him. "Let's wait on the ceremony, Al. Until you're getting your new salary regular-like."

Al's face was stricken. "Minnie, no, I want you to be mine now. I want the whole world to see how you're mine. No more chasing off nazy coves in fancy breeches. No more snarling at mongers looking at you all wistful-like. I'd put a wedding ring around your neck if I could — keep away from mine, it would signify."

Minnie put her hands to her throat. "No need fer a choker and I can wait on a ring. Although that big stick you're carrying," she pointed, "would suit me to a T."

Al snorted, shifting himself so his trousers were not bunched up around his erection. "You're a naughty buttercup. Me stick gets bigger whenever I think of you."

A modern curricle drove by at top speed, the brisk mechanical horses nearly silent. The two gentlemen within had seen them touching. "What's all this?" shouted one of them, in high good humor. "A cock and hen club on the very street? Go in of doors, you brazen strayers!"

Minnie was spurred to make a choice. Taking Al's hand, she pulled him in the direction of her place of work and residence. "Let's chance it. Can't use me room, I'm bunked in with Cook. The cloak alcove, maybe. Or no, I got it! The butler's pantry, where we can shut the door. Moan quiet, like mice in cheese."

Al let himself be jerked in a new direction, crossing the road and heading towards the posh side of town. "I think I can be quiet. You bet I'll try. But if we're caught lying bread 'n' butter, where will you go? No place for a woman at Mr. Dart's."

"There are boarding houses, Al, until we find our own place. And I'll find work soon enough."

"Boarding houses? Right up there with accommodation houses and introducing rooms! Just call 'em what they are, and that's brothels! I don't want you living someplace horrid, Minnie. It would shame me if you had to."

Minnie placed her hand on his crotch. He muffled his strangled outburst of excitement. Under her touch, she could feel him growing harder, if that was possible. He was already a great rock jutting out, fit to burst through his mustn't-mention-'ems.

"Minnie! Oh, oh, Minnie! When you touch me there, you put me smaller brain in charge, and it has no care for how we will live!"

Minnie left her hand where it was, enjoying the strength of him. "We have cast the dice, Albert. Let's see what comes up."

"I'm feeling very optimistic at the moment." He mumbled some endearments, his hand straining to cup what he could reach of her breasts as they loped through the dark towards her master's house.

Once there, they buttoned their lips. She opened the back entrance with deliberate care, turning the key and twisting the knob with elaborate stealth. Shaking off her outer clothing and hanging them on her usual pegs, Minnie led Al through the unlit hall to the butler's pantry. Familiarity guided her steps, as it did every morning at blue o'clock when she went about her duties, conserving on candles.

Inside the pantry with the door firmly closed, her lips found their blind way to his, and her hands fumbled with his buttons and tabs. She divested him of his coat and hat, draping them over the pantry's stepladder by feel, then going back for his waistcoat and breeches. At first she was tidy, folding his garments as she removed them, but in a short time, while he was eagerly pulling at her own frock and petticoats, she let everything drop.

Their clothes littered the pantry floor. Their eager hands, their searching mouths, their heated skin, bumped, rubbed, and caressed.

"Crack-golly, what a prodigious yard! You're as big as a prize bull!" exclaimed Minnie fervently, sotto voce.

Al tried to position himself between her legs but tripped over his own breeches. He blundered against a shelf, knocking down something heavy and soft.

Minnie smothered a giggle and whispered, "Never mind it, just a sack of flour. I'll sweep up after." She felt around with her foot until it touched up against the stepladder and she plopped herself down on a rung to unbutton her high-topped shoes. "Pity we don't have a candle. You could be looking up me skirt."

Al was pawing through the layers of her clothing in the lightless little room, his fingers disgorging buttons and disengaging ties as they came across them. "Not too much of a pity. I'm fixing it so you won't be wearing a skirt." He sucked in his breath each time his touch discovered another patch of her naked skin. "You're like a jigsaw puzzle, Minnie, where I take the pieces away instead of fitting 'em together."

Minnie, concentrating on her task, had enough of his clothes off to get on with it. She took hold of his handle and pulled him towards her. Al shuffled, his pants around his ankles, getting closer to her, and still closer.

This time he tripped over the fallen bag of flour, tumbling against the back wall's shelving and dislodging several pots of jam. The crockery smashed into brittle pieces on the pantry floor, the sound only slightly muffled by their viscous content. Minnie and Al froze like statues at the sharp sudden smacks, which to them crashed as loud as thunder. Stiff with fear, they listened for footsteps, upraised voices of consternation, or cursing coming from outside their cramped hiding place. Al was subdued, his arousal repressed by fear of imminent discovery.

The house remained silent. Minnie started breathing again. She scrabbled for the cleaning rags which were stored close to the doorway, tossed a few over the corner where the jam and pot shards fell, then reached for Al, or rather blundered her hands forward. Blindfolded by the dark, her hands bashed into his chest and then followed across his manly, bristly thatch of chest hair to grip his shoulders. "Let's get us settled-like, so we don't bring down the house. You lie on the floor. Mind don't bump your head." She pulled him to the middle of the cramped room, then traced her hands down to his pleasingly lean derriere, made trim and supple by the cross-legged seating typical of tailoring work. She grabbed handfuls of this flesh and pull downward until he was seated on the floor, then guided him until he was stretched out full in the limited space. Once he was where she wanted him, she moved her hands to his rod, which although only partially erect from the recent scare, was plumping again under her caress. If he could have seen her face at that moment, he would have known by her mirthful expression she had an amatory plan. She was whispering. "Let's say I will play the dragon. You play St. George."

In the dark, he nodded assent.

"Look out, George!" Minnie whisper-shouted, "the dragon is upon you! Now the fray begins!" Gleefully she flung a leg over to sit astride him, dropping her dripping muff to his taut belly, and lolled up and down until she found what she was seeking. "Ha! Draw your weapon now, Georgie. Can you feel the dragon fire? Hot and dripping on you, I am. Take courage! Get to stabbing part!"

Al was shaking, partly with repressed laughter. "Woe is me, no!" he crooned in falsetto tones, stalling for time, rubbing his engorging prick along her thighs, teasing her in return. "Stab such a mighty creature? Never!" He squirmed as if to flee from her, moaning as he felt her press her honeyed lips against him. There was no room on the floor to move away from her, even if he had intended to. The frottage of her quim and thighs encouraged his cock to regain full vigor. A groan burst from his throat, which he squelched to a quiet moan. He clutched her writhing body to his, his hips grinding, his hand sliding up her spine. He reached the tender spot at the nape of her neck, his fingertips invading the deep thicket of her braided and coiled hair, dislodging her hairpins. Her heavy braids broke loose and lashed down across his bare chest and loins. He strangled a gushing shriek of intense pleasure. "Ye gods and little fishes! Your dragon hair spiked me. Me innards are ript open!" He was panting harder now, his truncheon fully stiff again. "I'm a-goin'. Goin' to meet my death at the dragon's mouth. Make it a little one!" His voice burst beyond a whisper, lost to their circumstances.

"Hush." Her whisper was harsh with impatience. "'Nuff talk. Put it where it belongs." She fitted herself above him, pressing her nether lips along his shaft until she found his tip with her moist waiting introitus. She squealed with ardor and weighed down on him, biting to hush her own wail of sliding pleasure. She near swooned with delight, feeling his prick penetrating deep inside her.

Albert joined in sync with Minnie's wail, expressing himself with full voice.

"Shhh," she huffed. "Mustn't wake anyone. Moan like a dove." She demonstrated, giving voice to a soft spate of incoherent sounds and meaningless words while arching her back and closing her eyes. She rolled up and then leaned forward on her hands, lifting her hips so that she might slide up his pole and slip back down.

Al's moan was quieter this time, but no less intense than before. "Minnie."

"Mmmm, yes, Al," she said, rocking her body over his, pressing down, commingling their short hairs in their conjoined dew, and rising up again.

"Minnie, I want – marry me." Al had to gasp out his words, but he concentrated. He had something he wanted to say.

Minnie did not seem to be listening, but she responded when he said her name. "Yes, Al. I said I would." She roiled on top of him, sifting her hips, squeezing his cock inside her, rising up and down with quickening rhythm.

"Now, Minnie. Say it. Do you." He could not get all the words out in one breath, but he soldiered on. "Take. This man. Oh, oh!" This last when she dropped her head and shook it to let her hair lash across his face. "To be your wedded husband?" He finished quickly, fearing he would lose track of the fateful question.

"Man, Albert? Do you mean this maypole? This mighty baton? This great ruddy column of a prigging staff you got here?" She was trying to giggle but her breath was getting too short. "It is magnificent, Al, it is," she told him, shuddering as she drew up to his very tip, and sunk down again with force.

135

"That too, Minnie. It's yours. Say I never need worry about rogues, jarkmen, or swadders giving you the eye. Say your mine, Minnie. Say it now, before I explode!"

Minnie screeched under her breath as she began to lurch home, her thoughts aswim with desire. "What's that?" she said distractedly, banging harder now, with wild desire, her body in charge and having only one purpose, one goal. Her thighs lifted her up and dropped her back down with unrelenting lust. Her knees pressed hard to his hipbones and her walls gripped his engorged cock; her lower lips kissing its tip and gobbling it back up inside her to its very depth, their bodies smacking together, faster and faster.

Al felt her dire intent crackle through his body. "S'help me criss-cross, Minnie, you will drive me to blow!" He slid his hand across her plunging buttocks and gripped her waist in an attempt to slow her down. "Roll off now, Minnie. I can't let go inside you. Not till we're ready for babies."

"So long," she murmuring feverishly. "I've waited so long, Al. Give me. Give me!"

Al mewled, both with need and sudden fear. "No, Minnie, I must pull out." His mouth quivered, trying to form the words, nearing paroxysm. His feet scuffled in the restricted space, his hips thrust upward against hers, and his fingers tried to prise her thighs off him, all while his prick plunged on in spite of his noble intentions.

"Minnie, let me up!" Al tried to buck her off, but she only dug her heels in harder. He was thrashing now, torn between his frenzy of need and his desire to do right. "Stop! Stop!!"

It was at that moment that the door swung open with force, and a candle was thrust inside the tiny room. Mrs. Buttons was behind the flame, her eyes wild and triumphant under her ruffled nightcap. "Aha! Caught you, you blowsy bit of baggage!"

Minnie pulled herself roughly off of Albert, feeling somehow like she was leaving a part of herself behind. She stumbled to her feet to face the bitter woman, who was blocking the pantry doorway like a vengeful wraith, a single frizzled braid falling over the shoulder of her primly buttoned nightgown. Al scrabbled backward like a crab until he bumped his head on the far wall. He clawed up the first bit of clothing within reach and used it to hide his still throbbing member.

Mrs. Buttons continued to crow like a cock at dawn. "Now you will get what's coming to you! Always looking down on me, acting the duchess. We will see what kind of noble you look when you're out on the street with your belongings in a bag."

Albert took a step forward, a snarl sounding. He held out the fabric he had grabbed up in his haste, holding it up between his fists as if to ward off the offensive woman to protect his beloved.

Minnie shoved herself between them, one hand behind her to hold Al back, assuring him she had the situation under control. "Please don't shout so, Cook, you'll wake the dead with that tone." She was breathing deeply in her attempt to regain control of her speaking voice.

"I'll wake the quick and the dead, too, if it please me! You're spilt milk now! Won't Master will be appalled at what his mincing minx has done this time!" Mrs. Buttons was prancing with delight, her candle dripping wax precariously.

Minnie modulated her tone, pretending a calm she did not truly possess at that moment. "No need to be in a bad skin over this, Agnes." She spoke as if to a skittish child, holding her hand out in a conciliatory fashion and standing upright, even though she was fully naked except for one stocking fallen around her ankle. She refused to let the woman see her cower.

"I'll be in any kind of skin I like! You and your John-A-Nokes have done it this time. Fair torn it, you have! Perkins will turn you out in the snow with nothing but what you've got on your back! Oh wait, ha! You've nothing on your back!" Mrs. Buttons hooted. Minnie thought, rather uncharitably, it surprising that Cook's face didn't crack when she laughed.

"I'm going to wake Perkins." Mrs. Buttons sneered at Minnie. "I want to see his face when he hears of this!"

137

Al stepped forward again with righteous anger. "Mrs. Buttons, you're a ruddy moo! Me Minnie will be well rid of your kind of poison." He was drawing breath to go on with his tirade, but just then the door was wrenched from the bright-eyed cook's hand, and Mr. Perkins himself, in his old-fashioned nightshirt and cap, thrust his own candle into the little room.

"When I hear of what, Mrs. Buttons?" None of them had heard the butler's footsteps as he came down the stairs. Now he stood in the doorway, candle held high, a sleepy-eyed, elderly man of frail frame and proud prowess, even though he did look somewhat less imperious in his sleepwear than he did in his starched livery. "What's all this ruckus in the middle of the night? We can't be having..." he stopped mid-sentence, his mouth hanging open, seeing the untidy state of the pantry and the undressed state of the couple within.

Surprise made all four of them motionless, a tableau set up for a painter's sketch. The artist would depict the lovers huddling in startled dismay, the cook in a posture indicative of glee and triumph, and the old man the epitome of disbelief and confusion. Minnie snatched a folded apron from a shelf and shook it out, trying to make it unfold and cover her breasts and monosyllabic unmentionable. Albert stood transfixed with Minnie's dainty lace petticoat draped over his elongated but quickly deflating pole. Mrs. Buttons was beaming, her smile malevolent, her countenance more radiant than it had been in a donkey's age.

The butler's words had trailed off as he beheld the two insufficiently-clad lovers and the jubilant Mrs. Buttons in his private pantry, but he remained speechless only for seconds. He prided himself on quick thinking, and indeed he had dealt with plenty worse, both upstairs and down. He turned away from the lovers, composed his face, cleared his throat, and squarely faced the cook. "Buttons, what is the meaning of bringing one of your paramours home with you? This is utterly unacceptable. I insist you send him away at once!"

Cook started to protest, but he silenced her with an abrupt hand pushing palm outward. "I will hear no more on the matter."

"But, it wasn't — I didn't —" stammered Mrs. Buttons. Her expression could not have appeared more astonished were Gabriel to blow his trumpet inches from her ear.

"No more!" Perkins' voice was barely raised, but its authority was undeniable. When he turned to Minnie, he looked her exclusively in the eyes, not wavering an instant to her undressed state below. "Minnie, you must do me the favor of keeping a better watch on Cook. I know, I know, she is young and full of vim and vinegar, but I wish to keep her employed here as long as possible. Master has many a time remarked on the perfect crunch of her pickles, the delectability of her ham and watercress tea sandwiches, and above all the fluffiness of her dinner rolls that sop up sauce like a sponge."

Minnie blinked, leaning forward to check Perkins at close hand, ascertaining that his spectacles were unsmudged and his sleep-rimmed lids were open. Before she could speak, Perkins had returned his attention to Cook. "It would be a sad day for the household, Buttons, if I had to dismiss you, so please take my advice to heart, and work with Minnie to keep the household running smoothly. And if possible, pleasantly."

Cook glared at Perkins. Perkins calmly, but imperiously, stared back. Her mouth worked as if to come out with words spiteful enough to put him in mind of the truth, but in the end she saw he held all the cards. This was an ultimatum. She pouted, but then acquiesced with little grace. "Very well, Perkins. I shall endeavor not to humiliate the house in future." Her glare raked over Minnie, but she said nothing more.

"Thank you, Buttons," said Perkins graciously. "I appreciate your willingness to cooperate." If he were going to say more, he refrained. Keeping his face resolutely turned from the man in his pantry, he drew a shilling from the rim of his candlestick, where he kept coins to feed the gas meter, and handed it over to Minnie. "Take this, use what you need to put this young buck on a conveyance homeward, and then give half of what's left to Cook. So she can take her fancy fellow elsewhere in the future."

One of his old eyes winked briefly, letting her know he was well aware of his mistaken assumption. "When you return, Minnie, clean up this pantry and start the morning fires. Buttons, begin preparing Master's breakfast tray at once." Sternly he shifted his gaze back and forth between the serving women. "Both of you make no mistake. If I catch Cook being naughty again, dinner rolls or no, you will both find yourself without employment or lodging!"

Minnie, Al, and Mrs. Buttons all stood dumbfounded, watching the back of the butler's nightshirt as he marched up the staircase and out of sight.

"Well I'll be jigger'd," said Mrs. Buttons at last. She turned to Minnie, but only looked hungrily at the coin. "Half that is mine," she said, lifting the bag of flour from the floor and heading to the kitchen to start up a batch of her freshly praised rolls.

Mogambo, Or The Red Dust

Mogambo,
Or The Red Dust

"IT WASN'T SUPPOSED TO happen that way. I must tell you I truly am devastated. And I owe you a heartfelt, abiding, and deeply humble apology."

Archibald was standing in the doorway to their shared tent. He was fully dressed in proper jungle attire with his trouser creases sharp and all his buttons buttoned despite the heat. His wife was just now waking up, stirring in her single cot, blinking her eyes open and then shutting them again to ward off the already blinding sunlight. At the sound of his voice, she startled awake. "What was that you said, Archie? What time is it?"

Archie looked over his shoulder distractedly. "A bit after dawn. A relief team has arrived from the village, and Harris has sent along supplies and new bearers. The kitchen device is brewing tea and cooking up rashers, eggs, and toast with marmalade." He redirected his gaze at her and quickly looked away again upon glimpsing her night clothing in disarray. "I do beg your pardon," he said formulaically. Then added with fervor, "I really, truly, genuinely do beg your pardon. For yesterday. My dastardly behavior. After the volcano erupted and I..." his voice faltered.

Clara stretched, mumbling something about 'exiguous circumstances.'

Archie's words tumbled out, speaking out to discourage her from articulating her thoughts before he could apologize at length. "No, no, I was a cad. I am unbelievably embarrassed by my behavior, even under the circumstances. You are such a kind, inoffensive creature, and I know you would excuse anything, given your impeccable upbringing, but you must allow me to apologize with utmost candor. To expiate my faults. To expose my inexcusable comportment and atone, as best as possibly can be, for the sins I have laid at your door."

Clara's rumpled morning face took on a strange expression. A small crease appeared between her brows and one side of her mouth curled. Was it a lopsided frown? A grimace of confusion? A sneer?

Archie interpreted the expression to be one of repugnance. "Oh my precious darling, please, please know I cherish you so profoundly and would go to the veritable ends of the earth to make you happy. I humbly beg your forbearance and forgiveness for my inexplicably uncivilized actions yesterday."

Clara stirred herself, half sitting up and searching for her spectacles on the tiny campstool beside her cot. "Archie," she began.

"No, no, my beloved, do not speak yet! Let me throw myself at your feet. Beg you to forgive me and my trespasses. Implore you to allow me back into your exalted company. I will never do anything so forward and wayward again. I promise you that. I don't know what came over me! The eruption was just so sudden. With the smoking volcano, quiescent since we arrived months ago, with barely a hiccup in a month of Sundays, exploding without warning, raining down burning death on us, exhaling poison so thick we could not inhale, I was overcome. Which is not an adequate excuse, and I do acquiesce to that point without protestation, as well as with great personal embarrassment."

"But," Clara tried to interrupt. She positioned her spectacles on her face, fitting each side of the frame over each ear, and made motions to sit up on her cot.

"Not a word, my pet!" Archibald stepped forward with his hands outstretched, almost as if he meant to cover her mouth. "Hear me out before you condemn me. Before you banish me from your side and sight forever." Now standing on the naked ground beside her cot, he knelt down and bowed his head in shame, and continued speaking to her knees, still covered by a coverlet and her gown.

143

"We were fortunate at that very moment it happened to have been only a step from the shelter of a fractured cleft in the path on the mountainside. The little cave gave us an air pocket where we could breathe when the volcano unexpectedly evulsed its molten interior. I had little hope for our lives as our native bearers before and behind us on the path cried out, coughed, crumpled, grasping their throats and slipping from the narrow footpath, tumbling down the precipitous slope and dropping to what would be their deaths if they were not dead already from the gaseous exhalations of the pyroclastic flow. Our mechanical beasts rolled onward gamely, until the lava melted their treads and then they too tumbled. Our providential cavelet protected us, but my mind cried out 'for how long'?"

Clara, now awake and bespectacled, sat herself upright on her camp bed and fixed her attention on her husband of many adventurous years. As bidden, she did not speak, listening to him as he had begged.

"Our dire situation was almost but not quite as frightening as that time our balloon was swept off course over the rift at Fourteen Falls, when we were caught between the rocky cliffs endangering the envelope's tender skin and the hard spears of the natives pursuing us for daring to penetrate the lair of their sacred idol. Do you remember that time? Oh how my heart pounded in my throat then! But I digress, and I must pour out my confession. My expiation, my apotheosis of despair, my abject apology.

"There we were, in little more than a fissure in the igneous slope of the dread volcano, clinging to life by little more than our toenails, when a singular sensation ran through me. Perhaps you felt it too, as I huddled beside you with the volcanic avalanche trapping us both against our rocky outcropping. It was like a great knife stabbed me in the general area of my Adam's apple and eviscerated me down to my pubis. My manhood leapt to life, all of its own, and all my years of civilized culture were cut away from me. I don't remember stripping away my outer garments and pushing aside my undergarments, but I do remember to my great chagrin and consternation how I pawed at your magnificent bosoms, fingers tearing at the seams of your bush jacket, roughly pulling apart the fabric protecting us from the elements, the cloth veneer that separates humans from the rest of the animal kingdom.

"In my haste and clumsiness I tore off your clothes, and parenthetically I do additionally apologize for the damage I evinced to your wardrobe, and I placed my skin next to yours, nipple to nipple, pressing your body to my own, feeling your heart beating wildly, as mine was, in response to the great danger to our continued existence.

"I pulled you roughly to me, my lips bruising yours, my hand that was not occupied by smashing your body to mine was roaming your tender parts, my manhood poking at your belly, too hard and out-thrusting to bend between us. Oh my darling, I was so bold as to lift you up bodily and pin your slender self between me and the unyielding rock face, my woody shaft stabbing along your tender thighs, shoving aside the raven curls of your delta, seeking an entrance, a place to bury itself, a place to hide, its own cavern and place of safety in the ensuing madness of the natural world.

"How odd it seems to come to my memory now, how your delicate valley was as moist and inviting as a jungle orchid, full of sweet nectar, all wet and entrancing, drawing me inside its velvet depth. Perhaps it was just overly warm in our environs, what with the lava flowing around us and all.

"I heard you moan, as if in pain or fright, as I continued to press against you, opened your mossy entrance, and slammed myself into you, up to the very hilt, flush to my furry shot pouch, where I felt your fluttering walls stroking me, stoking me. I felt the fire outside us, but my brain only registered the pyre between us, the flame inside me roaring out of control like a Fawkes bonfire.

"Did I hear your stuttering protest or was it the volcano sputtering? It might have been my heart hammering and my breath coming in short pants of intense desire.

"I felt myself plunge and plunge again, over and over, with a sense of urgency such as I have never recollected before. You were my blanket, my glove, my refuge, and I drew you around me, covered myself with your divine embrace, and dove into your depths. You were my entire world, and I was enthralled, subsumed, part and parcel of your personage, a mere portion, a component, small but integral, of that which was whole within the two of us. Then came the moment I thought our bodies had caught ablaze from the molten flood.

"I remembered snatches of memories of our time together. The brazen picnic near Briarwood where you first showed me your ankles. The fumbling tenderness in the darkness of your parents' front porch swing that was situated just outside the parameter of the gas lamp's glow. And that time we scaled the peak of Kilimanjaro some moments before our guides, and we dared to kiss as if no one was watching us.

"Was this death, or was this nirvana? From within me my own lava flow spurted, gush after gush of energetic spunk, overflowing the tender cradle of our love, rushing down the mountainside of our flesh to coat our co-mingled hairs and slicken our tightly pressed thighs. My awareness plummeted into the inky depth, unknowing, unheeding, uncaring. My eyes fluttered shut in ecstasy. My mind slipped away to somewhere I never can describe or fully recall.

"It was some time, a minute or three perhaps, before I realized were we not dead. I opened my eyes and the rapidly cooling drifts of the volcano's lava were steaming and hardening to either side of our rock cleft. I heard the crackling as the pumice broke away from the partially molten rock beneath it. It was only then that I came to my senses. I disengaged my now flaccid member and took stock of what I had done. The torn remains of my trousers mocked me, singed where they lay on the ground, tossed aside when I precipitously freed myself of their impediment. Your button-less blouse and ripped corset seemed to reproach me. Your own tailored jodhpurs, undone around your ankles, told the whole sordid story of my guilt.

"And so it was brought home to me, my dearest, most precious helpmate and match to my very soul. I am a thoughtless, filthy cretin. I am unworthy of the lofty heights you occupy. What I deserve is to be cast out of the heaven of your angelic presence. But I beg you. I beseech you! I prostrate myself humbly on my knees, with my bleeding heart in my hands if you were to so ask it of me. Can you ever contemplate a time, perhaps in the far-flung future, when you might excuse my dereliction?

"Maybe not forgive immediately, for I know that is asking too much for such a hideous trespass. But if it is within your tender breast, might you offer me forbearance? In time? While I endeavor expeditiously to prove myself to you again, might you find it within your heart to offer me hope?"

Clara, still sitting upright and attentive on her cot, waited for some moments longer, making sure his torrent of words had run their course. She stood at last, and placing her hands on his shoulders, gently urged him to rise from his abject position at her feet. Moving one of her hands up to his cheek, she drew back a few inches and swatted him lightly.

"There. Consider yourself appropriately punished."

She planted a kiss on his chin. "I very much enjoyed our impromptu lovemaking yesterday. A lovely tup, if I might be so square in expression. Let's do that again soon, although without the disaster part. What say?"

STEAM GEARED

A La Carte

A La Carte

THE YOUNG MAN IN A suit of high fashion was sitting at the end of the platform. He was smoking his pipe and reading The Times, occasionally looking up and along the length of the station, appraising the milling passengers. He seemed to be looking for someone in particular. Now and again he would stand, walk about slowly, and venture to the newsstand to purchase a later edition or some sweetmeats. Anyone watching him would see nothing more than a young swell killing time.

Finally one of his glances was rewarded. He stood up, folded his paper, tucked it under his arm, and made his way toward a lone woman wearing black. She wore no veil and her eyes were clear, so one might imagine her loss was no longer fresh. She carried one smallish suitcase, much bedecked with old traveling stickers, having just handed off her portmanteau to a porter, giving him a coin from a soft leather purse. Now she stood somewhat uncertainly on the deck, as if business matters were settled and she knew not what to do next.

The young man made a beeline for her. "May I be of service, madam? You seem a bit lost, and I would be happy to assist one in need. My name is Jerome Smythe," he lied, and inclined his upper body respectfully.

The widow hesitated, but only for a moment. A lady traveling alone in polite society was permitted to allow a man to carry her luggage. "Thank you. It is very kind of you to offer. Mrs. Clementine Banister." She made a polite curtsy in response to his bow, and proffered him her suitcase to carry.

"This is the Brighton train coming in now. Would that be your destination?" Jerome seemed only to have eyes for her, although peripherally he was wary, ready to fend off any other offers of aid. He puffed out his chest when another young chap seemed to be coming towards her, but stood down when the fellow hailed a comely matron carrying a muff and a sewing box.

"Brighton, yes. A seaside holiday." Clementine's eyes were on the train pulling in, watching it chuffing and snorting, aligning its massive body alongside the station with a juttering jerk.

Jerome adroitly hoisted her valise and offered her his arm. "Allow me to help you settle in a carriage. I am going to Brighton myself." Glancing at the ticket in her gloved hand, he noted with satisfaction it was for a first class compartment. Smiling at his fortune, swaggering with a confident air, he led her along the platform to the cars marked First. "This way."

Jerome handed her in and followed along the gangway with her suitcase. "Will you need anything from your valise? Otherwise I will stow it above so that it does not rattle about while the train is in motion."

Clementine shook her head in the negative. "I have my book and my reticule. I will be fine for the hour or so." Jerome smiled in return and patted his newspaper, now rolled up and protruding from his jacket pocket. After placing the bag in the luggage netting, he unobtrusively locked the carriage door and settled himself on the bench opposite her. A passerby rattled the door but finding it locked, moved on. Jerome mocked surprise when he heard the rattle, but once the passenger was gone, he dismissed the matter from his mind. Pulling out his paper, he pretended to peruse the pages, having a smile ready for the lady should she look up at him, which she didn't. Once the train started up and the sound of the conductor calling for tickets could be heard, Jerome stood and peered out the window into the corridor. Surreptitiously he unlocked the door so his deception would not be detected. "So Mrs. Banister, is this your first visit to Brighton?"

Clementine had removed her traveling bonnet and placed it on the bench beside her. She was reclined in the tufted velvet upholstery as if exhausted. Her head was turned to look out the window at the scenery, but not really paying it any mind, and her book was unopened in her

151

lap. She roused herself when he spoke. "No, no, I've been many times. My late husband much enjoyed travel and the seaside was a favorite of his. Brighton, Bath, Scarborough, Budleigh Salterton." She smiled a bit, a tinge of sadness showing. "And you, sir? Mr. Smythe, was it?"

"Do call me, Jerome, madam. No, it is not my first time. I travel often on business." At that moment the train rounded a sharp bend and threw the unsuspecting lady forward, towards his lap. Jerome, as he had called himself, was on the edge of his seat, arms out and ready to catch her. "Ups-a-daisy," he sang out, incidentally cupping one hand around her breast and the other under her bustle as he helped her settle back into the bench seat. "Trains do make for the oddest of situations, don't they?" He released her reluctantly, his fingers trailing low across her belly as if by accident.

There was a brief interruption when the collector came to take their tickets. Clementine handed over the paper she had purchased earlier and Jerome handed the man a large bill. "Brighton, please," he murmured, ignoring the man's suspicious expression. "Mrs. Banister, do you think the nice weather will hold up in Brighton? Sunny days are best for strolls along the beach, to my mind, but a brisk walk in the rain suits me near as well." He nodded pleasantly when the collector handed him his change and punched ticket, busying himself with the newspaper until the man was gone. "Will you be staying long in town, Mrs. Banister? I usually stay at The Drunken Griffin myself. It is a cheery place with a decent cook. Although I'll only be overnight this time."

"A week, I think," said Clementine, picking up her book and paging through it. Not reading. Maybe looking at the pictures, or perhaps just turning pages to occupy her fingers while her mind was far away. She did not volunteer information about her accommodations.

Jerome was prepared to talk at length about 'his business,' which he would say was paper mills and sales to stationery shops, if only she had inquired. In fact, he had never worked a day in his life and everything he knew about the paper trade was learned from a garrulous stranger in a pub a few days back. He smiled encouragingly at Clementine. "A week then?"

"Or perhaps two." She drew her thoughts back to the carriage where she sat and to the present. "I have no engagements in London to return to." A rueful kind of smile lifted her lips slightly. "A single woman is so difficult at dinner parties, where everyone must be paired somehow, and single men are at a premium."

The train's rhythm, now that they were past the curve around Battersea, was monotonous and lulling. Clementine's eyes drooped, whether from the motion or an inner sorrow would be difficult to discern.

"Oh, now, that's not how it should be! A pretty woman like yourself should be in great demand." He reached out and touched the back of her hand, gauging her reaction to his flattery. His lips twitched as he watched her delicate jet necklace bump gently against her throat with the train's motion, thumping against her tender skin. She did not seem to heed the flattery, nor the touch. On the other hand, neither did she draw back. Jerome was emboldened.

"You must be lonely, Clementine," he said quietly. His hand moved to her wrist and clasped it gently. His thumb slipped down into her palm, paddling the sensitive flesh.

Clementine looked down at his hand as if not fully comprehending, and then up at his face. No fear showed. Just a mild surprise. Her lips started to form words and hesitated. His thumb massaged the mount of Venus below her thumb. She spoke at last. "Yes. I am rather. Lonely, that is to say."

He slid forward in his seat, his knees pointing directly at hers, or where he hoped they might be under the billowing armory of skirt and petticoats and who knows what else a widow might keep secret underneath. He hoped there were garters rather than suspender clips. He so loved to take a single garter as a souvenir. Gentle pressure on her hand pulled her toward him. Their knees, good guessing on his part, and their faces touched. He could feel the fire kindling between them.

He kissed her lips tenderly, and then half rose to unfasten the straps and allow the compartment's curtains to close. His deft hand slid the lock home once more. He was back in a trice, this time by her side on the same bench, nudging her hat into a corner.

She initiated the next kiss, leaning into him as he seated himself, her lips full and plump on his, pressing insistently. The veneer of civilization had been tossed aside. Gratified he would not need to importune her any further, he let his hands roam over her personage with his fingers caressing nooks and crannies. His tongue tip touched her teeth and she parted them to admit him. Their hungry tongues danced together, not in a stately waltz, but already a wild gypsy dance of urgent yearnings.

Her fingers traveled his chest, pulling at his cravat tie and picking at his waistcoat buttons. He smiled, pleased that the lady knew what she wanted and how to get it. He moved his own hands down the front of her traveling jacket, freeing the frogs from their loops and tugging at her blouse underneath, releasing it from the tight waistband so his fingers could travel upward to her nipples, under the rough canvas corset. He was mildly surprised not to find silk, but when on a journey…well, one does what one can. He found her nipples, protruding and hard, much as his own growing protrusion below. He slid one hand down to the hem of her skirt and with a single practiced sweep unveiled her legs from ankle to hip. There were garters! His insistent fingers made their way to her garden of downy hair and nuzzled into the warm hollow within, soft as the inside of a fur slipper, and decidedly damp.

His own middle was crowding out the front of his trousers now, and Clementine, seeing his need, nimbly aided his instrument's release. She gasped as his member snaked out, full and long. "What a prodigious animal you have there, sir!" she exclaimed, and her hands cupped around its girth. "Such a great and steely steed, indeed," she praised, heaving a sigh that ended in a moan, and repositioned herself on the bench with her legs wide, making room for him to move between them. "Won't you join me?" Her voice was raspy with emotion, and her fingers fondled along his length. "I have a fitting haven for your jaunty Jack right here. Willing and waiting for you."

He needed little encouragement to place himself upon her. The train was due in the station soon enough. They must be quick. They were both ready. He poked his stiff sinew against her cloven inlet, accompanied by soft cries from both of them. Her groans of pleasure grew more strenuous, and mutely he offered her his cravat to bite upon, feeding the cloth between her teeth, feeling her playfully nip and lick his fingertips. Down below, inch by inch, he fed his iron horse into her ripening, inviting tunnel, pressing his mouth hard against her neck and the padded back of the bench so that he might not immoderately exclaim his own rapture.

Before long they were rutting like animals, beating their parts together like pistons in time to the clacking of the wheels over the tracks, faster and faster, as if the train was hurtling downhill, unable to stop, without possibility of braking, until the urgency of their desire, abetted by the repressed sounds of their ardor, tumbled them pell-mell into spasms of supreme heights and paroxysms of utter joy, ending in spurting jets of molten love which transported them both to another plane of existence, far removed from a mundane day-tripping ride on a steam-powered train.

She stirred first, disengaging herself gently from him, allowing his slack member to slump limply to the velvet seat. Adroitly she pulled a handkerchief from her bag and sopped up the remnants of their ardor, then occupied herself with the rearranging her clothing, hurrying when she felt the train slowing, nearing their station.

Jerome blinked several times. Brought to his senses by her resolute movements, he smiled lazily and tugged up his underthings. "Let me help you with your toilette, my dear. The duty of a gentleman and all that." He buttoned his trousers, straightened his waistcoat, and helped her tuck her full breasts back into her corset. Together they made her blouse orderly again and fastened her jacket, arranging her apparel as best as could be, given that the train was nearly to their destination.

"There now, all proper and as fresh as one can expect after a sooty train ride. You will want a nice warm bath once you reach your inn in any case." He stood, tying his bitten and damp cravat in place, just as the train pulled into Brighton station.

Jerome fetched her valise from the rack. "Allow me to assist you in descending from the train, my dear." He hurried out of the car and onto the platform, hailing a porter with an imperious gesture. She had followed a bit behind, shaking out her skirt and checking that her nether clothes were all tucked up out of sight. Oddly, she could feel one of her stockings slipping down.

Her luggage now deposited and the porter sent on his way, Jerome turned to Clementine. "Forgive me, Mrs. Banister, but I think I must press on to Portsmouth from here. I have a meeting in the early bright, and it would be better to overnight there, now I think of it. I've arranged a porter for you. Ta-ta. A pleasure to have met you." He tipped his hat and reboarded the train quickly, giving her no chance to reply, catching only a fleeting glimpse of her bewildered expression upon his hasty departure.

"Toodle-loo," he heard her say belatedly, sounding perhaps resigned, as he marched down the corridor into an adjoining car, finding a seat in an empty carriage and sitting at the far side, so that he might not be seen through the window from the platform. He buried his face in his now tattered paper, hiding his broad grin from view. As the train was pulling away, he put one hand into his pocket to toy with the jersey garter he had purloined while he helped her re-dress.

It was only when he heard the conductor jingling his box and calling for tickets that he noticed his wallet, previously ensconced in his inner jacket pocket, was missing. "Son of a biscuit!" He looked back reflexively in the direction of Brighton. "Expensive bit of jam, she was, all said and done. I must remember to hide my money in my shoe next time."

STEAM GEARED

Wouldn't You Like To Be Beside The Seaside?

Wouldn't You Like To Be Beside The Seaside?

"THE PELLINGHAMS ARE due to arrive today," called Mrs. Thacker to her husband as she sliced up rashers of bacon for the inn's breakfast table. "Would you ask Hazel if she has smartened up their favorite cabin yet?"

Mr. Thacker, having stacked an armload of firewood, attempted to place a tinder-sized piece into the open vent on the cast iron stove. Mrs. Thacker let go of her knife and swatted his hand away. "Stop that!" she warned. "The heat is just right now. I'll add more fuel where and when I want it." She leaned over to give him a quick kiss in recompense for the swat. He grinned at her.

"As you say, Mrs. Thacker. You know I only do it for to help. And for the kiss." He started out the door. "What time are the Pellinghams due? They are such a bright and bubbly couple. It will be jolly times at the dinner table tonight with those two visiting again."

And indeed dinner was merry. Mr. and Mrs. Thacker laid out a table of Palestine soup, potted lampreys, roast goose with port gravy, clementine sorbet, Dory-fish en croute, saddle of beef with mustard sauce, steamed potatoes, stewed cardoons, stuffed marrows, blazing mince pie, mango cream, and several molds of colored jellies, ending with Stilton, celery, and pulled bread. Most of the guests were on holiday and the Thacker Inn served dinners to fit the occasion.

Mr. Thacker presided at the head of the table, his round belly showing the result of eating grand meals every day. "And how was your trip up from London, Mrs. Pellingham?" he asked, to keep the conversational ball rolling. "Pleasant, I trust?"

"Oh, it was most entertaining! At one point there were sheep on the track and the train stopped momentarily. Being as it was lunchtime, some of us passengers took our sandwiches and tea from the dining car, hopped off, spread a picnic blanket, and ate al fresco. A very delightful minted tea it was. I meant to ask the porter where we might purchase the same."

Mrs. Thacker spoke up with some alarm. "The train was delayed? I cannot believe the effrontery of the rail lines these days, not running on time! I say, Mr. Thacker, do you think we should write a letter to the Transport Authority?"

"Oh, not a bit of it!" Mrs. Pellingham continued, her vivid blue eyes sparkling, her hand brushing over her perfectly coiffed golden hair, as if remembering how the lunchtime breeze had dislodged her locks. "The train only was only stopped for some seconds. They blasted some new kickshaw whistle, a marvel of modernity, which sent the sheep skittering off like their tails were afire. Near as good as a fence, said the conductor. The delay, I fear, was caused by us passengers. Rather froward we were about it, refusing to return until our picnic was all eaten up. The conductor was quite put out." She showed her dimples.

Mr. Pellingham spoke up quietly, supplying the missing nomenclature. "A piezoelectric transducer emitting vibrations in the ultrasonic range to which we mere humans are oblivious, but distressingly irksome to the ears of many animals. Fascinating technology." Mr. Pellingham looked relieved to be interrupted from his conversation with Miss Spritely, the spinster seated on his right, regarding the assorted details of her fossil-hunting expedition that morning.

"Yes, that is what they called it! Thank you for the words, darling. Inventors these days are so clever, are they not? The picnicking was a divine break from the monotonous clackety-clacketing." Her lively azure eyes locked on her spouse, and reminiscent smiles passed between the two of them. Mrs. Pellingham took a bite of goose and made appreciative moans. "So, so good," she said, her eyes still on her husband, a heavy-lidded and dewy look having come over her face. She broke away after a moment and addressed the table in general. "Your cooking is superb, Mrs. Thacker."

General agreement arose all around. Mr. Thacker asked Mr. Brompton about the article in the Times concerning the possible ramifications of a new emperor in Europe, which Mr. Brompton had mentioned was a topic of high controversy at his club, The Pelican. Mr. Thacker was blinking, a slight as if attempting to call to mind which club that was, but it was clear that Mr. Brompton was most proud of his membership there. Mr. Pellingham and Reverend Learmonth discussed the decline of sailing ships for shipping. "Sails haven't got a patch on steam power," the Reverend proclaimed. "If the train lines ran to South India, the price of pekoe would be much improved."

The weather was also remarked upon. Worldwide, if one were to believe what one read in the newspapers, there had been record hail in India, record snowstorms in North America, a devastating earthquake in Brazil, and a volcano erupting in the Orient for the first time in a thousand years. Fortunately, remarked Mr. Thacker, the weather in Brighton was always mild.

If any of the ladies had an opinion on emperors, steam, or the weather, they kept it to themselves, and discussed the latest trend in parasols, with lace awnings still the rage this season, the health benefits of pills versus cordials when it came to a household's ailments and afflictions, and how best to collect of seashells without tattering the hem of one's gown.

The next day was sunny, as Mr. Thacker had advertised, and the Pellinghams went for a long walk on the beach. Mr. Pellingham even changed into a bathing costume and waded out a few yards into the sea, turning around often to wave at Mrs. Pellingham, her honeyed coiffure shaded by a becoming lace bonnet. "Don't catch cold, dear!" she called out. "We don't want to stay in bed with a cough."

Mr. Pellingham laughed and splashed water a few inches in her direction. "Never, my darling. I shall be ever so careful in this invigorating surf."

As was their custom later in the afternoon, the Pellinghams retired to their cabin for a rest. It so happened that Mrs. Thacker recalled the wild iris might be blooming out by the little stream at the very back of the inn's property. Basket and garden secateurs in hand, she passed along the pathway between Cabin 17, which was occupied by the Pellinghams, and the old stone well. It was there that she overheard a little cry. Naturally she was concerned should there be any kind of distress upon her property, and she detoured to investigate. Peeping in the window, she saw a startling sight.

The Pellinghams were deeply engaged on the cottage's living room sofa. Mrs. Pellingham, naked to her waist, was kneeling on the floor before Mr. Pellingham, seated on the cushions with his breeches undone and crumpled under his bottom. Mrs. P was just drawing back to sit on her heels, her hands in position to catch Mr. P's long Tom as her lips withdrew from its length. Her smile was impertinent. "Would you like some more, Mr. P?" she asked. Mr. P, writhing in near paroxysm, could scarcely speak. "Mmm..mmm...mmmore," he managed to gasp out. Whereupon Mrs. P engaged his ivory wand again, taking it in to its hilt and then drawing her lips upward to its tip. And again and again. As Mrs. Thacker watched, the inevitable began to occur. Mrs. P bobbed her head more quickly, and Mr. P's quiverings were more pronounced and erratic. All of a sudden, Mrs. P drew back with a start, closing her eyes, and Mr. P's fountain erupted forcefully, spattering pearly effluvium over Mrs. P's face, neck, and bosom, as well as portions of the sofa and carpet.

Mrs. Thacker made a mental note to direct Hazel give the upholstery and carpet extra special attention once the Pellinghams departed. She started to right herself, having knelt at the window for an unobstructed and advantageous view, when Mrs. P stood and undid the fastenings on her skirt. Her lobster tail bustle, and then her petticoats and then her drawers, dropped to her feet, leaving her naked except for stockings held in place with pink-bowed garters.

STEAM GEARED

'I wonder what she can expect now,' Mrs. Thacker thought to herself. The man was clearly spent and would need a nap or fortification with oysters before he would be useful again. Mrs. Thacker knelt down at the window once more, peering through the glass to see how the couple would proceed. She also made another note to herself to serve oysters at dinner if there were any fresh to be had.

Mrs. P had a determined look on her face. Mrs. Thacker was pinned in place under the window by guilty fascination.

Positioned on the low faux- Provençal side table was Mrs. P's sewing basket, and it was to this that Mrs. P sidled, dragging it back to her place between Mr. P's now relaxed knees. She opened the box, undoing two clasps and a strap to reveal the contents. Mrs. Thacker rose up some from her crouch to get a better angle. Inside was a jumble of threads, patchwork, paper, and bits of fluff. What an odd time for Mrs. P to think of embroidery!

Mrs. P brought out an assemblage of the colored fabric and placed it over her fingers to uncrumple it. It was a sock puppet of some sort. A finger puppet, more to like. Once the puppet was fully plumped out over two of Mrs. P's talented fingers, she smiled at it with satisfaction. Mrs. Thacker's mind finally grasped the significance. Oh my goodness, truly not!

Mrs. P held the toy up for Mr. P to see. It was a tube of grey watered silk with a miniature elephant head fashioned at the tip. Its flexible trunk was made of India rubber and its short blunted tusks were of flexible whalebone.

Mr. P., still flaccid, his eyes nearly closed, laughed to see her wiggle the puppet. She was pretending the elephant was enraged, tossing its head and flinging its trunk. "Do tell me," Mr. P murmured, "when do you have time to make these enchanting little creatures? Eh, my darling, dearest one with the bluest of blue eyes? The azure blue of the Aegean Sea at sunset?" He grinned at her, as if enjoying a private joke.

She pressed her lips together in some small displeasure and used the elephant puppet to thrash in front of his face, a minor rebuke for his

164

comment. Her pressed lips softened almost immediately and she answered. "There are times I cannot sleep. I creep downstairs and play with my fabric scraps until I am ... relaxed."

They laughed. Mrs. P threaded the puppet over Mr. P's limp dick, uttering encouraging words, little grunts, and elephant-like trumpeting sounds as she inched the fabric towards his root, stuffing the slack flesh inside. "Make it move, my darling. Show me how the proud African elephant stomps through the jungle in search of his mate."

With desultory movement, Mr. P shifted his hips on the sofa cushion. "Tramp, tramp," he ad-libbed.

Mrs. P took hold of his hips and rocked them forward and back. "The elephant travels more earnestly than that. Make bigger stomps."

Obligingly Mr. P's hips lurched forward and back under her cajoling grasp. "Galumph, galumph, galumph," he said in synchronization with each thrust. His listlessness was less pronounced now, although the elephant's body was still somewhat slumped. "Such a clever engineer you are, my dear. Where is the switch on this one? Are you ready?"

Mrs. P considered the question of readiness. Her head tilted and her eyes gazed upward as if in deep thought, but her mouth was pursed in a repressed grin. "I suppose I could be." She slid her forefinger along the underside of the elephant's body, that is to say in a line under Mr. P's phallus, and massaged a spot at the base. Mr. P uttered a moan of pleasure in response to her touch. The puppet purred into action, lifting its snout and nodding its head. Mr. P's moan turned into a pronounced groan. "Oh heavens above, my precious angel, how ever do you create that vibration? Gads, it rips through me like bolts of lightning!"

Mrs. P studied the puppet and his emphatic reaction to it. "A voltaic cell. A tiny one. I hired a clocksmith. You should have seen his face when I explained what I wanted!"

Mrs. Thacker at the window gasped aloud with astonishment, but fortunately neither Mr. nor Mrs. P noticed the sound beneath their own laughter and coos of delight. Mrs. P. petted and praised the elephant, whose name it seemed was "Jumbo," asking it about its day, the

165

weather in the jungle, and the effect of a new emperor on the price of mangoes in the wild jungle market. Mr. P. answered for the elephant, a jumbled account of ongoing foolishness. All the while his elephant straightened, grew stouter, and reared upright.

Mrs. Thacker found herself squirming a bit as she crouched outside the window, watching the animalistic play.

Mrs. P had moved closer, continuing to hold a conversation with the elephant, her own eyes shining brighter and brighter. She climbed up onto the sofa, her stockinged legs embracing Mr. P's bare ones between them, and her quim could be seen vividly flushed and rosy in the center of its thatched nest.

"Look out, Mrs. P! The elephant is rampaging," shouted Mr. P.

"Rampaging? Do you mean, Jumbo is looking for his favorite hollow to have a kip?"

"No, no," panted Mr. P. "He is on a tear, looking for something to bang!"

"Oh my goodness, I must take care!" Mrs. P, despite her innocent words, was also trembling and panting now. She shimmied forward on her knees, her quim quivering and parting. "Come along here, Jumbo. I have just the place for you. Your very own special garden, Jumbo. Don't be afraid. Press through the thicket." She had crept forward until her inner thighs touched the puppet. She fumbled with the elephant's head, positioning the tusks just so. She sifted her hips to rub the blunt tusks against her button, the rubber trunk flailing below, the whole assemblage vibrating, eliciting utterances of pleasure from her.

Mr. P made trumpeting noises and lifted his hips to press further into her opening, held in check by her hands on his thighs. When he would thrust too vigorously, she merely drew back to sit more firmly on her bended calves. "So impatient, Jumbo. Your cavern is not quite ready. Just a trifle more. Very close." She pressed her velvet to the tip of the puppet's head, shivers running through her, her nipples growing harder and more distended. Her ribs heaved with her panting. "So close," she crooned, in between heavy sighs and strenuous moans. The elephant's ears were starting to flatten against its head from the dew dripping from her cave.

"Now," she breathed between groans, "Now, Jumbo. Press on! Press on! Bang on!"

Mr. P needed no further encouragement. His erect elephant plunged forward into the inviting depths. He cried out with pleasure, the elephant now smothered by undulating walls and melted dew. Gasps and shrieks ensued from the animals. Heaving, groaning, and the slapping sound of flesh on flesh punctuated the air, as together the pair were transported to paradise.

Mrs. Thacker, outside the window, felt her own warm glow erupt, and she slumped against the cottage wall, keeping a grasp on the window ledge so as not to fall, biting her lips to silence her own cry of release.

Some time afterwards, Mrs. P disengaged the silk elephant and placed it in a miniature bamboo cage within the sewing case. The elephant's ears were flat and sodden. Its tusks were shining and dappled with dew. Apparently its vibrations ceased when the mechanism was pressed upon at full penetration. "Tomorrow," she said in a voice still husky, "I have a giraffe. With two ball bearings affixed to its head."

"My ravenous darling," Mr. P sighed, pulling her close to cuddle beside him.

It was later that afternoon when Mrs. Thacker, dusting the parlor, heard a man making inquiries at the front desk. His tone was near frantic.

"Have you seen her? She is about so tall. Blonde. With the bluest eyes you can imagine. Like the Aegean Sea at sunset." Mrs. Thacker couldn't see the man at the desk, but she was sure his hand was indicating the approximate height of Mrs. Pellingham. "My business meeting concluded early, so I thought to take the train up and surprise her at her aunt's home, but she was not there. Her aunt tells me she usually takes residence at this inn when she visits. Are you sure you do not have a Mrs. Pickerel registered for this week?"

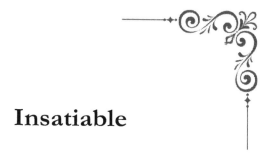

Insatiable

Insatiable

ALLOW ME TO SET THE scene for us. We are deep underground, beneath a fashionable house in an upscale neighborhood. You know the kind of place I mean, with gas street lamps gracing every block, manicured hedges separating tall mansions from the freshly cobbled streets, and self-powered steam locks softly hissing on the iron scrollwork gates.

We are standing in a clandestine chamber, which we reached by sneaking down a series of descending staircases. At the beginning of our trek, the walls were papered with quaint cottage roses and delicate stripes, but along the way, the wallpaper gave way to naked wood planks and the scent of burrowing earthworms. Around us now are crisscrossed shelving, dusty with disuse, which embrace many waxed and corked bottles. It is the kind of wine cellar one might expect in a great lord's castle or a fine dining establishment like our gentlemen's club, The Pelican. There is a table with decanting appurtenances and a fancy-sprocketed uncorking implement, an open cupboard with serving salvers and embroidered linens, and a dry sink, scrupulously cleaned more recently than the rest of the room.

Come look over here, on this tiny sliver of wall that is not covered by furnishings. Do you see this small nodule in the plaster? It is deliberately unobtrusive. Run your hand along the wall about shoulder height and you will feel it. Press hard, for it is a knob that works the mechanism that releases the covert door. Your pressing hand will activate a lever, which will ratchet a cog, which will draw back a peg, and with a metallic clink, the shelving alongside will shift slightly. Take hold of the cross-section and push inward on the central swivel. It takes a bit of effort, but worthwhile things often do. At last you will see into the secret room. Which is our destination for this evening.

As I mentioned, we are at least two stories beneath the basement of the grand home above, so it is not possible for voices to be overheard. If any of the servants were to wonder why the wine cellar was so far below the house, they would certainly have kept such thoughts to themselves. Even the trustworthy butler does not have a key of his own. When necessary, he is given the master's, which he returns with celerity. Is it not fortunate that I thought to take an impression of this key? I did so the other evening at the club, while the master was preoccupied with the gaming tables.

But back to the secret room, now that we have opened the door. The walls are rammed earth with rough timber framing. There is an odd scent above and beyond the bitter dank, something exotic. Cinnamon oil? Machine oil? The floor is flagged stone with a deep-piled Turkey carpet covering most of it. In one corner is positioned a comfortable leather armchair. To its side is a generous occasional table. On the table a glass pitcher of still water, two snifters, and a glass bottle recognizable by shape as fine cognac. Additionally the table has a single drawer. Should we snoop inside? Yes, we should, for our curiosity is greatly piqued! Some unusual implements rest within, such as one might expect in a stable, a linen closet, or a physician's cabinet.

The walls, although rough, have a series of gilt-framed paintings arranged in pleasing juxtaposition. They depict scenes mostly allegorical in nature, illustrated with scantily-clad females and males in full dress. I recognize this one with the shining knight rescuing the damsel in diaphanous rags, and also this one with an attractive lady on a picnic, sitting naked upon her bunched up clothing with men lounging casually near her. A wooden, ladder-like piece of furniture stands near the leather armchair. The style is called a 'valet,' because it puts up clothing neatly when not needed for a length of time. Such a witty term, the furniture servicing as if it were a domestic.

In the opposite corner from the armchair, fortunately for us, there is an oriental-style screen of lacquered rice paper, with brush-

171

calligraphy drawings of — oh my lord, look at them! Little men with very large members. So huge they need walking sticks and even bamboo carts to carry them. How very droll!

But we have skipped over a critical element in the center of the room. A large, commodious brass bedstead, adorned with an intricately quilted silken coverlet and artfully displayed decorative pillows. Recessed in the gleaming headboard is a panel of levers, buttons, and dials, glowing discreetly. And an inquisitive eye will discern leather straps with matching brass buckles nearly hidden in the folds of the bed-skirt.

Oh, let us step out of sight now, for I hear footsteps! We can crouch here behind the screen, in the corner opposite the armchair, where we have a good view of the bed and one set of the ominous straps.

The hidden door revolves open. (Thank goodness we had the forethought to close it behind us!) We see the master and the mistress enter. He is leading, and she follows. He takes hold of her arm and helps her over the rough threshold. "I hope you are not having second thoughts, my turtle dove? Your betting at cards was particularly reckless this evening. Indeed you lost by a farcically large margin. Thus, we are here." He gestures grandly, stretching out his arms to encompass the entirety of secret room. "You might call it your forfeiture. I call it my boon." He leads her across to the wood valet and armchair. His steps are impatient and eager. Might we guess she is reluctant? Her steps are measured. Seemingly composed.

Of course it would be the master. I mentioned, did I not, that he has the only key? But that his companion is his lady wife somewhat astonishes me. To be honest, I took him for something of a player. A rake, it is often said. A dissolute rapscallion of base and scandalous habits. Would it be amusing to put out a rumor at the club that he is faithful to his marriage bonds?

Although on second thought, it is not all that surprising, for she is a comely woman, with fashionably pale skin, inky-dark hair, a mouth drawn like a Cupid's bow poised to strike and possessed of other charms of a prodigious nature. How fortunate for him that his bride was also his joy.

"Shall I undress you, precious apple of my eye?' he asks. "Or will you disrobe while I watch?" He waits for an answer. In response she unbuckles her high-collared bolero, that currently popular bit of fabric that covers only the arms, shoulders and a strip of the tender neck, leaving a woman's upper chest and indeed often most of her breasts to the open air. She looks up into his face. His back is to us, so we cannot see his expression from where we hide, but we can see hers through the cracks where the divider hinges. Her eyes are searching for something. Does she find it? Abruptly she turns away from him, and us, exposing the laces at the obverse of her bodice to his administrations. Now we can see only their backs and his hands attending upon her.

He chuckles. There is a sinister tinge to his mirth. His fingertips fiddle with the tidy knots and finesse the strings apart. Once they are loosened enough, he reaches around to detach the bodice at the front. He removes the article and drops it carelessly over a wooden rung. She starts to turn but he catches her shoulders and keeps her facing away. Pin by pin he unwinds her artfully styled hair. Wavelets tumble down. He pauses now and then to finger the lengths, seemingly enjoying the feel of the coils draping around his naked fingers. Oh, did I mention he stopped to remove his gloves at one point while he was unpinning? He did.

With her hair now undone, hanging like a dense swag over her exposed shoulders, he loosens and unfastens the corset as he did the bodice. We can hear the silver singing of the laces dragged through their eyelets. We see her shiver as each pull stimulates a little stripe of skin, rippling along her back. Next the brocade skirt, which he unhooks, tugs over her hips, and allows to fall to the floor in a circle around her. He pauses, looking down, perhaps admiring the symmetry. Then he begins on the petticoats. A goodly number of them, although to be fair I was not really counting, preoccupied as I was by watching the dramatic unveiling in progress. The petals of petticoats drop one by one, and at last her rounded rump emerges, visible beneath her chemise. There was a bustle in there somewhere, but he tossed it aside carelessly. It bounced on the Turkey carpet and wobbled some feet away, its structural integrity compromised. This caused a small whimper from the lady, to which the master murmured a quiet promise of a shopping trip on the morrow. At the end she stood in her shift, pantaloons, and stockings.

Allow me to pause a brief moment here to expound again how handsome this female is, both clothed and in the altogether. Do you see how proud is the prow of her arching breasts! How seductive the outline of her sensuously padded buttocks — nearly a bustle unto themselves! Such consummate grace engendered by her startled limbs as she flinches from his insistent explorations. It is hardly a wonder the man is aroused by her, even though she is his wife.

The master begins prowling around her, leisurely, taking his time, letting his hands drift across her body and roam inside the openings of her underthings. Little gasps escape her as he fondles delicate parts, while sighs of pleasure and anticipation are heard from his own lips.

A swift change seems to come over him and he yanks at her drawers. Harsh ripping sounds are heard and he flings the flimsy fabric aside. Roughly he grabs the hem of her shift and pulls it off over her head, her arms perforce drawn upward as well. More ripping. He grabs at her stockings, now fallen to her ankles, nearly knocking her over as he snatches them down and off her feet. He then grasps her slender arms, pulling them together behind her and holding them in one hand. In a trice he has his neckcloth dislodged and is binding her with its length, tugging her wrists across each other and making them fast with multiple turns around and between, finishing with an intricate knot as a final flourish. Such a tidy package he makes of her. He picks up the torn shift, fingering it as if examining its fineness, before ripping off a rough strip along the hem. So much ripping! He doubles the torn fabric and positions it with care across her eyes, standing behind her with his body close to hers, her anticipatory trembling evident even from our hiding spot across the room. He whispers to her. "How is that, dear heart? Can you see? No?" His tongue darts out, licking her scalp behind her ear. "I can tell by your quickening breaths that you are ready. We will proceed."

Tying off the blindfold, he embraces her bodily and wheels around, spinning so that her sightless eyes now face the bed. We can see both their expressions now. The flush on her cheeks is charming. All of her is charming in fact. Delicate pink and erect nipples, blushing roses, and below her plump lips peek from a frame of dark curls, all set in a canvas of milky satin skin, the entire expanse of which is now exposed to prurient view. From behind her, he crowds her with his body, nudging her in our direction, to the bed. We duck back a little, fearful they might see us, but he is deeply engaged and she is blindfolded. I think they would not notice our presence unless we were a herd of trumpeting elephants. Maybe not even then.

I perhaps need hardly mention that when he turns, we can glimpse the front of his trousers straining outward. He pushes her forward until she stumbles and flops down on the mattress with a startled cry. He smacks one bare buttock with his open hand. "Be still, please, precious gumdrop!" His tone is light, but there is an undercurrent of menace. "Remain silent as long as you possibly can. I find it excites me to hear your squeaks when you struggle to muffle your cries." He is undressing himself now, kicking his shoes in the direction of the valet and dropping his trousers, weskit, shirt, stockings, and undergarments to the floor.

She lies helpless where she fell; half on, half off the bed, perhaps not daring to move. Once he has undressed, the master positions her firmly on her belly, drawing her ankles to each lower post and fastening them with the straps and buckles. "I think of these as jewelry, my heavenly pearl. Or like the straps of costly evening shoes. I love shopping with you for shoes, you know? When you button and buckle them to your foot, I smile, thinking of these very moments, where I snug these buckles to your deliciously formed ankles." She squirms in some discomfort as he pulls at the leather and slots the metal prong through its eyelet, stretching her to make the fit tight. With her feet thus anchored, he drags her bodily to the center of the bed, one hand on a bound wrist and the other entwined in her hair. He chuckles softly as she bites back an outburst of pain. "That's better. I need to be able to tell the extent of your discomfiture by your sobs. That only hurt a bearable amount, did it not?" She starts to nod, but his hand is still tangled in her hair. She arrests her movement to prevent her hair from being pulled out at the roots.

He smiles at that. "You are such a quick study, my tantalizing peach." His teeth flash in a sudden grin. On the bed's panel, he turns a knob, watching attentively as the ankle chains ratchet taut. Then he is standing up, crossing to the little table. Her head turns when she hears the little drawer pull open, her eyes unseeing, but her ears alert.

"What tonight for us, tender tulip? Here is the riding crop, but I used that last time. Would you prefer a change of pace? I think you would. You usually do." He rummages through the contents in the drawer. "A paddle, perhaps?" He holds it up, turning to the bed, as if showing the implement to his blindfolded victim. We can see his face clearly from our hiding spot. His eyes are hard and seem to glitter. He smacks the wooden blade of the paddle on the palm of his other hand with a great resounding thwack, his grin growing wide when she startles at the sound. There is a quiet measure of time while he seems to deliberate, giving her time to imagine what is upcoming. Then a solid thud lets her know he has dropped it back into the drawer. "A hairbrush?" He mimics bringing the brush down with the bristles up, and another test in the air with the bristles down. He shrugs and another thud is heard as the brush is dropped back in the drawer. "A flogger?" The bedsprings creak as his bride seems to jerk away from him, recoiling from the suggestion. A happy smile springs to his face. "Did I hear a yes, sweetling?"

He lifts out a leather-wrapped handle with drooping cords. Some of the cords have knots at their ends. Others are frayed, as if the knotted ends have been worn away from long use. He dangles it, swaying it a little. Gently he draws the cords across his own naked chest. His erection bobs upward with the stroke. The ankle chains rattle as she kicks, squirming, perhaps trying to free herself.

"Just the ticket!" he gloats. "A superlative choice on your part, my passionate flower." He bangs the open drawer shut with his naked hip and approaches the bed.

For some long moments, he stands quietly above her, as if drawing up his plan of attack. The general with tin soldiers in hand, standing before his diorama, plotting his next strike. The painter poised with brush and palette knife before an unblemished canvas, envisioning the best placement of strokes for his masterpiece. The sculptor coming to grips with the nature of his block of stone, holding chisel and hammer in readiness for the first blow. Where to begin this work? This is the master's challenge. And the victim's agonizing suspense.

He flings the cords forward and then jerks them back in the air above her, letting the business ends fall onto her shoulder with a strand or two kissing her ear, earning a lengthy shudder from her. He draws the leather cords along her achingly beautiful, exquisitely pale, tenderly resilient skin, dragging from her neck to her buttocks. He picks up, flings, and lets fall again. Dragging across her slender waist this time. Her groan is barely audible as the soft tendrils trail across her flesh. Next the cords drop on a hip and are dragged crosswise to her neck. Dropping and dragging along her un-stockinged thighs and across her calves, leaving pink trails on the canvas of her skin. She trembles, anticipating the strokes. She shudders, enduring the draggings.

The master continues this way for quite some time. Now and again his other hand rearranges her hair or limbs to suit his artistic eye. She trembles less and less as he strokes her, caressing her with the lengths of cording.

From our hiding place I had just come to think this was a mock performance the couple was playing. That they were enraptured by the gentle flicks and drawn out drags, and there was no intent to inflict or receive pain. Thus it is a sudden and unexpected instance when out of the blue he rears back and lays the cat out full on her gluteal mound. The strike breaks her skin cruelly.

She screams. I must admit I nearly did too, lulled as I had been by the prior hypnotic movements. With lightning strokes he transforms into a madman, flailing at her with the flogger, all along her body, her desire-inducing thighs, her well-formed back, her sensuously curved arms, the provocative soles of her feet. Her long hair catches in the cords and he pulls savagely, ripping small tendrils from her scalp. When she twists to flinch away from the blows the cat strikes along her sides, biting into her rosy tipped breasts, and digging deep into her shins. He moves all around the bed, wielding the flogger high above his head and bringing it down in a fury, leaving long streaks of reddened skin irregularly across her body and droplets of blood where the knots had torn deeper into her flesh. The mistress is thrashing to avoid the master's hand, hampered by the bindings on her wrists and the restraints on her ankles. She is panting and her eyes are squeezed shut. She gasps, weeps, and whimpers, unable to cringe very far from the flurry of blows.

All at once, the master grows quiet. The cords had left a particularly deep mark across the mound of her lower cheek, wrapping around into the tenderest flesh where her body branched. His hand drops to his side and he stands looking down at her as she lays twitching, gasping and quivering, from her clenched toes to her mussed hair. Her face, now turned to the side we can see, is a like a mask, resolutely absorbed with keeping her feelings from showing. One might guess she is mortally afraid to let her features show the fear she might feel. Rivulets of tears glisten on her flushed cheeks and her body shines with perspiration.

Master is also trembling, and has worked up his own sheen of sweat from his efforts. Mixed scents of ardor, shock, and exertion waft through the room. He brushes the side of his hand along the brass panel until he trips a lever and a slender projection slides out, clearly designed for the convenience of keeping the implement positioned for easy retrieval. With one hand Master caresses his stiff manhood, which is now standing out very proud and glistening at its tip. He moves to the foot of the bed, still holding himself, and bends down to nip at the mistress's one ankle and lick along her calf. Then he turns to the other foot, tickling its sole with his tongue and marking her with little bites and harsh kisses as he works his way upward, crawling up onto the bed to reach higher. Once he gains her knees, he uses both hands on her, letting his manhood dangle against her skin. Upwards he continues, tasting her with his lips and tongue, his hard prick poking along behind. He reaches her fork and meanders for some time along her valley, murmuring sweetly with evident delight as she shivers under his ministrations, bombinating his lips to vibrate her tender hidden parts, dandling his tongue upward, over her little pea in its sheltering pod, which surely was heated and plump by now. He pulls her bound hands towards him, forcing her upper body to lift up off the bed. His teeth nibble at her ear through her tousled hair, and he then bends her to his liking. Now she is kneeling, her ripe posterior uppermost. He places himself behind her, his knees inside her spread ones, and leans across to pick up the flogger.

Suddenly he flattens his body on top of hers, pressing his weight upon her, knocking her flat on the bed again, and knocking the wind from her. We can hear her startled exhale. He whispers to her. "I know you can't see it, but it is there. A button on the panel, glowing red, next to the metered grid identifying the amount of tension on the restraining chains. It waits for you and you alone. All you need do is say your safe word and the bed will release you. Merely utter the sounds." He opens his mouth wide to bite a large mouthful of her silky hair. He jerks the strands, wrenching at her roots, and then releases them to whisper again. "But do you wish to say that word? I think you do not." He pauses barely seconds before he bends her over again, and the lashings begin anew.

The cords come down across her belly. A light stroke. She recoils and a small shriek of renewed surprise is drawn involuntarily from her lips. His own protuberance can be glimpsed between her spread thighs as he surges forward. He is whispering some more, perhaps to reassure her, or perhaps to incite. I cannot hear the exact words from our hiding place, but I would describe his tone as coaxing. Almost pleading. I see her face, determined to endure, her lips tightened to repress further outbursts.

The flogger comes down again. Lashing her loins. She cannot fully suppress a muffled groan. He raises and lowers the implement repeatedly. Thighs, breasts, delta. Deliberately at first. Individual beats. And then more swiftly and with greater force. Her compressed lips fail after a short time. Her cries rise in pitch and fervor. Her attempts to wrench herself from her bonds, to wrest herself free of his grasp, become more urgent and passionate. He adjusts his grip, pressing her unrelentingly, his arm still rising and falling. His ruddy sword chaffs across her thighs and pokes upward, grazing her valley and entering now and then the secret depths of her private hollow.

The tension is now reaching penultimate heights in the room. Her buttocks are heaving and pitching, rocked by his hard-driving body. His hand strikes a continuous rain of blows, almost as if he is flagellating himself. Both of them gasping, her moaning and thrashing, him plunging with hands and hips, both slippery from sweat, and her with some trails of blood dripping. It could not last much longer. (I could not last much longer!)

The crisis peaks and he cries out, a spasmodic burst of pent-up joy. Pearly lava explodes from him, spurting out onto her nether region, spilling out onto the bedspread, spray after spray as he pumps convulsively against her, his seed shooting glistening threads over her flushed skin and the flogger he is still holding tight against her middle.

In due time, his furor fully spent, he gently lowers her sagging body to the bed. He drops the implement and loosens the bond on her wrists so she can slip free. He unleashes one ankle and lays himself out beside her on the soft and soggy bedding, pulling her close to him in a tender embrace. "That was magnificent, empress of my heart. Truly. I could not ask for better." His voice is frogged and distant. He stretches himself to reach the panel at the head of the bed. A small tray clicks open, steam rising. He lifts out a warm towel and offers it to her solemnly, like a badge of achievement.

She stirs at that, her eyelids slitting open. Her fingers are rubbing at her wrists where deep red creases mark her. She pushes his hand to drop the towel back in the tray. Her elegant finger finds the button and the tray recedes. "More," she says softly.

He does not respond at once, his essence still floating in nirvana. She picks up the flogger he had dropped, pries his sticky wet fingers apart, and places the handle in his palm.

"But," he protests, his voice cracking. "Precious owner of all that I am, please, I beg you. Rest."

"More," she tells him firmly, forcing his hand to close on the flogger's grip.

STEAM GEARED

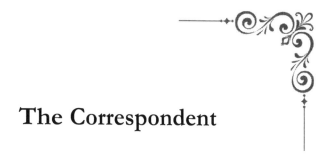

The Correspondent

The Correspondent

THE LETTER WAS RESTING on the carpet beneath the postal slot in the front door when he went down to breakfast. A frisson of anticipation shivered through his body, ending with a spark in his gunnysack. He went on through to the dining room, letting the notion of a letter from her sift through his awakening consciousness.

Baxter kissed his mother's cheek dutifully. "A pleasant good morning to you, Mater." He took his seat at the breakfast table and grunted a good morning at his father. Behind the daunting facade of the Metro Financial Times, his father grunted back. The maid stepped forward with the coffee pot. Now that he had reached his majority, his parents allowed him to choose his breakfast drink, and out of some contrariness he chose coffee instead of tea. "Toast, eggs, and kippers, sir?" the maid asked deferentially as she poured.

"Yes, Hester, and some of that excellent marmalade we had yesterday if there is any left. I'm afraid I made rather a piggy of myself, but it was so good. Do give Mrs. Laveller my compliments." He smiled at his mother, and at his father's newspaper.

His mother smiled back. The paper did not.

"Baxter, dear," his mother began gently, employing a tone that caused him to sense she expected a confrontation of some sort. "We have received a dinner invitation for next week, from the Wallingford's. Their little Amanda will be at home for visitation in the coming week. It seems she has not found a suitable boy this season, so I want you to be especially pleasant to her. With a sizable fortune of her own, she is not a bad catch, and it is about time for you to think of your future." Mother picked up a corner of toast and examined it as if it was the subject in question. "Personally I'm surprised she wasn't snapped up as soon as she was presented. But then again, she is a little headstrong."

"And pug ugly," said the newspaper, fluttering slightly as a page was turned.

Mother glared, affronted by the newspaper's pronouncement. "Reginald, that is so unkind! I will not have you speak so disrespectfully in front of our son. And the servants." She dud not look at Hester, who had returned from delivering the breakfast order and was standing motionless against the wall, seemingly as insensible to the conversation as the sideboard.

Father lowered his wood-pulp defenses. His sharp eyes and hawk-like nose surveyed the scene at the table first, and then he spoke in clipped tones. "Our son is of age and has likely heard much worse. Not to mention, he is capable of drawing his own conclusions." The paper wall rose again.

"Honestly, Reginald!" Mother's exasperation was rendered with a sigh and a sniff combined. She tossed her head, dismissing what she could not change, and returned her attention to Baxter. "Do try to engage her in conversation, please, Baxter, for my sake. You are a fine young lad, and the time has come for you to be choosing a wife and settling down. I'm especially looking forward to grandchildren. I am sure Mrs. Wallingford would yield to persuasion and arrange for you to be seated to Amanda's left, so that you might be the preferred dinner conversationalist."

Baxter gave his mother a munificent smile. "Of course, Mater. For you, I would walk through fire."

"All she is asking is that you talk to an ugly girl," quipped the paper.

Mother darted a baleful glare in the paper's direction. "She isn't ugly. She just has a certain height. And her nose is a bit big. But think how graceful she is. And so talented! She plays the flute like a bird, it is said. And she is clever too, although not in an overly pretentious way. I hear she all but ran her father's airship factory after he had the stroke last year. Of course she will have to find a foreman for that once she marries."

Baxter chuckled. "I'd lay long odds on that!"

"What are you saying, Baxter? Odds? Evens? I'm sure there are many good foremen she could choose from. You, for example, might be a good fit for the position. Your job at the Airship Terminal, as chief mechanic, would stand you in excellent stead. To my way of thinking, it is high time your talents and skills should be better compensated than Maycombe-Springerham currently affords you."

The paper mumbled something about Mother's way of thinking but didn't dare express itself too distinctly. Mother resolutely faced forward and would not deign to offer the paper even one iota of her attention.

Baxter's breakfast arrived and he applied his cutlery to it, letting the subject drop entirely. "How is the financial market this morning, Father? Any word about the bobble in the fresh rubber prices?"

AFTER BREAKFAST, AS Baxter left the house attired in his starched collar shirt and his nattiest batwing bow tie, he noticed the letter had been retrieved from the carpet and placed on a silver salver for that evening's perusal. He could have snatched it up and tore open the ivory paper with eager glee, but instead, he let it rest unmolested for the time being. The possible delights awaiting him within the envelope filled his day with a certain amount of cheerful merriment.

Easily he weathered the gloomy morning meeting full of dire predictions about the shortage of India rubber, which some thought to be temporary, but which the timid management interpreted as proof another bubble year was in the making. He laughed when oil leaking from a key shaft spurted out when he adjusted it, drenching the left side of his face with grunge. He joked with his co-workers at lunchtime about synthetic rubber, and what possible uses it could have besides airship flotation. Some of the suggestions were rather rough-hewn, but Baxter grinned and did nothing to quell the language as a supervisor might. He was well aware of the consequences of not releasing steam when necessary.

After lunch he retired to his office, the plans for a newly redesigned internal combustion engine on the drawing table before him. The VP's called it an "infernal combustion engine" and were certain it would fail. They would point with pride to the century of progress from burning coal to heat steam to power engines. It was a perfectly reasonable process, a proven system that had fueled nearly a century of progress.

He did not oppose this argument, at least not yet, however when the moment was right, he intended to put forth the precept that an engine capable of internally producing power would indisputably provide for unprecedented conservation of resources. More compact. More transportable. No longer reliant on the humongous repository of coal which external engines needed, the enormous tinderbox to burn the fuel, the exorbitant manpower to replenish the voracious box, and the complicated and potentially dangerous linked apparatuses to capture and manipulate the steam. Baxter was alive to the mechanical possibilities. For management, likely all he need say was one of the resources conserved would be money.

Even as he marveled and brooded over the blueprints, his mind could not help skipping back to the morning's letter. The return name and address were falsified, of course, but the handwriting, so upright and persnickety, as if written by a maidenly and strict schoolmistress, never failed to elicit within him a warm glow. He mulled over the pleasing contrast between the text's unwaveringly sharp ascenders and its writer's voluptuous figure. The no-nonsense penmanship was seemingly at odds with her lively tropes and amusing internal rhymes. Like Elizabeth Barret Browning, namesake of his pet name for her, she wrote fresh, strange music, exquisite pathos, and brave thoughts. Although what he most enjoyed was her degenerative similes. It was not long before his loins were incensed. Resolutely he picked up his toolkit and headed to the repair bay. Surely there was a timing chain he could tighten. Or release. Maybe both.

For the rest of the afternoon he busied himself in the bay, hands-on with the company's swiftest dirigible, Intrepid Bumblebee, which had

187

developed a small, but persistent leak. "Let's just start over at the beginning with her. See what ails her."

Airships, as he explained to his mother when she inquired, were simple at their heart. It had to do with hot air being lighter than cold air. When the burner heated the air inside the balloon, the lighter air lifted the ship upwards. A skilled airship captain would ride the wind currents, aided by flaps, rudders, and the occasional burst of steam. In time the air inside the balloon cooled, and unless reheated, the craft descended. What more could one desire in the way of transportation? His mother had laughed. Thank you kindly, but I will take the train, she told him.

Inspecting the Bee's envelope for damage, he ably scrambled across the rope spans. But he found no leaks. Next he disassembled the burner so he could reassemble it anew. "When all else fails, start from scratch," he quoted himself. His nimble fingers stroked a recalcitrant valve with the finest synthetic emollient. A rough patch was tamed with the finest of files, and a tangle with cabling was re-threaded with fresh. After which, the airship performed like clockwork. He grinned, waving off the accolades of his crew at his accomplishment, secretly pleased by their praise.

At quitting time, while shedding his mechanic's apron and redonning his jacket and hat preparatory to leaving for the day, the managing director called to him. He bit down his reluctance at the delay in his ride home, his mind yearning to muse on the diverting possibilities the letter might hold.

"Baxter, my boy, you were unaware of it, I'm sure, but the chairman of our board was in the office today, watching through the portholes in the top office. He was quite impressed with the way you work. Such diligence! Such attentiveness! Your interaction with the men and how you gained their confidence was that of a consummate manager! You are just the kind of man he thinks should be given more responsibility. And of course, more pay. Do come to our executive dinner next week at the Tanqueray Club. It is after hours, but that's a small price to pay for advancement, wouldn't you say?"

Baxter blinked a few times as the director's meaning punched through his incipient reverie. "Oh yes, sir. I mean no, sir. I mean, of course, sir. I would be thrilled to attend, and I would say a small price, yes, sir." He took the director's outstretched hand and pumped it twice with emphasis. "Thank you, sir, and good evening."

On the steam tram on the way home, he allowed himself the luxury of basking in his good fortune. His mother, as usual, was correct concerning the timing of when his talent would be recognized. Once that luxury had been indulged, his thoughts promptly returned to the letter. And its writer. Amanda of the upright hand and crooked smile. How could Father think her ugly? True, she seldom took a parasol when out in the day, and often forgot her bonnet, so that her skin was unfashionably sun-drenched. If staying indoors and taking precautions were at the root of beauty, then his Mandy could indeed be called drab.

What kind of mischief would she have invented for him this time? It was usually a puzzle of some sort. He hoped it was one of the jigsaw puzzle kind. Like last spring when she cut up a map to the Zoological Gardens in Regents Park, and they met in a dark glade behind the Water Fowl Lawn, unseen by the flâneurs on the beaten path. On the other hand, he would be inordinately happy with a cipher, like the one that when decoded led him to a seldom opened book in the circulating library with one of her fantastical schematics inside the cover, depicting an invention that traced out heart shapes with an electrically-resonant transformer circuit. Or indeed, even something as delicious and delicate as the clockwork butterfly she had sent, which had one wing that did not open properly. When he disassembled it to modify the chittering flapper, there he discovered a tiny metal heart engraved with letters so small it required a magnification glass to read the endearing sonnet she had written in his honor.

At her insistence, they had met only secretively since their first chance encounter at the antiquarian bookstore, where they both inquired after the same book at the same time. Together they carried the store's one copy of "Sonnets from the Portuguese" to a secluded alcove, and read it sitting side by side. By the time her aunt and his mother came looking for them, their hearts had melted like candles, muddled all together into one pool of wax. On that enchanted day when their souls engaged, they began to plot, for they knew their families would keep them apart. 'A boy from that begrimed industrial family? Parvenus!' would say her parents. 'A girl from that kiss-fingers dynasty? Neversweats!' would say his.

Amanda's parents were utterly peevish on the subject. Baxter's were no less obstinate. Even so, Mandy assured Baxter that by the end of the season, both their mothers would be driven together, fearful of their respective offspring going stale on the shelf. Thus far the plan was working. But in the meantime, how could they bear not to touch? They lived for each other's missives.

Speculation regarding the contents of the letter kept Baxter rapturously preoccupied during the ride home. Once safely inside his domicile, he grabbed up the envelope and holding it to his bosom, carried it up to his private rooms. Taking care not to make noise, he turned the key in the door, and settled into his comfortable armchair with the fading light of day seeping in through the high window. From under the nightstand, he opened a panel and withdrew a glass tumbler and his secret stash of single-malt. With drink in one hand and letter in the other, he began to read that which had held sway over his imagination all the day.

And indeed the missive did not disappoint.

It opened with an enigmatic salutation. The better to explain it away were it to be opened by another by mistake. Baxter had warned Mandy that his mother on occasion snooped, reading his mail. Mater would write silly excuses on the envelope, like 'opened by mistake to see what was inside,' a ruse she had borrowed from the American author, Samuel Clemens. The letter began:

"My beloved ersatz Robert,

"I am writing to you, my dear man, to let you know of a dream that I had the other night. Do you remember the time we escaped my chaperone and found our way to a back staircase at Madame Tussaud's? We spoke of our namesakes, Elizabeth and Robert, and what we might have done in their circumstances, which after all, was somewhat like our own. Prudish parents. Inflexible in the face of our modern world. Insensate of our professed desires. Although I am far from an invalid, and you are far from a penurious suitor.

"Now let me tell you what I dreamt. From that back staircase, we fled from the museum and hid in a wild garden, a very dense garden of a kind not found in the city. I was very bold, in my dream, I must warn you now, and I will use indelicate words to describe my actions. Herewith I will expound on what kind of bold I was!

"For in my dream, I sensed a sort of tension in you. A yearning beyond that of a young man coming up in the world who longs for an erstwhile companion to join in matrimony. And I dared to think I might do for you what I had seen the parlor maid do for the groomsman out in the kitchen garden behind the back gate.

"Thus I stroked my hand along your beard, tracing through your silky pelt, letting my fingers dally along your lips, follow the outline of your cheek and stroke under your chin. I then allowed my fingers to flutter ever downward, over that sensuous bump of your throat and across the neat folds of your bow tie. I won't untie it, for there is the matter of the time it might take to do it up again without a valet's assistance, but I do continue on my path, letting my fingers pop open some of your shirt studs, allowing my bare fingertips to make free with your freshly bared skin. Oh, the impure thrill of it! I dally some here, raising the hackles of your chest hair, tickling you. Tickling my senses. Next I leisurely continue my hands' journey, finding the band of your trousers at last.

"Oh, how naughty you must think me! Saying that word! I will say it again. Trousers! I giggle at myself. Am I not the very model of a forward and wanton female? But to the point, in my dream, I use both

191

hands to take hold of your inexpressibles and release the secreted buttons from their imprisonment. Like the parlor maid, I fumble within and draw out my treasure, fondling it, admiring it, and bringing it out into the open where my eyes can feast upon it.

"What a handful it is! Soft and furry as a kitten, but when I pet it, quickly it develops a stern stem, growing, expanding, pointing upright, and exhibiting what kind of a stout fellow you are! I cradle the soft leather satchel below with one hand while my other caresses the ruddy shaft.

"I cannot help it! It affects me so that I must kiss it. Just like the maid did her groomsman. I bend down to kiss the proud, prancing steed, and then bring myself to my knees to kiss it again and again.

"Parenthetically, my beloved Robert, if you are not playing along with yourself at this juncture, please put this letter down for a moment and catch up. I am imagining your hands engaged upon your firm, blue-veined, roseate-tinted marble column with its magnificent smooth helmet as I write. You shall have to imagine my kisses. They are fervent and earnest. Do you feel them now? Good, then I shall resume my narrative.

"Now I am on my knees before you, my bum bustle sticking up behind me like a beehive. I must look a fright! I hope your attention is focused on your lap instead of my arse. My tongue is curling around your phallus. My nose pushing your stick upright so I might lick the tickling tendrils at its base. I draw back and enclose my lips on your tip, letting my tongue tease the tiny opening, sensitive, like my own opening, but in miniature. I have heard whispers that there are words for this. 'Fellatio.' 'Dog's portion.' 'Gamahuche.' I suspect not all of these apply in this particular instance, but I say them anyway. Like saying 'trousers,' it excites me somewhere deep and primal inside.

"As I move my lips and tongue up and down, I hum phrases from a cheery tune. I feel your member twitch and dabble inside my mouth. I smile, drawing my lips tighter to your firm flesh, enjoying the iron rigidity underneath. I love feeling your phallus jiggle and dance under my ministrations. My hands instinctively reach for your hips and beyond, my fingers digging into the clenched muscles of your cheeks. I feel you pulse. Rock. Shudder. Quake. Shiver in eagerness for the fray. My tongue and lips work faster, taking you in rapaciously and letting you out only so that I can draw you in again. Faster and faster. Harder. Our movements are like that of one of my company's airship's internal engines, finely aligned, with a seal so tight there is a mere sheen of lubrication between the piston and the chamber.

"Vigorously we work our way to maximum propulsion, maximum exertion, maximum acceleration. There is danger we will overheat. Steam begins to escape as the pounding piston quivers and shakes outside of tolerance. I keep my lips tight to the moving part. I feel all boiling over. Like the milkmaid I gasp, pull back, but then again press forward, feeling the pearly shower spew forth. I hold out my tongue and swallow the liquid proof of my labor, the emulsion of my devotion, the treasured dew due to me. I am drenched with the proof of fruition. The exultant attainment of the summit. Salty sweet reward.

"Afterwards I feel a heaviness in you, as your body sinks and sprawls languidly. I unclench my hands from your relaxed bottom, and slide them upward, over the bumps of your ribs, across your muscular chest, the ivory column of your neck, and finally take your face in my hands. I tilt my head to kiss you, the salt of you still moist on my lips.

"Robert, my lover, can you hear me murmur to you? Was it good for you, too? Take up your pen now and tell me how it felt. Tell me in great detail. And use some naughty words for me. Please?

"With the greatest affection and deepest sincerity,

"Your Ersatz Portuguese.

"P.S. Hurry!!"

STEAM GEARED

Albert and Minnie, Part III
Or
The Consummation

Albert and Minnie, Part III
Or
The Consummation

THE SUGGESTED ADDRESS was down a darkish lane, with discreet lights emanating from a coffee house, or what might have loosely been defined as one, located in the middle of the block. Albert kept his arm tight around Minnie's shoulders. Their heads were down, partly due to the droplets of cold rain blowing at their faces, but also in some embarrassment.

"What did your mate say again, Al? This doesn't look like a street where respectable people would be." Minnie shrank back against him, flinching from a haggard man going in the other direction, who was openly staring at her as he lurched by. She thought she heard him say something. She imagined it was offensive and crude.

"He said it was a well-run hostelry, clean, and the proprietors were not overly inquisitive of their guests. He wasn't sure of the cost, but he thought sixpence." Al was grinning. "Think of it, Minnie! An hour alone together, in a cozy room, with clean sheets!"

Minnie nodded her head against Al's chest. "I'm thinking on it, Al. I'm a-thinking." Her hand pressed on her pocket, nestled inside her skirt, where all her coins, plus the ones Al had given her for safekeeping, were hidden. She was still wearing her uniform dress, minus her apron, but she had taken time to tie the pocket carefully beneath her petticoat layers.

As they approached, they heard voices raised in good cheer. On the pavement in front of their destination was a soldier holding hands with a woman wearing a dress hemmed so as to display her anklebones. He was in high spirits, telling a joke for which he seemed to have forgotten the punch line. The woman, whose shortened skirt was a beacon brazenly advertising her availability, was smiling brightly and waiting patiently for the appropriate moment to laugh. She assisted her tipsy soldier in climbing up the half-flight of steps to the closest entrance, where an attendant in a checkered jacket stood waiting.

The attendant made a courteous bow in greeting. "Good evening, Major! Good evening, madam! Have you come for the meretricious pleasures of our Judge and Jury Club tonight? Present company could use a bit of military-style discipline, if you've a mind to play the punisher tonight, Major."

The corporal, his rank clearly signaled by the double chevron insignia on his shoulder, laughed pleasurably and did not correct the fellow. "No, not tonight. We have come to dance!"

The checkered man stepped gracefully in front of the entrance, barring their way. "Ah, then you are looking for the door just a few steps onward, leading down to the ballroom and libations of an alcoholic nature." He was pointing. "This is the coffee house, for those wanting their pipes, conversation, and games of chance." He looked pointedly at the woman. "Perhaps Madam would prefer the sure thing for her soldier?"

The woman drew back awkwardly as if suspecting he had insulted her, even though she could not be sure how exactly. "Let's try the other door, Jocko," she responded. The couple did an about-face, and Al and Minnie stepped back to let them pass. The doorman gave Al a knowing wink, and Al nodded shyly in return before hurrying to catch up with the couple again. It was convenient to have the soldier breaking the ice ahead of them, since neither of them knew how to discreetly negotiate a room for an amorous tryst. At the next door, which was down a half-flight of steps, stood another attendant in a similarly checkered outfit. His smile was less genuine than his counterpart's, and his eyebrows were lifted in disdain to see the soldier arriving with his own slattern. "Welcome to Merrimen's Ballroom. Might we possibly be of service?"

The soldier started to raise his hand in a salute to the man's imperious gaze, but quickly recovered himself and performed a social bow instead. "Good evening to you as well, young man! We have come for waltzing. I understand you have a superlative dancing floor and a grand orchestra for just such entertainment? In addition," he smirked conspiratorially at his companion, dressed as she was for sport, "we would like a room for some private conversation."

The man nodded brusquely and held out his hand. "We got rooms."

The soldier put a coin in the man's hand. Minnie leaned forward, hoping to learn the cost, but the man disappeared the coin with a magician's flourish and produced a key in return. "Room 7 for an hour. Up the steps to your left, down the center hall, lock the door after ya. No waking snakes in the hallway, but once you're locked in, you can scream all you like." The man's eyes moved on to Al and Minnie, having no further interest in the soldier and his paramour.

"Pleasant evening to ye. Are you looking for dancing as well?"

Al hesitated, not sure if dancing was a euphemism. "We'd like a private room," he said carefully. He looked at Minnie, who was already pulling out the small quantity of coins they had saved. The man held out his hand the same way he had for the soldier. Minnie swallowed to wet her suddenly dry throat, not sure they had enough between them. She began counting, running out of pennies after five and starting to pay with ha'pennies.

"That's enough for a room," the attendant said after she had counted out two half-pence coins, "as long as you don't want dancing. Room 29, top of the stairs, turn right and then left, down the hall to almost the end. Walk quiet, lock yer door. Then the world's your oyster." He grinned at her, pocketing their payment and handing over a key with a motion reminiscent of a pickpocket.

Minnie and Al moved together, in what they hoped was dignified haste, toward the staircase flush against the wall, but their eyes couldn't help giving the ballroom a lingering look as they climbed. Many feet drummed on wooden floorboards in the smoky room, to the accompaniment of a trio of ill-tuned musicians. Raucous voices boomed, and brightly colored dresses whirled, showing stockings and even flashes of flesh. Against the far wall was a long table, around which barmaids circulated with pitchers in both hands. Another man in the establishment's checkered livery was presiding over those seated. "No taps or daylights, my fellows and ladies!" he shouted. "Drink to the dregs and we'll pour more!"

Al, holding Minnie by her waist, for once not out of line with the etiquette of the denizens around them, let his hand dally downwards, along her ample hips until her thin bustle interfered with his reach.

"Nearly there," Minnie whispered.

By the time they got to the landing and found the right hallway, they were all but running. Albert thrust the key in the lock and fumbled to turn it. Minnie put her hands firmly over his and assisted, the lock giving way to their combined efforts. Once inside, they slammed the door shut, and looked deeply into each other's eyes. At almost the same moment, their faces registered shock. The key was still on the outside!

Hastily Minnie stepped back while Albert opened the door and withdrew the key from the keyhole. This time Albert's hands did not fumble, closing and locking the door from the inside. They were alone at last.

Minnie launched herself at Al. The fervency of her body weight hurled against him flattened him to the locked door. He opened his mouth, intending to say how much he loved her, but his words were stopped by her lips pressed to his, throbbing and urgent. Words no longer met their needs.

He slipped the key into his pocket so he had both hands free and kissed back, tilting his head to explore the depth of her soft lips, pressing along their length, parting his teeth, eager for more. His tongue slipping out to taste the tender juncture where her lips met.

Minnie felt his tongue touch, and she advanced hers out to meet his. Together their tongues tapped each other, introducing themselves, then stroked, licked, and explored their curved edges, their slightly raspy tops, their smooth yet crenulated undersides.

Al could feel Minnie's buttoned boot rising along his leg, its heel curling behind his calf. He sighed deep in his throat, vibrating their embracing tongues. He was stirred down to his solar plexus, and his manhood rose to the occasion. He was shaken down to his root by the thought of Minnie, his Minnie, who would soon be a part of him, who would soon be the other half of him.

Minnie entrapped his lower lip between her upper lip and tongue, mouthing him, her teeth coming in to nibble. At her belly she could feel his organ bulging forth, pressing into her. She shimmied her front against him, rubbing his rocky outcrop and teasing her nipples through her layers of clothing, feeling her body heat rising, desire coiling, and honey forming, dripping from within her to wet her undergarments.

Al reached between them to unbutton his fly, the tension on his cock having grown uncomfortable. He continued to kiss Minnie's lips, bobbing his head to give room for his unfastening hand, then drawing close again, lips finding their mates, sucking at them and parting with a little smack of temporary release.

Minnie cupped his cheek and chin, arching her body so Al's hands could strip away the fabric imprisoning his growing ardor, but still keep his lips where she wanted them, close to hers, fluttering and gripping, their tongues now exploring each other like wrestlers engaging with dire purpose.

Al unbuttoned his fly, his great shaft now jutting out and claiming its place between their middles. Both his arms found Minnie's hips, fondling beneath the edges of her bustle through her uniform dress. The thin dark skin of fabric barely contained her tantalizing curves. Jubilation ran through him like a razor-sharp shears through silk. He lifted his head from their kiss, struck by the sensation tearing through him, dumbfounded by the raw emotion scissoring its way along his flesh.

Minnie, her lips, tongue, and teeth suddenly bereft, found the tender spot beneath his chin, and kissed along his Adam's apple down to his bow tie. She bit the fabric savagely, jerking her head to untie the thing. One hand let go of his face to disentangle the encumbrance from his neck.

Al snorted in surprise. The jerk at his throat only intensified the rippling pleasure racing through his sinews. His hands left her hips to assist, and once the tie and collar were undone, he plunged his fingers into her plied and piled hair, unmindful of her hairpins, his fingertips tracing along her sheltered scalp, dislodging her maid's cap, which she had forgotten to remove in her haste to meet him, and which might have explained the doorman's crooked grin.

Minnie too was unmindful of the pins as they pulled her taut braids and prickled at her skin. Her hands were racing down his shirt and waistcoat buttons, grabbing roughly at the edges, yanking to each side, trying to divest him of all his upper garments at once. Somewhere, somehow, his hat had already been knocked from off his head.

Al disentangled his fingers from her curls, drawing his arms out of shirt and jacket sleeves, dimly recognizing that his waistcoat and prized pocket watch were sandwiched between. He felt a chilly draft spread over his naked arms and nip at the edges of his undershirt. Hastily he stripped it off as well, so that his bare chest with its sprinkle of dark hair, unbleached by the sun, was exposed. His hands returned to her, embracing what he could reach of her breasts, thinking he could feel her nipples growing erect despite the protective armor of her dress and corset.

Minnie gazed at him, breathless. She had never seen a man without a shirt before, although she had felt his chest pressed to hers in the past. The sight amazed her. His nipples were darker than her own in color, and although flat to his chest, the tip-tops of them were beaded up and aroused like her own. His muscles under his pale skin moved in a way that made her giddy, heaving like waves surging onto a shore when his arms stroked across her front. The bristly chest hairs, which she had felt but never seen, were darker than those on his head. She gazed, transfixed, captive to the novelty his near nudity presented.

Al, naked above, hurried to make the rest of him so. While Minnie stood looking on him with wonder and delight, he pushed down his trousers, which dropped to his feet and then caught, his sturdy brogues bigger than his cuff openings. He would have to sit down to remove the shoes, but he wasn't going to step away from his Minnie. She was still fully dressed. There were no buttons on her front, so he moved past her delectable mounds and reached behind her waist, hoping to find strings tucked under her bodice. His pole reached forward with him, bumping his knob against her skirt. He groped furtively at the small of her back, his fingers grouping for laces or buttons. How did this confounded dress come off?

Minnie reached behind her back, meeting his rummaging fingers, guiding him to the bodice hooks at her neck. She left him to unlatch the top ones while she started at her waist, her fingers twitching the hooks open with the quick rhythm that came of a daily chore. When their fingers met, she whisked the fabric away. She was wearing her prettiest corset cover, the one with tiny sprigs of embroidered roses, and her favorite corset, with cording that laced down the front. She looked down at herself as he untied her, but her eyes were drawn as if by a magnet to view his manhood standing out below. She reached for it. Her juices, she now realized, were overflowing. Her thighs were damp, her nectar having dripped through her drawers and soaked into her gartered stockings.

Al was wresting her clothes away, lost in his desire, unmindful of the dress she must make last until she could afford another. He groaned when her hand gripped his member and redoubled his efforts. He wanted her free of impediments. He wanted her secreted skin. He wanted her all for his own.

Minnie would not let go of him, but her free hand assisted in undressing herself. She shook her hips to encourage her unhooked skirt, untied petticoats, and dislodged garters to drop at her feet. She swapped hands while she lifted her shift over her shoulders and head, shrugging the garment away, leaving herself bare before him. She placed her still-shod feet on either side of his brogues, tethered as they were by his smashed-down trousers, and raised up on her toes to place her dripping quim within reach of his cock.

Al felt his throbbing member graze her belly, poke her belly button, and then prod an inch lower. Still far to go before his peg met up with her chamber. He felt her hand clamp onto his, placing it under her buttock. Taking the hint, he cradled her in his arms, lifting her bottom to give them the final inches they needed. He imagined there was a clap of thunder, for he felt as if lightning had struck them when their genitals matched. He pushed into her, feeling her moist and yielding flesh part for him. Another blinding, deafening bolt seemed to strike home when both sets of short hairs at last smashed to each other.

Minnie's body was aflame, feeling his virile shaft poke its way along her flesh to her waiting folds. She moved his hand to grasp beneath her fanny, heaved herself into his compliant arms, and took hold of his shoulders, pulling herself towards him, pressing his tackle into her empty channel, ramming their parts together, inwardly screaming in anticipation and then shouting joyously, out load, full gusto, shrieking to the heavens and anyone else who might have been nearby that she was splendidly, willfully, deeply and utterly filled by her Albert's thick hungry cock.

By now they were pounding turbulently against each other then, her rocking frantically in the cradle of his embrace, her hips hanging low and posting upward; him curving his body to her, thrusting like a needle into a garment, making a long row of even stitching, stabbing with persistent rhythm. The ache in their loins tightened, stiffened, twisted, encompassed their entire bodies, their entire beings.

Al stepped on the crotch of his downed trousers, wrenching his other foot from the stricture of its cuff, tearing the seams to free himself. He thrust his foot forward, lunging with Minnie in his arms, setting her down as gently as his need allowed, placing her on the floor, his legs between her open knees, his insistent shaft nary missing a beat as it lunged in and out with consistent and urgent propulsion.

Minnie felt herself swoon, at first thinking it was her passion that caused her to dip towards the floor, but then understanding that Al had made them horizontal. She thrust her breasts, her nipples sharply pointed by his caresses, into his hard chest, feeling a pair of small prickles near her shoulders that were his aroused man nips raised in tribute to her frenzied yearnings. Her back felt a thin rug quavering under her as Al's thrusting pushed her against its fringed edges. She raked her stocking-clad ankles upwards along his thighs, digging them into his backside, giving her purchase against his flesh to press her eager purse deeper over his pulsing prick. Her gaze was swimming, her quim gripping, her thighs wet. She was panting, gulping air when he pulled up and expelling when he thrust.

Al could hear his own breath quickening, his heart pounding, his thoughts lost to recollection as he gave everything he had over to wapping. The harder he plunged, the more she tightened around him, her walls squeezing him, undulating, working up to a climactic release. How long could he last like this? Keyed up like an overwound clock. He would burst. The coil would break, fly apart, and release all the pent-up energy in one, unsprung, blinding, expulsive moment.

Minnie felt it, that dancing friction reaching its zenith. Her panting became a low groan. Turning to a yowl. Rising in pitch. Changing to an unabashed, unleashed shriek of ultimate pleasure. Her eyelids squeezed tight, her pubic bone arched up, strained to his, grinding, their bodies blurred in their overwrought beating now fused together into one. One glorious, soul-stirring, heart-striking, belly-wrenching waterfall of gushing, exhilarating bliss.

Spurred by her precipitous shriek of pleasure, Al cried out in his own sharp release, his body quivering over hers as jet upon jet burst forth, his bollocks contracting with the force of expulsion, his body a mere appurtenance to the peerless event attendant upon ejaculation.

The silence in the room was sudden. Their conjoined bodies went lax, Al piled on top of Minnie, both inert, both lost to the tiny sands of time that were only of import those not temporarily transported beyond all worldly care.

In time, Al clumsily tipped his drowsy body to one side, so as to remove his manly weight from Minnie's more diminutive personage.

Minnie rolled with him, her body not ready to release him. This brought her to her side, facing him. Her eyes blinked slowly, her mind, in no hurry to return to the quotidian world, gathering up brief flashes of reality between her lashes. Eventually she totted up all the pieces, put the world outside her senses together again, and recalled they were happily within each other's embrace, lying on a rug in a rented room. Gently leaving the wisps of their recent visit to paradise behind, she whispered. "All that money for a bed and here we are on the floor."

Together they giggled, then laughed, and then guffawed. They were like finches in a hedgerow, hidden from prying eyes, but chittering joyously to proclaim their triumph.

STEAM GEARED

ROBINETTE WATERSON

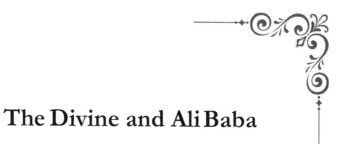

The Divine and Ali Baba

The Divine and Ali Baba

IT DID NOT TAKE LONG before everyone knew Miss Sarah Bernhardt was traveling on the very same train as they were. The presence of the illustrious actress, sculptress, bon vivant, and muse to Victor Hugo, Alexandre Dumas, (and the Prince too, some whispered!) was electrifying.

Some passengers surmised her proximity when they saw the dozens of much-experienced portmanteaus, their surfaces papered over with numerous exotic shipping labels, being brought on board in Brighton. Others heard the mellifluous voice echoing down the passageways, the arresting modulation that famously mesmerized her audiences even if she were to speak gibberish. Still others saw the extravagant dress, plumed hat, and oft-celebrated fiery red hair of the actress herself as she traipsed down the corridor, dripping with adornments so rich and over the top that it had to be – it just had to be! — The Divine Sarah, the greatest thespian of their time. Indeed of all times, some would put forth the argument.

Passengers peeked from their compartment windows, and many thronged into the aisle to greet her, agog with admiration, gushing compliments, begging for autographs, or plain just swooning with delirium to catch sight of her august personage. Understandably it took some time for her to make the journey through the corridors to her private car. Were this truly an inconvenience to her, she could have boarded her car directly and avoided such adulation, but it was evident that an inconspicuous entrance was not her intent.

And so it was to be expected, considering her mere presence caused such a stir, that her shrieks of consternation ratcheted the tension on the train to a carnival pitch.

"My Ali Baba! He is missing! Oh, help, help, help, help, help!" Her sonorous cries resonated from one end of the train to the other.

The conductor hastened down the walkway, pressing passengers out of the way as gently as he could, given the urgent necessity. "Madame Bernhardt, I hear something is lost? I am Percival Pelton, conductor for the Great Western Rail, at your service." He bowed with careful dignity. "I shall do my utmost to find your missing luggage. Pardon me, but what, pray tell, is an alibaba?"

After some histrionics, understandable in one so highly strung and so highly praised for being so, the Divine Sarah clarified herself, in charmingly accented English. "Ali Baba is my pet alligator. I have had him since my latest visit to America, and I do so love the little creature. Although he is a bit too fond of champagne." She pointed to an empty bottle on the floor. "I have the suspicion that he drank up my welcome gift and has left my compartment to look for more. That, or he is kidnapped. I cannot imagine who would do such a dastardly thing; however, there is the possibility of ransom. I believe there is a word for villains who steal pets for ransom?"

The conductor passed over the vulgar terms for pet nappers. "I shall initiate a search immediately. Have no fear, Madame. We shall find your missing pet." Percy picked up the empty bottle, examining the remaining foil cover which was wickedly slashed, indicative of a thorough gnashing by sharp pointed teeth. He fingered the gnawed foil with growing trepidation. "Let me gather a few details." He set the bottle down gently, upright on a high table. "Would you describe the missing person, er, animal?" Drawing a small notepad from his jacket pocket and a short pencil from his hatband, he made ready to take notes.

"Oh you can't mistake him, Mr. Pelton. He has the cutest little expression on his face, with one eyebrow higher than the other."

As he stood close to her in the confines of the private carriage, he found it hard to focus on his task. Her perfume was evocative and compelling, somehow delicate and raw at the same time. She projected a self-assurance that wafted from her body like a golden aura, often commented upon in reviews of her performances. He felt her almost as a vibration, a wave of unfettered sensation, sensual, savage and visceral, yet tender and romantic in some manner, all jumbled together. Percy found himself leaning too close for decency, and he gulped and straightened his backbone at once. This lady, he told himself sternly, was a traveler in need of his assistance. Yet all he could think, as he looked into the luminous eyes in her delicately painted face, was how this traveler was the embodiment of Cleopatra. Of Camille. Of Delilah. Of the enigmatic and lecherous Sphinx. She wasn't merely pretty. She was far more dangerous than that. His base animal lust bestirred itself. Metaphorically he took himself in hand so that he might do his duty, both as a conductor and as a gentleman.

"Very well, cutest expression..." Percy scribbled on his pad, concentrating on recording the altitude of the missing animal's eyebrows. "And about how tall is he? Or long, should I say?"

The Divine Sarah spread her arms out to each side, her hands flat out, suggesting as far as she could reach and then some. "About so long. Maybe a foot tall, or a foot and a half." She paused, posing herself poignantly in an attitude of deep thought. "Rather small for an alligator. I think traveling has stunted his growth. Or perhaps his diet of milk and champagne."

The conductor's eyes opened wide when considered the length from one hand to the other. "Hair color?" he asked out of habit, following his list of inquiries for lost children. Recollecting the present situation, he shook his head. "Pardon me, no hair I would guess."

"No hair, yes. Just dark umber scales. I would describe his color as a raw umber with some greenish undertone. Maybe towards sepia, but definitely on the darker side and with a touch of terre verte."

The conductor's bedazzled mind struggled to stay on task. "Last seen wearing?" he asked and this time corrected himself immediately. "Ah, well I don't suppose many reptiles dress for traveling."

The actress shook her pretty head in the negative. "No clothing, but how odd you should ask that," she gasped out as a fresh round of sobs wracked her. "He does not know it yet, the little dear, but we are on our way to see the new exhibition at the Kettering & Putterham Steamworks, and I have commissioned them to make a custom set of a gilt-edged collar and cuffs. Four little matching cuffs! The company is adept at making entertaining mechanisms for the stage, and he will look so much the gentleman in them!" Her sobs increased in volume and shrillness. She wailed, loud enough to wake the dead and evince deep emotions from the living.

"There, there, dear Madame Bernhardt, do not fret so. We will find your Ali Baba. Is there anything else you can tell us to aid in our investigation?"

The lady dabbed at her eyes a moment and then drew breath as if for an oratory. "His snout is about this big." The conductor's eyes grew wider still as her hands moved apart. "He has a rather blunt nose, you know, not narrow like a crocodile, if you are familiar with them." She circled her hands expressively about her jaw. "And one lip tends to curl over his left incisor." She leered in imitation. "It gives him a perpetual smile. He is a jolly little dumpling, always happy. His tail is rather short for his size, and he swings it a great deal. Often I can find him by the path he leaves, knocking things about as he walks by." She pointed to the skirt of a nearby occasional table, which showed a tenting inward. "He decidedly went that way, but after that? We are bereft of detritus bearing witness to which way he swished."

Like a breaking rain cloud, she unleashed a torrent of tears, hiding her face in a lace handkerchief. Her maid hurried to her side, patting her hand, and holding smelling salts at the ready.

The conductor returned his pad and pencil to their respective pocket and hatband. His eyes fell upon the mangled champagne bottle. "Perhaps he just went down to the dining car for a snack. I'll check there first." There is no response to his attempt at humor. "I don't suppose you would consider him dangerous? I mean to ask, might he bite things? Or people?"

The Divine was weeping deeply into a second handkerchief, the first now limp and discarded. Her maid answered for her. "Yes, he jolly well would bite, the nasty little brute. He enjoys the attention. Given his druthers, he eats meat." Although the actress shook her head at this statement, she did not leave off crying to contradict it.

Percy looked down at his crisp uniform and tidy gloves, hoping their covering would make him appear sufficiently unlike meat. "I'll get right to this then." He bowed and backed out of the small compartment, closing the door gently but firmly before him. If the gator was still within, he wanted to keep it so.

His first course of action was to walk through the train, his eyes on the ground and his ears listening for cries of alarm to indicate a hungry predator was making its way through. Reaching the engine room without any sign of the scaly runaway, he turned back. "Now if I were a jolly yet hazardous interloper, where would I go to ground?"

The tension on the train was higher than ever, now that the story was leaking out. The chatter, instead of the typical desultory snippets engendered by the lulling clacking of wheels crossing tracks, was fervid and vivacious. Percy himself felt invigorated by the altered mood, in addition to the close contact with a celebrity. A pity there was a ferocious beast aboard.

If he were Sherlock Holmes, from one of those engaging stories from the pulp magazines, he would eliminate the impossible and deduce the improbable. Was an alligator loose, unescorted, and unconstrained, aboard Her Majesty's most excellent steam railway as improbable as deducing military service from tanned hands and a limp? Or unmasking a murderer evidenced by a wedding band and cigar ash? Or outing a King behind a mask to recover a cabinet photo? Very well then, Mr. Holmes might label this puzzle a simple one. If only the man himself were here to help him search!

In the baggage car, he took down a pole with a blunt hook on the end, configured for snagging luggage handles, and poked into the sardine-sized spaces between the packed paraphernalia. Could alligators squeeze into tiny cracks like mice? He thought not, but poked anyway. Keeping the hook, he proceeded to the engine compartment, stirring

212

the heaped coal and joking with the brakemen and engineer. No, they said. They had seen a pink flamingo and a will-o-the-wisp, but no alligator.

Percy chided himself. 'Think, man, think! Where would a hungry, and purportedly drunk, member of the crocodilian order betake itself?' He made for the kitchen car and began opening cabinets.

"Peckish, Percy?" asked the chef as he sidestepped the porter intruding in his small workspace. "I recommend the roast goose with bread sauce and mushy peas, with Battenberg for afters. For what do you hunger?"

"Alligator," Percy replied, grinning at the look of astonishment that crossed the chef's face. Quickly the man recovered and sallied forth with his own jest. "Closest I can do is some potted hippopotamus. Must it be alligator?"

When Percy explained himself, the chef looked pointedly at the tiny strip of exposed flooring in his domain, a rail car that held multiple stoves, an extended cooktop, plating counters, and high cabinets. "I assure you the animal hasn't passed through here without my notice." They laughed together, brothers in uniform, fighting the good fight, protecting the traveling public from fray and follies, even though most of the mishaps were of the traveler's own making. Percy moved resolutely onward.

He continued in this manner, stopping to inspect uninhabited nooks and corners until he came full circle to the private car again. He knocked with his professionally deferential rap. When her attendant opened the door, he could see the actress at her vanity mirror, applying a scandalously red shade of lipstick. He looked down quickly and shielded his face, so as to afford her privacy in her intimate boudoir deeds, but not before she caught his eyes in her mirror.

"Any news? Have you found my little Baba?" she asked. Hope, fear, and many sorts of excessive emotions were redolent upon those red lips, embodied by her rich and full-voiced inflection. She was trembling too, no doubt due to worry over her lost pet, but to Percy's imagination, her quiver suggested a current of erotic promise, raking over his senses like a suggestive and intimate chant, enticing him to partake of her secret depths, pungent with passion. Did she know the effect she had on him? Surely she was aware of it. Presumably she was inured to it. Expected it, even demanded it, from each and every member in her sold-out performances. Her livelihood depended on that implicit invitation. The hinted offer of sex behind the curtained divider, just out of sight of society's prying eyes.

He stepped inside the carriage and closed the door so that gossip-hungering ears would not eavesdrop, but he conversed with his shy eyes on his shoes, swallowing his ungentlemanly and scandalously vivid ruminations. "Has your pet returned, Madame? Alas, cursory inspection indicates he is not in plain sight, but the hunt continues. No need to overly fret yourself. Not yet."

Once the door was closed again, Percy released an extended sibilant expression of concern. There was no help for it then. He would have to enlist aid from the passengers. Inevitably this would cause more negative reactions. Likely there would be a panic. With trepidation, he started to make inquiries of the travelers.

"A what?! You don't say! And it is loose?" There were cries of excited alarm. "What does it look like? What kind of teeth does it have? Oh dear, long and sharp, you say?" A child wailed, "Don't let it eat me!" Its siblings took up the cry, and neighboring children in other compartments joined in. As Percy went from carriage to carriage, the train took on the atmosphere of a holiday carnival with enlivened chatter and raised voices, punctuated with catcalls and shrieks. People spilled out into the walkway to gossip about the latest installment in the ongoing drama that was the Divine Sarah. He stepped through them with spoken pardons and gentle nudges. They were raucous, loud, and out of control. A regular Bartholomew's Fair, he thought, pressing through the ear-assaulting din.

The couple in the car with the drawn drapes hastily covered their private parts when he knocked. "Pardon, but you haven't seen an alligator about, have you?" The man's retort bordered on rude and did not bear repeating.

Likewise the two gentlemen in the dining car, holding hands under the table and whispering endearments to each other, shook their heads, saying they had not seen anything out of the ordinary pass by.

Even the car with the large family, when Percy knocked, was preoccupied with amorous inclinations. The staid couple stopped playing footsie to look up at him in surprise, but could contribute no substantive evidence to further his search. Their children were leaving sticky nose prints on the windows and trailing their boiled sweets along the upholstery. He frowned slightly and moved on with no further word to them.

Did no one take the train just for transportation anymore?

Perhaps the presence of Madame B had entranced them all. Her open sensuality, in all its ambiguity, mystery, and abundance, was powerful and bewitching. She, both by reputation and stagecraft, would incite primal urges to be expended whenever, wherever, repeatedly, and as often as was humanly possible. Percy himself felt a quiver somewhere deep inside him. No doubt about it, the thought of her got him right down to his tallywags.

With effort, he bent his mind and body back to his task, reassuring and placating along the way, but without further clues to the errant animal's whereabouts. His alert eyes darted into dark corners and unused alcoves for covert reptilian movement. There was only one compartment where the sole occupant seemed unaffected by the disturbance. He was a rather low sort of man with clean clothes but unkempt fingernails. "Haven't seen anything," the man said sullenly and looked out the window again, dismissing the conductor peremptorily.

Something odd about him, thought Percy. If the conductor had not been wholly occupied with the rescue of the hide-bound pet, he might loiter in the passageway and watch this man closely. A single male departing Brighton was not unusual, but being sour-tempered after a visit to the holiday town was a bit out of the ordinary. Maybe had a row with his sweetheart, he conjectured distractedly, abandoning further rumination on the matter in his haste to return to task.

A screech in the open seating section caused him to run to the source, but it was just a young woman affrighted by her companion's telling of a ghost story. The jokester had reached his arm around her. "I'll protect you from the phantom and its menace," he told her, pulling her close. "Give us a buss."

Percy gave the man a flinty glare. "There are no ghosts on this train. Her Majesty does not permit them. And young lady, if I were you, I would give this masher a hatpin to the knee instead of a kiss."

By the time Percy reached the engine compartment again, he was starting to smell something rotten, and not in Denmark. How could no one claim to have seen or heard anything suspicious, when an inordinate length of scales with a toothy grin was lurking about? Could it still be in the lady's private compartment? Surely Madame B and her maid would have uncovered the fanged darling in very short order. If it had been found since he was last there, he would expect the diva's exclamations of joy would carry past the moon and stars, much less to the ends of Her Majesty's rail line. If it had been drawn out by the scent of food, exclamations of terror would be expected in the dining car. If it was merely out for a stroll or had chosen a cozy corner to sleep off a hangover, Percy's scrutiny should have discovered it by now.

Thus having eliminated all possible factors, the one which remained, however improbable, must be the truth. Thus it was evident that Ali Baba had been kidnapped. Was a ransom note being composed this very instant? Would it shortly be delivered to Madame B's temporary abode? He passed through the throng again to the lady's private car and stationed himself outside its door.

So ensconced, a positively horrendous possibility assailed him. Dog my cats! What if it had hunkered down in some out of the way place and cast off the strife and suffering of this ephemeral world? Laid down the knife and fork? Turned down its cup? Shuffled off its mortal coil?

Took up residence in Abney Park? Dropped the cue? Jacked it? To be plain, what if the alligator were dead?

He looked heavenward. Perish the thought! Poor Sarah would be utterly bereft! He barely noted he was forming an unwarranted informality with the thespian's given name. The conductor gave himself over to calculating how long it might be before an offensive odor was reported.

As he pondered such morbid possibilities, Mr. Filthy-Fingernails opened the connecting door. On sighting Percy, the man performed an abrupt about-face and hoofed away at high speed.

"Stop right there, you miscreant!" Percy cried out and began to run after the fleeing felon. Through the length of the train corridor, the two of them raced, milling passengers shoved aside, and startled faces left in their wake. The disreputable fellow stopped when he saw the engineer and his staff charging from the opposite end of the train, pipes and shovels in hand. The would-be kidnapper gave one last furtive glance behind him at Percy, whose face was livid from effort and hardened in a determined grimace. The ruffian, his expression equally determined, yanked open an outer door and flung himself bodily from the moving train. There he was seen to have rolled, arse over teakettle, into the open countryside.

Percy reached the flapping door and stood in the breach, helplessly watching the evil-doer come to his feet and dust off his trousers. "Blackguard!" he shouted in vain. Noting the next marker number, he mentally composed a telegram to be sent at the next station. Be on the lookout for a man with muck under his nails. But most importantly, the scoundrel decidedly did not have an alligator about his person when he jumped.

Percy hurried back to the car where he first encountered the malefactor. There was a long thin case, such as might be carrying expensive polo mallets, in the upper rack. He brought it down gently, keeping the case as level as he possibly could. It was inert, much to his dismay. By now he had an audience in the passageway. They murmured shouts of "Look out!" and "Oh the poor little creature, locked up in that box for who knows how long!" Percy waved them back. "Watch yourselves! Give the wretched reptile some air."

The crowd complied, stepping back and watching in strained silence. Percy positioned the case with its hinges facing away from him, towards the window side of the car. There was no movement from within. He considered asking the actress herself to come and open it, hoping her presence might placate it if it were riled. The alligator was likely frightened and might strike out at anyone within easy reach. And that anyone would be him. Howsoever, with the box quiescent, he feared the worst. He would behave as an agent of the Great Western should, and take it upon himself to ascertain if the alligator was breathing before he subjected the great lady to the possible pain of its loss.

Cautiously, with his arms as far away from his fingertips as he could manage, he pressed on the two latching mechanisms, which sprang open with a click, sounding inordinately loud to him in the hush. He lifted the lid slowly, so as not to aggravate a living creature should there be one within.

Ali Baba, curled into a semi-circle in the enclosed space, opened one eye and glared as if Percy was disturbing him in his morning-after kip.

"Well I'll be deuced," Percy said softly, ignoring the oohs and ahhs behind him and addressing the animal directly. "You do have a sort of a grin on you, don't you, little fellow? Ali Baba, I presume? I am Percival Pelton, at your service." Behind them in the corridor, the exclamations, celebratory utterings, and general hubbub were increasing in volume, and gently he lowered the lid to allow the alligator the privacy it seemed to crave. Besides, from the size of the one formidable tooth outstanding, Percy felt it perfectly reasonable to be in fear for his person.

The dulcet tones of the songstress were soon heard over the crowd. "You have found him? Mr. Percy, you clever, clever man. I owe you so much!" The madding crowd parted for the much-lauded actress, and she entered the compartment to kneel beside him, all a flurry. She planted a kiss on each side of his face before her dainty gloved hands reached towards her pet's prison. Percy was overcome by her nearness, paralyzed by her fluttering lips on his cheeks.

The Divine Sarah lifted the lid and cooed at Ali Baba. "Why you little scamp! How ever did you get in there?" She lifted the animal up, with one arm holding his scaly front feet and the other under his belly, leaning her behatted head to his snout.

If it could be said that an alligator snuggled, this he did. He flattened his neck, or rather the underside of his rough head, to her cheek and made a burp-like sound, which perhaps was his equivalent of a purr. Percy turned his head to give them privacy in their intimate embrace.

The maid came forward with an embossed leather leash, and the lady cooed effusively while she tethered her pet and coaxed it out of the polo box. His tail thrashed about, sweeping the full circle of his mistress's garment into a crescent shape. With the pet's safety now put to right, the Divine turned her gaze on Percy. Her eyes, famously large and fringed by kohl-enhanced lashes, regarded him appraisingly.

"You brave, brave man. I must reward you. What would please you? I have offered a monetary reward, and it is yours of course, but I owe you très beaucoup! So much more than mere financial compensation." She tipped her head in an enchanting fashion and blinked at him coyly.

Brief scenarios flashed through Percy's mind. Ruffles rustling, scampering fingers, her cooing voice, and her heavy-lidded look. He imagined her in a wrapper and nightgown and blushed furiously. It was too much for him. He stuttered. "Just doing my duty, Madame." His mind cursed himself for the reflexive phrase.

"Oh but you were so heroic, approaching Ali in spite of his vicious appearance. He has been known to be overly liberal in flashing his teeth. I insist that you receive recompense for the Herculean effort you have undertaken on my behalf." She smiled prettily, and a pert expression came over her face. "He can be quite menacing when vexed. I've paid for stitches for the careless. I can't count how many times."

Percy gulped. "But I thought you said..."

The Divine's lilting laughter carried a great distance. She stepped even closer to him and lowered her voice. "Meat," she said without a trace of a smirk. "He is not supposed to bite, but sometimes he can't help himself. Let me show you something." She tapped her painted nails on Ali's snout, producing a hollow metallic echo. Sliding her fingertips along the alligator's spine, she pressed a hidden button, and a small handle emerged from a concealed compartment. "Sad to say, and please don't tell anyone, but Ali passed on many moons ago from his champagne indulgences. I had Kettering & Putterham Steamworks recreate him." The Divine shifted her automaton pet by its handle and passed it off to her attendant, who carted it back to the private carriage.

"The replica is perhaps a bit too life-like. I truly do owe you something more." She took his hand, brought it to her ample bosom, looking deep into his eyes with unprecedented familiarity. "I know!" she cried out suddenly, her gaze locked to his. "I know just the thing!"

Percy watched her hand, taking his hand, and bringing it to her exquisite décolleté with the provocative cleft in its center. Once her gaze arrested his, he found that could not look away again. Might he dare to hope? Dare he to ask? He was trembling with anticipation; unable to utter the words he longed desperately to speak.

The Divine seemed to have deduced his innermost thoughts. "I know what you must want most of all. The tabloids scream of it — my long, long list of men! And yes, of course, I will add you to the list. Even move you to the top, if that pleases you? What do you say to Tuesday next?"

Percy stuttered, his lips having gone numb. "Tuesday? Heaven is that close?" Her nearness emboldened him, imbuing him with a thespian exuberance. "I would be superlatively honored! Bless me, thrill upon thrill! Yes, yes, and yes again - a myriad of times, yes!"

The Divine Sarah smiled benignly, having seen this kind of timidity rise to lark-like exaltation many, many times before. "Very good then. The Palladium, Argyll Street, make-up at six in the evening, performance at eight. There is no need to prepare. All you need do is lie still and play dead."

Percy blinked.

"The role of my dearly departed paramour merely requires you to sprawl becomingly and lie motionless on the platform. The stagehands will assist in placing you, and then crank you up from below for the final act."

She patted his hand where it rested on her bosom. He was riveted in place, overcome by the munificence of the gift she had bestowed upon him. To play the lover to the grand actress, on a stage where thousands would witness their performance, and gaze upon him at the pinnacle of his glory! The thought utterly beguiled him. Madame B eventually took his hand from her apple basket and placed it back by his side. With a flourish of her broad-brimmed hat, she turned to make her way back to her traveling abode. The crowd parted reverently, whispering words of undiluted adoration.

Percival Pelton looked down at his hand. The one she had touched. The one she allowed to rest on her intimate and private personage. Surely he had just died and passed into the realm of paradise.

STEAM GEARED

About the Author

Robinette Waterson began writing stories at an early age. Given her predilection for literature and history, especially of the Victorian era, it is not surprising that she ventured into the alternative historical style of steampunk. From there, she detoured down a quaint alleyway into Victorian steampunk erotica.

Read more at https://RobinetteWaterson.com.

Printed in Great Britain
by Amazon

36141709R00135